Turn Back Time

Eleanor Tucker is a writer and journalist who has written on subjects including culture, feminism, parenting and beauty for publications such as The *Guardian*, The *Observer*, The *Independent*, *Grazia*, *Red* and *Marie Claire*. Originally from Oxford, she lives in Edinburgh with her husband and two teenage children. This is her first novel.

ELEANOR TUCKER

turn back time

First published in the United Kingdom in 2026 by

Hera Books, an imprint of
Canelo Digital Publishing Limited,
20 Vauxhall Bridge Road,
London SW1V 2SA
United Kingdom

A Penguin Random House Company
The authorised representative in the EEA is Dorling Kindersley Verlag GmbH.
Arnulfstr. 124, 80636 Munich, Germany

Copyright © Eleanor Tucker 2026

The moral right of Eleanor Tucker to be identified as the creator of this work has been asserted in accordance with the Copyright, Designs and Patents Act, 1988.
All rights reserved. No part of this publication may be reproduced or transmitted in any form or by any means, electronic or mechanical, including photocopy, recording, or any information storage and retrieval system, without permission in writing from the publisher.
No part of this book may be used or reproduced in any manner for the purpose of training artificial intelligence technologies or systems. In accordance with Article 4(3) of the DSM Directive 2019/790, Canelo expressly reserves this work from the text and data mining exception.

A CIP catalogue record for this book is available from the British Library.

ISBN 978 1 83598 395 9

This book is a work of fiction. Names, characters, businesses, organizations, places and events are either the product of the author's imagination or are used fictitiously. Any resemblance to actual persons, living or dead, events or locales is entirely coincidental.

Cover design by Lisa Brewster

Cover images © Shutterstock.com

Printed and bound in Great Britain by Clays Ltd, Elcograf S.p.A.

Look for more great books at
www.herabooks.com | www.dk.com

For Ma.

Part One

Chapter One

Rabbits are surprisingly muscular

How did you show kindness to yourself yesterday?
TYPE YOUR ANSWER HERE: Cheese

This 60 Days to Confidence app is a bloody nightmare. The idea is that by answering one question a day, you can 'micro-journal your way to self-belief'. Which sounds unlikely – and also, *sixty* days? That feels like a lot of days. The features editor at *Glowgetter* will have moved on before I've written the review up. As will I. And the majority of *Glowgetter* readers too.

Frankly, I could save everyone the bother and just *tell* them what's wrong with my self-belief. How about the fact that I'm pushing fifty and have to scrutinise my face every day so I can write about anti-ageing creams? Hold on... you aren't meant to call them that anymore. Somebody finally worked out that 'anti-ageing' is nonsensical – because everyone ages, and a cream isn't going to stop that. If you *aren't* ageing, you're most likely dead, or an alien or supernatural being. So nowadays it's all about 'pro-ageing', which is much more positive and inspiring. Allegedly.

The truth is, writing about beauty products all the time was fine when I was in my twenties and had those 'pretend' signs of ageing, like teeny tiny lines under my eyes. The kind that look adorable and charactertul, like having freckles or owning a Dachshund. But when my whole face started sliding down my neck like a Salvador Dali clock in the desert, I realised I could slather on as many peptides as I liked, but I was never going to look twenty-seven again. Even getting 'tweakments' (as they call them these days) doesn't really make anyone look young – I should know, I've tried most of them. It's all about looking 'Fresh' or 'You – but rested!'. And if you go too far, you end up looking like you're in *The Lion King*, all wide eyes and a face so filled up it's like you've got a muzzle. No thanks.

It's Tuesday morning. Through the living room window, I can see the postman approaching with his red trolley, and no doubt the usual stack of parcels for me. He's taking ages so I turn back to my phone and google 'Erica Pells' to see if my article about some supermodel's botched hi-tech beauty treatment has gone live. *'I'm done hibernating,' says Celeste, after being disfigured by CryoSculpting*. She doesn't look disfigured to me, but then supermodel disfigurement is probably on a par with how regular people feel when they walk to the garage without make-up on. It has an M&S Food section (the garage, that is) as of this March, so it's worth the twenty-minute round trip, even if you haven't had time to put on a Bobbi Brown Five-Minute Face, which I usually swear by for leaving the house. You never know when you're going to run into Paul Rudd, after all.

I go back to googling my name and spot a new search result, but my excitement that it's the 'by-line' of an article I wrote is short-lived because, as per usual, it's about a memorial service in a US retirement home. Why is my name so popular with elderly Americans? I stand up and adjust my kimono so Lewis or Laurie or whatever the postman is called (definitely begins with an L) doesn't think I'm trying to flirt with him. There's nothing more unsavoury than a middle-aged woman wearing poolside casual in Wiltshire during the autumn, other than maybe the same but with three inches of cleavage.

'Been online shopping again, Ms Pells?' he says when I open the door.

I take an armful of packages. 'Nope. They're for my job.'

'What is it you do again?'

'I write beauty articles for magazines and websites. About skincare, treatments, things like that.' I feel I have told him this before, many, many times.

'Right... And they pay you for that?'

'They do indeed.' I smile. 'Well, usually. Sometimes I do it for exposure.' I yank my kimono up again. 'Anyway... is there a parcel from Slay PR?'

He looks on his phone-meets-scanner device. 'Have you got the tracking info?'

I hold up my phone for him to scan the barcode. Just as I do, a notification appears at the top of my screen.

> **BEAT PERIMENOPAUSE BELLY FAT** has followed you back!

The postman glances at me.

'I get lots of spam because of my job,' I say.

He is young and won't even know what the perimenopause is. And who cares, I can never remember his name anyway. Maybe it's Liam. Maybe not.

When he's gone, I sit on the living room floor to unpack the parcels, pushing aside a saucer containing the remains of some Taleggio from my latest Say Cheese subscription box. I often sit on the floor, and consider myself well designed for it, with short legs and a big bum. It's like an inbuilt seating system – who needs a chair?

I'm making three piles of packages: *Need Now For Imminent Features*, *Quite Fancy Trying For Myself* and *Give Away As Presents*. On the first pile are four body scrubs I've been waiting for, all to be tested out for a feature in *Grace* magazine. As it's due to be filed by five p.m. today, I'm contemplating the best way to give them all a genuine evaluation: probably one shower, and a limb for each scrub. No time for any lasting effects but honestly, who has? Every product must be tested, written up, posted online and – the horror – shared on Instagram reels, all within forty-eight hours... if you want to keep the editors (and PRs) happy, that is.

I'm interrupted by a call from 'Sally Pells'. I know, it's weird that my own mother is saved in my contacts under her full name. But as 'Mum' with no surname looks a bit lost on its own, what else could I have it as? Not 'Mum Pells'... Actually, how about Mother Pells? It makes her sound like the old wise woman in a mediaeval village, one successful herbal poultice away from being burnt as a witch. I quite like it.

I let it ring three times, almost fou...

I can hear that she either has a cold, or is crying, and immediately wish I'd let it go to voicemail, because then she would try my brother, Simon, who would be better at dealing with whatever is causing the sniffing and an unscheduled ten-thirty a.m. call. Mother Pells normally sticks to after six p.m., believing, perhaps, that it is still cheaper, as it was in the days of landlines.

'You okay, Mum?'

'It's Carol, Erica. She passed away last night.'

I squeeze some Tuscan Tomato and Sea Salt Energising Body Polish (which smells like pizza, incidentally) onto my leg and think how to respond. I'm not particularly good at this sort of thing. Carol is my mother's closest friend, who's been ill for a while. Simon would probably know what to say, annoyingly.

Rather than condolences for the grief-stricken, my forte is more a punny title to a beauty product round-up. I'm already mulling over *Take The Rough With The Smooth* as the headline for the body scrub feature I have to write today, although this isn't really my finest work. How about *Yes Scrubs*? Like 'No Scrubs', but the opposite? But then, I suppose if you have to explain it, it probably doesn't work...

'Ohhhhh,' I say, aiming for sympathy-mixed-with-a-bit-of-surprise, plus a touch of inevitability, as Carol has been in a hospice for a few weeks and was definitely on the wrong side of eighty. But it comes out more like the sound someone might make when they discover a three for two on Zinfandel, which wasn't quite what I was aiming for.

'Is that the best you can do, Erica? I knew I should have called your brother...'

Why am I so bad at this sort of thing? I get up and move towards the mantelpiece to get a sniff of a criminally expensive reed diffuser I was recently gifted by a PR. It's meant to 'shift energy' and has, according to the gold packaging, been 'energetically imbued by an in-house alchemist'. As I attempt to appease my mother by saying nostalgic but thoughtful things about Carol, I wonder if it works down the phone.

But I'm stuck for what to say as I can't remember much about her other than that, when I was a teenager, I was tasked with feeding her rabbit while she was on holiday. Or probably, thinking back, her children's rabbit – that would make more sense. I wasn't meant to get it out of the hutch, but I did, and it ran under Carol's decking. They never found it. Maybe it made a new life for itself under there, and was happy. But Carol and her family certainly weren't when they came back from Los Cristianos.

Thinking about this, I feel a wave of guilt. (Holy crap, is this the energy shift the reed diffuser promised? Remarkable.) I shake it off quickly though – best not to pick at the scab of feeling guilty about things that happened years ago. Anyway, rabbits are surprisingly muscular, not like gerbils or other smaller rodents one might keep as a pet, so maybe it wasn't even my fault that it wriggled free.

'So, you'll come with me then?'

I snap out of my reminiscence and realise I've agreed to accompany my mother to Carol's funeral, 'when it happens, which probably won't be for a while'. Why, I wonder... is there some kind of hideous dead body backlog I don't know about? I decide not to ask, having probably done enough damage for one conversation.

'Of course, Mum. And I'm sorry about Carol. She was a real...'

I go to say 'treasure' but feel this is a bit strong, so change it to 'doll' halfway through, because I was watching *Mad Men* last night. It comes out as something akin to 'troll' though. Thankfully, Mother Pells is now focusing on the funeral logistics and I'm pretty sure she doesn't hear.

'You know how I've been getting so confused about directions lately. *The Inevitable*, I'm sure...'

My mother has always been a bit dozy, and there has been absolutely no change to this as she enters old age, other than the fact that she constantly talks about *The Inevitable*, which I presume means dementia. It's as though she has been waiting her whole life forgetting words, names, places, keys, artichokes (a long story) to finally be able to shout 'HA! I told you. It's *The Inevitable*.'

The postman reappears at the window and squints in, waving a large envelope. My new-build home (well, newish) is in a 'cottage' style, but not the picture postcard cottages with paths lined with rose bushes and such like. It's more of a worker's cottage, with its front door right on the pavement, so every time somebody walks past, they look in, and apparently this is okay, because the house is on the street, so why shouldn't they? I have toyed with the idea of net curtains and wondered if they are so out they are back in, like mullets. I tell Mother Pells I need to go.

'It's a special delivery,' the postman announces when I open the front door again. 'That's why it didn't come with the other stuff. It's *separate*.' He seems somehow proud of this. I take the envelope and shut the door, even though the postman seems to want me to open it in front of him.

Back down on the floor, I'm surrounded by pots, tubes and packaging, but I can't be bothered going upstairs to my 'office'. My office is in inverted commas because it's really a small bedroom with a desk in it, as well as several large boxes overflowing with beauty products, and a Peloton (still being paid off), which currently has a duvet cover draped over it. It's probably dry by now, seeing as I put it there a good three weeks ago.

The envelope contains not the usual PR missive, but an invitation, on thick, grainy paper that smells quite strongly of pumpkin spice. *Oh My Gourd!* it proclaims, in curly, Gothic writing. *You're Invited to a Halloween Party at Luscious Magazine!*

I stare at the invitation. On the plus side, I haven't been invited to a fancy dress party at *Luscious* since 'The Good Old Days' when I wrote for them regularly, before my editor Merlyn moved to a non-executive editor role. And we all know what that means. Except we don't really, but we guess it means you don't do that much anymore but want to continue going to parties. If I'm getting an invitation, I might be in line for a feature, or even a column. Merlyn has always looked after me – defending my more niche pun headlines to the sub-editors, putting me on the guest list for PR events that were clearly just for the big-league editors, and sometimes even paying me upfront when I was short of money.

On the minus side, it means a trip to London, which I steer clear of these days. The magazine offices are full of twenty-five-year-olds into that Clean Girl look, which I don't fully understand, whose biggest issue is how to shape their brows to look 'this season'. I mean, COME ON. I'd shave off my brows completely for a problem like that. They probably look at me and think, 'Oh, well done that middle-aged woman for still making an effort,' but they know deep down that my jaunty neckerchief is just to hide my double chin.

And then there's the whole fancy dress thing, which I have avoided my entire life. Although... the right costume could make me look less, well, forty-seven. There's a thought. And as Cassia Carver will undoubtedly be there, being all perfect, I will need to either look my best, or unrecognisable, like a zombie. The latter seems more appealing, because who would ever tilt their head and say,

'How are you? You look KNACKERED!' to one of the undead. They're *meant* to look a bit worn out, surely?

Just as I have the beginnings of a vague plan, I remember. *Lucas*. Of course. Why was that so difficult? JEEZ. Unsure what to do with this new (or old, just forgotten) information, I jump up, fling open the front door and yell 'THANKS LUCAS!' in the direction of the red post trolley. By now it's halfway down the street, past Mrs Belcher's, near Josie's house (one of the few people in the town that I like, apart from Keith, and smiley Gabe Dix from The Perch, of course). Lucas turns back briefly, like a schoolchild at drop-off, embarrassed by his over-affectionate mother.

I shut the door, flop down on the couch and open my laptop to start my body scrub article, despite the fact I haven't tried any of them yet. I'm going to see how many puns I can squeeze in, just to amuse myself. They'll probably get taken out by that mean sub-editor at *Grace* magazine, but who cares? Makes it more fun to write.

Scrub Me Up The Right Way
By Erica Pells

> We get it: exfoliate can easily become exfoli-hate, because it's one of the most boring parts of your bodycare routine. But if you really want to be a smooth operator, this extra step can make all the difference, and that's not just buff and nonsense.
>
> So, which are the top products around at the moment for a really good glow job? The best ones use exfoliating particles (like sugar or jojoba beads) to get rid of dead skin

cells. The result? Nobody will accuse you of looking rough.

Exfoliating treatments can also help your body moisturiser penetrate more deeply (just let that sink in). The bottom line: if you haven't been using a body scrub regularly, maybe it's time to get your grit together and pick one from our line-up of the best. Everything will be smooth sailing once you've tried these.

I'm pretty pleased with that so far. I close my laptop, grab an armful of body scrubs from the floor and head upstairs for a shower.

Chapter Two

Almost floral and quite intriguing

It's hard for me to put my finger on what the smell reminds me of, but it's deeply unpleasant. Like when someone has a terrible incident in the bathroom, and then tries unsuccessfully to disguise it with a substandard air freshener. In other words, top notes of Monterey Vanilla, base notes of faeces. According to my beauty therapist, the 'odour' is caused by ammonium thioglycolate – and it's a 'Completely Normal Part Of The Lash Lift Process'. She talks like every word has a capital letter, which is exhausting to listen to, so I tune it out and deal with the weird sensation you get after you've had your eyes closed for ages when you can't work out if they're still closed or not. This is accompanied by an urge to open them really wide, like a feeling of claustrophobia – which is ridiculous, as all I'm doing is lying in a chair with miniature rollers stuck to my eyelids; it's not exactly comparable to being trapped in a lift.

The whole thing is less than enjoyable but it's a) free, as I'm reviewing the treatment for *Glowgetter* and b) all part of my preparation for the Halloween party at *Luscious* magazine. I've decided to go as one of the 'Infected' from *The Last of Us*. This is for several reasons – the first being that wearing a mask will hide my face in a room full of young and/or gorgeous people. Secondly, it will show how current I am (or that I watch a lot of TV). And thirdly, the aforementioned 'Infected' have the potential to look more attractive than a classic zombie, for example the ones from *Shaun of the Dead* (the only other zombie film I've seen). Obviously, they aren't attractive in a conventional way, but some of the fungus bits on them are almost floral and quite intriguing.

What the outfit will be made of, I am not yet sure. If only I could open my eyes right now to google LAST OF US ZOMBIE COSTUME. Damn having to suffer for beauty all the time. But my therapist says I have 'Unusually Stubby Lashes' so needs must. Cassia's are no doubt 'Unusually Fluttery'. She's probably done a reel to tell everyone how she doesn't need lash lifts, accompanied by a lash-related song by someone like Dua Lipa. While doing a dance. Really, really well.

My therapist (or maybe another one, I can't see) taps me on the arm.

'You okay hun?'

So, people really do say that.

'Yup.' I'm beginning to wish I'd ventured into London for this treatment rather than coming here, to Je Suis Belle, which is next to the sandwich shop FILLINGZ on the high street in my local town. I always think FILLINGZ would be a better name for a dentist surgery. I sigh and hear one Hun giggling with another Hun nearby. Maybe they're laughing at my stubby legs now, or my stubby hair. Stub off, everyone.

There must have been a point when it all just stopped being fun. I can't put my finger on when that was exactly. Being a 'Freelance Beauty Journalist' was my dream for a long time – I remember proudly creating an email signature using those exact words when I left my staffer job at *Beautique* magazine in the early Noughties. Far fewer people were freelancing then – it all seemed quite daring and independent, as did my move out of London. Looking back, it was all a diversion after what happened with Kofi – oh and Simon getting married of course. He's older than me but still, people started asking when I'd settle down too. They've stopped asking now.

I make a kind of harrumphing noise as though to punctuate this thought, prompting more tittering from the unseen Huns. This could possibly be the longest hour of my life.

Ricky Martin's 'She Bangs' comes on the radio in the salon. Instead of lifting my lashes, are they trying to break down my resolve in order to extract information, Cold War style? What next, sleep deprivation and the sound of a baby crying? I get that at home anyway, what with the perimenopause and my next-door neighbour's newborn. I'm so uncomfortable right now that if I didn't have to film a reel about this, I'd ask the Hun to come over and finish me off. Not kill me, obviously, just finish the treatment – whether my lashes were sufficiently lifted or not. But I don't want to rush to get home, just to sit looking at myself in my phone camera, holding my chin high in the hope of looking less like former Prime Minister Gordon Brown and more like Millie Bobby Brown.

Ahhh Millie Bobby Brown… She must still only be in her early twenties. Imagine being that young. I would have been at university in Birmingham. Happy, hazy days. Everyone I knew was young then (apart from Mother and Father Pells, of course) but we just took it for granted. All that beauty, energy, freedom… everything seemed to sparkle.

Back then, that Body Shop bean scrub that smelt weird but did a great job on blackheads was all I needed. Nowadays, it takes my face two hours to de-crumple in the morning, hence my excellent list of reasons for being 'camera off' on Zoom. I have so many I hardly ever have to repeat them. What will it be today: 'I'm trialling a confidence app and today's challenge is not to look at my own face <hearty laugh>!' 'My neighbour Mrs Belcher is doing her morning chair yoga and it's really distracting!' 'I read an article that said they use web camera footage to create AI influencers!' I'm so bloody chirpy nobody would ever know I'm sitting here wearing a hyaluronic sheet mask wondering if I should get a face lift or just start a new life with one of those tribes who revere their elders.

But nobody notices, and frankly, nobody cares. It's like I'm being reabsorbed into the ether, with no defined edges anymore – on my face, or anywhere else for that matter. Even my punny headlines aren't that sharp of late, although that's the part I like writing the most. It's as though *Six Degrees Of Curl Separation* in 2018 was my finest hour, and it's been downhill since then. Apart from *How Now Brown Brow* last year, but that was a blip, and I'm not sure everyone got it.

I can hear my phone ringing in my bag, then footsteps.

'Want Me To Give You Your Phone, Hun?'

'Yup. Sure. Thanks. Hold on... who is it?'

More scruffling and a faint giggle – possibly at something in my bag. There's a lot to work with here. It could be the Settlers Wind-eze Plus (a combined symptom of perimenopause and too much cheese), the playing cards (not a middle-aged thing at all; Clock Patience is very mindful), or the coconut, which I bought on the way here, having read that '*According to natural beauty Jessica Alba, the key ingredient to pristine skin is raw coconut.*'

'It's Simon Pells,' says the Hun.

'Just leave it then, thanks,' I say, deciding it will be something about our mother and the late Carol, and the only mournful thing I want to focus on right now is my own face when I do the lash lift Instagram reel.

I slip back into my thoughts... To have that life back, when I wasn't familiar with Settlers, and my vagina worked and was generally a fun place for people to be – and not reminiscent of one of those overgrown dusty cellars in horror films that everyone is too scared to investigate. Everything felt easier, every night was full of promise, because when you are young you are gorgeous by default, and everything just falls into place, including your vagina.

As it no doubt does for Cassia Carver. She seems to have taken middle age and run with it. Imagine that: your heyday is when everyone else is starting to feel depleted. That's quite the competitive advantage. Cassia and I worked together at *Beautique* in the late Nineties and were friends, well, drinking partners, for a while. We would share a round or two of Flaming Sambucas at the odd PR party and tell each other over the music how we'd 'NEVER FELT THIS CLOSE TO ANYONE BEFORE, WE JUST LIKE REALLY GET EACH OTHER, D'YOU KNOW WHAT I MEAN?'

Cassia's star ascended and ascended. Mine, on the other hand, was fairly dim with an occasional flicker, like one of those energy-saving lightbulbs. We both went for the assistant beauty editor role at *Beautique*. I put so much into that interview, with a mock-up of a whole magazine issue (an anti-ageing special) with the headline 'Young Ho!'.

It took me bloody ages, long before the days of Canva. I even glued an eye serum sample onto the cover, because in those days you got a freebie with every magazine. In fact, I've still got a pair of sunglasses from an old issue of *Red* somewhere...

But Cassia got the job, not me, probably because her dad was friends with Egon on the board. We drifted apart after that, aside from the occasional 'Hi sweetie mwah mwah' at parties, and after I moved out of London our careers diverged rapidly with Cassia moving to the coveted editor spot – with her own beauty and lifestyle blog *Cassical* on the side, still usually ranking top five, just behind *@LuxeLooksWithLily*. As video crept in, she took to it as much as I didn't – investing in a selfie stick way before anyone else, while I just hoped the whole thing would pass. I hated – hate – talking to the camera. For some reason my eyes dart about as though there's a fly in the room, and my voice sounds like I'm eating a banana. Seth Rogan has a banana voice all the time, but it's strangely appealing on him. Pretty sure it isn't on me.

And then came Instagram, the place where I feel like I'm at a house party with a bunch of much cooler people, and I'm in the kitchen. No, not even the kitchen – the queue for the downstairs loo. Scrap that – I haven't even been invited to the bloody party. Cassia, however, is dancing in the living room (this is still a metaphor, by the way). Even her profile on Instagram is cool. It just says 'Creator' with a cryptic emoji of some cherries and a quote from *Stranger Things* that I don't get as I've never seen it. Millie Bobby Brown would get it. They're probably following each other.

Cassia posts daily – more than daily if you include the chatty updates from her car on Stories. No banana voice for Cassia, even when ACTUALLY EATING A BANANA, as she was the other day. And it doesn't help that Cassia is the physical opposite of me: blonde, tall, with that posh physique that grew up skiing, playing tennis and being wholesome. The sort of person people describe as 'coltish'. I look like I grew up in an underground bunker by comparison: wiry brown hair, pale skin and a decidedly unathletic body. What's even more annoying is that we're the same age, although Cassia uses hashtags like *#wisewomen* and *#midyouth*.

I roll my eyes at an imaginary Cassia, then wonder if that's even possible when they're sealed shut. How much longer is this going to take? Cassia would make light work of the *Before and After* reel I have to do. Her videos are all dropping clothes on the floor, which then magically appear on her body. She makes vintage cocktails called things like gimlets every Friday – and only has one (*#mindfuldrinking*). She winks at the camera, but it isn't creepy, which I feel it would be if I did it. And she has 134K followers, while I have 2892. A large proportion of mine are American servicemen and pictures of bums in thongs with handles like *@savannah_5638*. I know you're meant to report stuff like that, and I will, but only once I get to 3K.

A tap on my arm from the Hun and finally, it's over – I'm ready to have the miniature rollers removed. The room is blurry and my leg has gone to sleep, which gives me an interesting gait when I head for the door, but at least my eyelashes are a modicum less stubby. Outside, it's tipping down, and my too-long-for-short-legs jeans absorb the rain off the pavement and start flapping about like wet flannels. I linger in the doorway of FILLINGZ and check to see if anyone messaged during my ordeal.

One person, it transpires: Nandy, or Nandita Choudhury to be precise, another of my former colleagues at *Beautique* magazine but unlike Cassia, a 'kindred spirit', as Anne of Green Gables would have said.

> Hey mofo. Are you going to the Twat Fest at Luscious HQ? Let's get BOLLOCKSED and tell them all we hate them. Thoughts?

I laugh, which turns into the coughing fit I've been hoping for since I left the salon, to remove the lash lift stench from my lungs. Thank god FILLINGZ isn't open – I have to lean on the door and make one of those retching noises to conclude matters.

When I look up, eyes watering, there's smiley Gabe Dix, Josie's friend, who I promised myself I'd say hello to next time I saw him. And this is my moment, standing in a sandwich shop doorway, jeans now pretty much wet up to my knees (damn you, osmosis) and zero make-up, as the Hun took it all off To Make The Treatment As Effective As Possible.

'Hi.' My voice comes out in a croak.

'Hi!' Gabe looks surprised then concerned. 'Are you okay?'

I mutter vague words about 'something going down the wrong way' to explain the retching without mentioning my lash lift. But instead of politely moving on, he reaches into his bag, pulls out a bottle of water and hands it to me.

'I just bought it. I mean, I haven't drunk out of it. Would it help?' He's like a hotter version of Gary Barlow, without the tax evasion rumours. I thank him and shake my head.

'Maybe see you at The Perch soon?' he says, putting the bottle back in his bag and, I notice, making quite a meal of refastening it. I also notice he has rather lovely, slightly freckled hands.

'Oh yes please.' My voice is still husky, so I sound like Rod Stewart, but not in a 'Do you think I'm sexy' way. And also – *please*? Why the hell did I say PLEASE? For a writer I have quite a talent for picking the wrong words. In the hope of ending this shameful interaction as quickly as possible, I mutter a goodbye and start walking home, waving over my shoulder. To appear busy and important, I get my phone out and google Halloween costumes. And that's when I spot it, as double-take-inducing as a coconut in a grocer's window: an email from my old editor Merlyn.

> Dear Erica,
> I hope you got the invitation to the party at Luscious that I asked the team to send over. Very much hoping you can make it, especially as I have an exciting proposition for you.
> Until then!
> Baci
> M
>
> Merlyn Vye
> Non-executive Editor, Luscious (UK edition)

I have a feeling. Well two feelings, the first of which can hopefully be remedied by a Settlers Wind-eze Plus. The second is a feeling that something might be about to change. At bloody last.

Chapter Three

Make mine a ham and cheese, please

It's a few days later and my neighbour Josie is in my kitchen. We're sitting where we usually do, but today we're drinking coffee, not wine, and there is a third person at my yellow table, Josie's ten-year-old daughter Héloïse. I feel I should like Héloïse more than I do, but I find her intimidating. There's something of the Wednesday Addams about her: a quiet judgement – and plaits. She also frequently points out what things smell like, which isn't always complimentary. For example, when she arrived today with Josie to help with my Halloween costume, she told me I smelled 'like balloons'. I didn't know how to react so said 'thanks'. Héloïse stared at me for quite a while after that.

Don't get me wrong, I'm grateful for the assistance – the party is next week and I might have non-stubby eyelashes, but the criminally expensive 'wet fungus mask' I got from Etsy covers them up, so requires some strategic trimming. Also, on its own, the mask makes me look like I have an omelette stuck to my face. So the plan is to do some clever body paint and maybe stick some fungal-looking things on my shoulders using eyelash glue. These will be on show as Héloïse has given the dress I'm wearing some apocalyptic 'distressing' with a pair of Ikea kitchen scissors.

The table is quiet as we sip coffee, munch on dark chocolate and sea salt cookies (Héloïse made them, not me, obvs) and mould fungus shapes out of modelling clay, dabbing on green eyeshadow from a Forest Fantasy Luxe Palette (*#gifted*) to make them look more realistic.

'This smells like zoos,' says Héloïse, sniffing the clay.

I ignore her this time and turn to Josie. 'I saw Gabe the other day.'

'Ooooh really?' Josie says. I look at her face. She's got absolutely no make-up on and I find it quite weird. I can't imagine just being out and about during the day having done nothing more than a thorough tooth brushing and an application of SPF. I want to put some contour on her and see what it looks like. She's forty-five, slightly younger than me, but not so much younger that she wouldn't benefit from a bit of help to look more chiselled, let's put it that way. But she does have nice skin, and in a way, I admire her for not feeling like she has to 'put her face on' before she leaves the house.

We've known each other since she moved in opposite a few years ago. We started smiling at each other across the street, then chatting... then became friends. Josie is a brilliant cook, whipping up big Ottolenghi feasts with very little notice, and she often invites me round for company as her French wife, Laure, travels a fair bit for work – something worthwhile to do with 'Médecins'. Sometimes we go to The Perch – a pub nearby, where I met Gabe for the first time. He's a music teacher who uses Josie (a bookkeeper) for his accounts. I watch her sculpting cordyceps out of clay for me, and wonder if I would do the same for her, or anyone. Must give her one of those body scrubs.

'Yes... not sure I was really looking my best though,' I say.

'Well, Gabe isn't the sort of person who would worry about that.'

He's a man, so I seriously doubt that, but I don't say anything, and go back to the green eyeshadow instead.

—

In the week leading up to the party, I spend fifty per cent of my time getting excited about Merlyn's email, and fifty per cent thinking about Gabe's freckly hands – or more specifically, Gabe putting his freckly hands on me, although I can't imagine why he would want to do such a thing. With that in mind, I've started doing a YouTube workout called The Change Challenge With Bethany which has No Jumping (important, as although I can jump, I'm not very good at landing) and focuses on weights, which is 'vital' because at forty-seven I apparently have 'wasting muscle mass' and 'reduced bone density'. Go me! I like Bethany though because she keeps telling me to 'listen to my body' and 'only do what feels good', which on most days is carte blanche to sack the whole thing off after about ten minutes and scroll through Cassia's Instagram stories instead.

Although the bone density thing is depressing, it's less worrying than the flapping bits under my arms, which now appear to have two matching flapping bits on my inner thighs. At least I'm symmetrical. Unfortunately, however, I don't have any weights, and they are too expensive for someone who has spent all their money on a fungus mask. So I'm improvising with two large, weighted fabric doorstops that my Auntie Viv gave me last Christmas. One says, *Remove your shoes or scrub the floor* and the other says *A house is not a home without a cat*. The first seems just plain rude, and the second is confusing, as I don't have a cat, and I'm pretty sure Auntie Viv knows that.

It's the day of the party and on my way to London, I message Nandy.

> In the bogs at Paddington reattaching fake mycelium to my shoulders. You?

> Same girl, same.

> No seriously, where are you? And what are you dressed as?

> Having a tightener in the pub round the corner from the Luscious offices. I'm dressed as a Bollywood star you won't have heard of. Thought I'd culturally appropriate myself. Hurry up will you, mofo?

There are mercifully enough weirdos on the Bakerloo line to allow me to blend in. That's the beauty of London.

However self-conscious you feel, there will always be someone within six feet of you either looking weirder or doing something weirder. It's like that urban myth about never being more than six feet away from a rat. But today that's no myth. There's both a rat on the platform (which looks at my face like I must look at Port Salut) and a man in the carriage with a wooden chopping board on his knee, julienning carrots. Thanks to him, not a single passenger gives me a second glance. I miss London sometimes. Nobody would stare through my living room window here; everyone would be too busy being weird to care what I'm up to.

—

I'm not prepared for how hot – and indeed cool – the party is. It's been a while since I've been to the *Luscious* offices and while other beauty mags have stayed the same, or not survived, *Luscious* has always managed to keep up with the times. For the party, they've opened up both of their office floors and turned them into a Halloween-themed labyrinth, decorated with real (and rattan, obvs) pumpkins and gourds, and crow-themed ceiling lights that give the impression of being constantly dive-bombed by birds, like in that Alfred Hitchcock film. Which is really relaxing.

As Nandy and I walk in, I get the same horrible sinking feeling I do when my brother phones me. The room is a sea of designers, models, journalists, art directors, stylists, influencers… all looking amazing. And not a single one of them has an omelette on their face like I do. I wonder why three Aperol spritzes in The Ox round the corner with Nandy seem to have had the reverse effect than usual on my confidence.

The idea – which seemed like a good one last week – was to hide my bad bits (jowls, sagging, hollowness, forehead lines, crepey lids... the list goes on) and show off my okay ones (shoulders) – but seeing Cassia Carver on the other side of the room looking effortlessly bloody amazing as Margot Tenenbaum, I wonder if there would have been a better way to do that. And I also wonder what Margot Tenenbaum has to do with Halloween, but I suppose one could argue the same about fungal zombies. And also, what was the point in having a lash lift when a) nobody recognises me and b) the first thing my costume makes you think is 'make mine a ham and cheese please'.

'Well, this is shit, obviously,' says Nandy, who looks incredible in a tight orange sari, a beehive hairdo and massive earrings.

'I feel like I might need to drink substantially more to be able to enjoy myself,' I shout at her over the inexplicably loud EDM.

Then I spot Merlyn in the corner. She's dressed as Frida from ABBA, in the curly mullet era, which is also not very Halloweeny. It is however very stylish, unsurprisingly for Merlyn. She waves at us across the room and Nandy and I head over.

'Watch out at three o'clock – Carver incoming,' says Nandy as we push through the crowd.

Cassia intercepts us at an angle, like a cheetah stalking antelope in the Serengeti. I watched a documentary about this once. David Attenborough is amazing. Cassia is just annoying though – she doesn't look remotely sweaty in that fur coat. I'd be at the 'drips on my top lip' stage of the proceedings by now. How does she do it?

'Nandy sweetie! How are you? How's that hot husband of yours?' she says.

'Ash. Ash is fine, thanks Cassia.' Nandy fixes a smile.

'And is that you, Erica?' Cassia pulls a fake bemused face at me.

'It's me, Cassia,' I say. We mwah mwah and Cassia does a kind of weird sigh.

'It's sooooo lovely that you managed to come up here from the... <pointed pause>... country, Erica. And what an effort you made with your outfit. What's the headline for this one? Something about how you couldn't make your Halloween costume without breaking some eggs?' She dissolves into laughter.

Nandy and I stare at her.

'You know, it's like a pun,' Cassia continues. 'You love puns! And your face is like an omelette!'

The exclamation marks are exhausting.

'Aren't the decorations... decadent?' She keeps going. 'Let's take a selfie together!'

I don't say anything, so Nandy takes over. 'No, thanks... We'll catch up with you later Cassia, we're just going to get a drink.' She drags me off in the direction of Merlyn before Cassia has a chance to reply.

When we reach her, grabbing drinks from a tray on the way, Merlyn looks at Nandy and grins. 'Are you Mumtaz from *Brahmachari*, Nandita? How fabulous.'

'I knew *you* would get it straight away Merl, you're such a legend,' says Nandy.

Merlyn turns to me and laughs, ABBA wig quivering. 'And Erica, that's quite the look, my dear.'

'I know,' I say. 'Not sure what I was thinking, to be honest.'

'It's wonderful,' says Merlyn. 'I so enjoyed *The Last of Us*.'

Merlyn has managed to make me feel like I wrote the screenplay, rather than just bought a mask on Etsy. I love her for that and feel better, or maybe drunker, I'm not sure. We stand and talk and laugh about people's costumes until Nandy wanders off to dance.

'So… what was the proposition you mentioned?' I say to Merlyn.

'Oh yes… well. The thing is…' she trails off. 'It's rather disconcerting speaking to you looking like that. But it certainly confirms your interest in transformation, which is promising.'

I smile underneath the omelette. Here it comes – a commission. Sounds like it could be a big one if it's going to transform my career, and frankly, I could do with the cash to buy some dumbbells.

'Erica, an opportunity has come up to try a new beauty treatment and I think you would be the ideal person to do so.' She scans my mask for a reaction. Behind it, my face has fallen.

'Hear me out,' continues Merlyn. 'This isn't like anything you might have tried before.'

'What is it, some new kind of Botox?' I sound snappy. But no wonder. Over the years, I've tested treatment after serum after supplement. There was the much-hyped DermaLift Pro™ facial in 2015, which promised the *age-defying beauty of Salma Hayek* – but left me with cheeks so lumpy I looked like I was storing acorns for the spring. Oh and Eterna®, that hand-held electrical contouring device that Jennifer Aniston was rumoured to be using. Thank god it was a freebie, as it did precisely nothing and I eventually gave it to Simon's kids, saying it was an angry alien robot. Then there was that plankton supplement I had to suck out of a sachet 'on rising'. I'd admittedly agreed to trial it due to the potential for a funny headline (*Licence To Krill, Krill Or Cure*... this one was like shooting fish in a barrel, pun very much intended). But it made no difference to my fine lines and uneven pigmentation, and tasted like the fish paste Mother Pells used to put in my sandwiches in the Eighties.

'Merlyn, I've tried it all. You of all people should know that. I'm not interested in looking "fresher". And the alternative is looking like Mufasa. So...'

'This is different, my dear. This is...' She leans in. 'Quite extraordinary.' She pronounces every single syllable: *ex-tra-or-din-air-ee*.

Maybe this is the revolutionary new treatment that I've heard whispers about from some of my editors... I soften a little, feeling special. 'Tell me more.'

'It's called WULT®, which stands for "Woke Up Like This". It's top secret at the moment, Erica, but seriously, Yuvana Labs who created it think they might have struck gold. It's nanotechnology. D'you know what that is?'

It rings a bell... then I remember. It's in *Ant Man*. Paul Rudd really is the gift that keeps on giving.

'Like mini robots?'

'Pretty much. They go into your stem cells and reset the ageing process. So far, it's only been tested on rats and a handful of clinical human trials, but Erica, my dear, we're all *very* excited.'

For some reason all I can think of is the rat that stared at me on the tube earlier. Was it a sign?

'That sounds very erm... *new*? I think I've heard about it though.'

'It is new, Erica. But it's ready. And safe. And...' She looks over her shoulder as if anyone listening would possibly be able to hear us over the music. 'We think it will make those who have the treatment look...'

I can't work out if Merlyn is pausing for effect or if she can't remember. But I'm quite invested by now.

'Twenty years younger.'

'Specifically twenty?'

'Specifically twenty. Which will make *you* look mid-twenties of course.'

'This sounds... insane,' I say. 'Totally insane.'

'But in a good way, don't you think, my dear?'

'I'm not sure, Merlyn. I mean how would people even recognise me if I suddenly looked that much younger?'

Merlyn purses her lips. 'Do you think anyone recognises you tonight?'

Good point. As I take it all in, Nandy reappears.

'Hello ladies, have you finished chatting? Who's up for a shimmy?' Nandy always ends up enjoying herself.

Merlyn laughs as Nandy spins her around. 'I'm definitely not too old for that.' As they head off, Merlyn looks over her shoulder at me.

'Think about it my dear. Yuvana Labs have got some promo ideas that could earn you some really decent money. And WULT® is going to cost £250,000 when it's launched, so this might be your only chance – unless you've got some savings up your sleeve...'

I very much do NOT have any savings, to the point where I even went through some old coats before I left this afternoon to see if I could find a tenner. Instead, I found some Extra Strong Mints, a Clinique Chubby Stick and what was either a shopping list with just 'bread' on it, or some kind of 'note to self' simply stating 'dread'. Who knows? And now, here I am, sweating under my omelette, watching Cassia out of the corner of my eye with her giant Hermès Birkin on her knee, holding court. Ahead of me, on the dancefloor, Nandy is teaching Merlyn some Bollywood moves, which go surprisingly well with the decidedly un-Bollywood music.

Twenty years younger? Holy crap.

Chapter Four

Every pore exuding Aperol

I'm googling *does the perimenopause make your breath smell* when Simon calls. I answer before I realise I haven't yet done my 'Morning Shed', so as I'm still wearing both my tooth whitening trays and mouth tape, my voice comes out like I'm inside a bottle.

A 'Morning Shed', incidentally, has nothing to do with those wooden huts at the bottom of the garden frequented by middle-aged men, and instead means shed as in 'cast off'. It's a viral trend from a year or so ago that I have got *very* into after I tested it for *Glowgetter*, due to its anti-... sorry... *pro*-ageing benefits. It consists of trussing (there really is no other word for it) yourself up at night with a variety of masks, tape to pull back saggy skin and to keep your mouth shut so you breathe through your nose, heatless curlers, a giant bonnet to protect your hair, and last but not least, a massive silk sleep mask. The overall effect is nothing short of ghoulish, I admit, but in the morning you 'shed' it all and I believe there is a chance that I look zero-point-zero-point-one per cent better and/or younger as a result. Which is enough for me.

'It sounds like you're trapped in a well, Erica. Are you still in bed?'

'I am Simon, yes,' I say, yanking out my teeth-whitening trays and immediately wishing I hadn't answered my phone. 'I had a very important work event last night and thankfully unlike you I don't have to get up for any children. And also, it's none of your business.'

'It's eleven-thirty a.m., Erica.'

'I realise that. I didn't sleep well.' I peel off my gold silicone under-eye patches, and then remove the tape on my nasolabial folds (smile lines to the layman) hoping Simon can't hear the weird noise it makes.

'Mum said you phoned her last night and it sounded like you were drunk.'

I take a second to try to remember if it was an accident or if I was calling my mother to drunkenly shout, I'M SORRY I'M SUCH A DISAPPOINTMENT TO YOU or similar. I decide it was definitely a pocket dial.

'That's ludicrous, Simon. I'm forty-seven years old. Why does everyone in this family treat me like a badly behaved child?'

'Because you've got previous, Erica, and you know it.'

'Ever heard of redemption, Simon? Anyway, why are you phoning? Surely not just to have a go at me?'

I say 'surely not' but that is exactly the sort of thing Simon would do.

'No, actually, Erica. I wanted to talk to you about Mum.'

Saved by the bell – the front doorbell rings, right on cue. Must be my Deliveroo from the garage. Twenty minutes round trip is too much for me today, with every pore exuding Aperol and the remains of some wet fungus on my shoulders.

'I have to go,' I say, hoping he heard the doorbell too. 'Someone important is at the door.'

It's true, M&S food can't wait. 'And they're here for a meeting,' I add, to give it some sort of credibility. 'A neighbourhood watch meeting.'

I think I took that too far.

—

I can't really remember a time when Simon and I were close. Four and a half years' age gap doesn't sound like that much but when Simon started school, I was still in nappies. 'We tried to get you out of them earlier,' according to Mother Pells, 'but it seemed like you didn't mind sitting on... *mess*.' After school and at weekends, Simon and his friend Martin would take over the back garden of the house in Saltford where we grew up. My earliest memories were of the boys making my Sindy kiss their Action Men, Martin pulling my hair, and Simon telling me he'd hoped he would be an only child before I came along – and worse, that Mother and Father Pells did too.

School was fine – the local primary in Saltford, then the academy in Bristol. Not a period I look back on with much pain, or indeed much pleasure. Simon was five years above me because of when our birthdays fell, so our lives rarely overlapped. When they did, I found him serious, condescending, never my equal. We were 'latch key kids' – our parents both working long hours for an aerospace company in Filton – although at least money wasn't ever much of a problem. But it meant that the minute we got home from school, Simon and I disappeared to opposite ends of the house until *Rentaghost* came on, our paths only crossing briefly in the kitchen where we would grill Findus Crispy Pancakes in silence (he favoured minced beef, I preferred Cheddar cheese) and plunder the biscuit tin for Wagon Wheels and Trios. It suited us both just fine.

I got through it, I did okay, I made some friends, some of whom I stayed in touch with for a while on Facebook, but nobody's really on that these days. My grades got me to Birmingham University to study social anthropology because, well, it looked quite interesting, and also most of the lectures started at eleven a.m. I probably should have done English, looking back. But unleashed from Somerset – and away from Mother and Father Pells, who seemed to prefer Simon (although Father Pells did sometimes dote on his 'funny little Erry') – it was as though I'd been waiting for freedom. Fuelled by *CK One* and Moscow Mules, 'Show Me Love' by Robin S became the soundtrack to my emancipation. Show me love – show me any strong emotion for that matter – after a life hitherto on the receiving end of indifference.

Simon did business and management at Exeter and made quite the name for himself at the surf club, but he'd graduated and moved back to Bristol before I even started at university. From then on, we only saw each other at family gatherings – until one Christmas, Simon came home with Alannah. Australian, always in a good mood, she brought something out in Simon that seemed to make my parents love him even more. Simon and Alannah married in Bath, settled down, and my nephews, Oli and Sam (now seventeen and fifteen), came along. Meanwhile, and by contrast (as usual), I was having that 'difficult year' after Kofi and I broke up. But, Alannah and the children seemed to soften everything around the edges, and I was briefly glad I had moved out of London to be an auntie and to be closer to my parents, who'd retired by then and moved from Bristol to the Wiltshire town where I now live. Things all seemed brighter, for a while at least.

—

Ten minutes later and I'm eating my M&S Farmhouse Cheddar Cheese Sandwich on the living room floor like that sea lion did with an unfortunate penguin on a documentary I saw last night. The phone call with Simon has put me in the kind of bad mood you only get when you have a stinking hangover. What is it with my family? Admittedly, there were some pretty crazy clubbing years when I went a bit Lindsay Lohan – then the awful thing happened, which led to the questionable move back to Wiltshire. But I am not exactly a lost cause. I'm just in a rut. In need of a change – any change. Something more interesting than watching *The Great British Bake Off* and eating a Raspberry Royale, which is what I'm about to do now.

This whole WULT® thing could be exactly the change I need. Last night, I pulled the mask off in the bathrooms of the *Luscious* offices at the end of the party, to avoid attracting any unwanted attention on the way home. Chance would be a fine thing – catching sight of myself in the mirror, I decided I looked more gruesome *without* the zombie costume. Seriously, what the hell happened to my neck? I hadn't really noticed before, but it seems to have developed lines that run right around it, like segments of a worm.

Then, sitting on the 22:49 to Swindon, I thought, you know what? Just do it, Erica. What's the alternative? Gradually retreating into higher and higher polo necks to hide my nematode neck? Constantly lifting my head up and smiling as much as possible to create some semblance of a jawline, like a meerkat who's had some particularly good news? And locking the door to my overgrown dusty cellar once and for all? I'm as out of date as those rotating electric face cleansing brushes that everyone had in the Noughties.

And now that I'm safely at home, working my hangover like a pro – M&S lunch and some Say Cheese Chaumes in the fridge for later, with every chance I will rewatch *The Good Place* – I am even more sure. I'm the perfect candidate for any sort of procedure like this: I've seen enough needles to be completely unfazed by them. When the nurse came round for Father Pells in his last few weeks, I'd watch when she got the stuff out to give him an injection, fascinated. Maybe I missed my calling, although I doubt it as I got a D in biology GCSE.

'With all these injections, I'm holier than thou, Erry,' Father Pells would say, sniggering.

He moved slowly in his recliner chair, with his hands bunched up and bent over like long paws, reminding me of a documentary I watched once about sloths. When I held them, the mottled skin seemed to slide about over the surface like a wet carrier bag. Life was ebbing away and all I wanted to do was transfer mine to him. Why hadn't anyone worked out how to do that yet? Like charging your phone from your laptop. You'd think it would be pretty elementary. Here, have my vitality, you deserve it more than me. I was his baby girl... never his old girl. I am becoming someone he would never even recognise.

Nothing like an Aperol hangover to put you in a good mood... I half laugh and half sniff at my own misery, then think about WULT® and smile. Why the hell not? It might even be what finally makes my parents – or *parent* I should say – take notice of me. And it's not just that. I've tried every other possible way to feel better about myself and I'm still practically a hermit. It's not going to get any better is it? We're all going to end up intravenously morphined out of our heads with sloth hands. Either that or *The Inevitable*. Oh god, now I sound like my mother…

The doorbell goes again. Excellent, the Deliveroo rider must have found my missing samosa. I haul myself up off the floor to open the front door. Why do my ankles seem to take longer to get going than the rest of me these days? I was hoping I'd at least get to fifty before needing to know what 'arch support' means. Mind you, if it's as groundbreaking as the rumours suggest, maybe this WULT® thing will fix that too.

However, it's Josie, who does not appear to have a samosa about her person, but instead a large Tupperware box and a bunch of those orange flowers that look like lanterns. 'I brought you some butternut squash gnocchi. And these.' She sticks the flowers under my nose. 'I can never remember what they're called.'

She looks like the personification of autumn, wearing brown cords and an oatmeal colour jumper with a roll neck so big it's like a scarf.

'Thanks,' I say.

'How was the party – did the magazine give you a commission?'

I'm not really sure what to say, and I certainly don't want to tell her about WULT® yet. I look at Josie's smiling face, the Tupperware glistening with condensation, the flowers… and it all just feels so kind and lovely – the polar opposite of the thoughts I was having about my depressing existence just minutes ago. So, I burst into tears. I don't think I've ever cried in front of Josie, except maybe that time when we drank all that Gavi and I told her why I broke up with Kofi, and about that terrible night.

'Erica – oh no… I'm sorry, are you okay?' She ushers me into the hallway and puts down the gnocchi and flowers so she can hug me.

'Yes. Sorry. Just the hangover… I'm fine. Ignore me.' I compose myself almost as quickly as I started crying. 'All good. And yes, I might have a commission.'

'That's great!' Josie throws her arms around me again. 'Well done you.'

'Yes, well done me…'

I try to shake off the self-pity that always bubbles up when people are nice to me at my most miserable, and focus instead on the possibility that the misery might change into something more positive soon. I go quiet and Josie seems to sense I would rather be alone and backs out onto the pavement, continuing to eye me with concern.

'Why don't you come to dinner on Saturday? Keith is coming too. We could go to The Perch after, if you like?'

The mention of The Perch immediately makes me think of Gabe, and the retching/wet-flannel-jeans incident, which then makes my eyes fill up once more, although more out of retrospective embarrassment than sadness. Josie looks alarmed again.

'Only if you feel like it, Erica,' she says, as if asking someone extremely elderly if they want to go for a walk.

I nod. Then I remember the goodie bag from the party, and grab it from the hall table. I thrust it at her, despite knowing she won't use half of what's in it.

'I got you this. There's a lip mask in it.'

'Thanks, Erica, that's really kind of you.' She doesn't look in the bag. 'Hopefully see you on Saturday. Oh, and the gnocchi just need two minutes in the microwave – and some parmesan on the top, if you have it.'

'Of course I do.' I manage a smile as I shut the door.

Chapter Five

Jameela Jamil is truly blessed

One happy day I got IDed in Sainsbury's while buying a bottle of Primitivo. 'What?!' I snorted with ill-concealed delight when the assistant came over and asked me for my driving licence. 'I'm nearly 50!' I wasn't, of course, I was only about forty-three, I just added that for a bit of drama. The shine was taken off the experience quite quickly when the assistant, who was a young man of about twenty-three, asked me to take off my sunglasses, which I was wearing indoors after trying the new Socket To Me™ rejuvenating eye treatment the day before (mainly because of the name). When I did remove them, he immediately said 'Oh yeah, that's fine'. I mean COME ON, take a second to have a look, it can't be so instantly obvious? I comforted myself with the fact that from behind, my outfit must have looked particularly youthful even if the top half of my face didn't. I also prayed that one day such a thing would happen again – but when I wasn't wearing sunglasses.

It never has. But today, as I stand in the self-serve checkout queue, it occurs to me that if I get this WULT® treatment, maybe it will. I wonder what the assistant will think then, when they see my date of birth, so very comfortably in the 1970s, on my driving licence? I guess for the moment, with WULT® not available to the public, I'll have to explain why I look so young. Something about 'drinking plenty of water', 'good genes' or 'always wearing an SPF', like celebrities who've had tons of work done. I've always wanted to tell the same lies as famous people.

I've been researching Yuvana Labs ever since I got home from the Halloween party and for someone who has become quite the expert at googling over the years (must add that to my CV), I am disappointed by how little I've been able to uncover. There seems to be a 'Dr M' involved, and also someone called Professor B, but Yuvana isn't registered with Companies House, and I can't find an address either. I hope they're not dodgy, but I'm sure if Merlyn is involved they won't be. I'll ask her when I speak to her – she said she was going to give me a couple of days to think about it.

The person in front of me appears to have never used a self-serve checkout before, or indeed money. My phone ringing is a welcome distraction.

'Yo, mofo.'

'Hi Nandy...'

'You okay? You sound a bit... weird?'

'I'm fine, I'm fine,' I say. 'I'm whispering because I'm in Sainsbury's. I also had a rough night. The baby next door. Oh, and crazy dreams. And peeing every hour. Getting older sucks.'

'Doesn't it just? You should get some bloody HRT and some of that vag cream I was telling you about. At least if *that* warms up again you can stop peeing all the time and even get some action. That'll put a smile on your face. Even if it's DIY action. IF YOU KNOW WHAT I MEAN.' Nandy cackles down the phone.

'Yes, I know what you mean.' I'm slightly self-conscious having this conversation in a supermarket. Although I do spare a thought at this moment for my Goop Ultraplush Self-Heating G-Spot Vibrator (*#gifted*), which is living out its life somewhere at the back of my pants drawer. Probably not what Gwyneth Paltrow had in mind for it.

'Okay, well... I won't keep you if you're busy peri-menopausing,' says Nandy. 'Just wanted to see what the latest was with Merl. Did she give you a commission?'

'Yeah... kind of.'

'Excellent.'

'Well, it's more like a treatment thing to trial for *Luscious*. A facial.' I decide now might be as good a time as any to gently introduce the concept.

'NOICE. Something super posh, I'm sure. It's Merlyn after all. She's got such a soft spot for you.'

'She's just kind.'

'To you, more than anyone.'

'Yeah, I suppose... I wonder why that is.' I feel like we're going off topic.

'I think you remind her of her daughter, I'm sure she told me that once. Or someone did. You know, the daughter she doesn't talk to who went to live in Canada or something. Anyway, so it's posh, the treatment?'

'Really posh. Could be a gamechanger.'

'Hark at you. Well, as long as you get to write a punny headline for it I'm sure you'll be fine. Right, better go, I'm on the *Metro* features desk this week. I just popped out for some Bonjela. Living the dream, my friend, living the fucking dream.'

'Aren't we all...' I mutter as I watch the person in front of me try to find 'Cheese Twist' on the bakery menu, and stop short of shouting 'IT'S NEXT TO THE CINNAMON WHIRL!'

I should have told Nandy about WULT®, I suppose. It isn't lying though, just withholding information... Not that I'm keen on that either. The only people I don't mind lying to are editors, about whether a feature I haven't even started yet is 'nearly finished!'. Speaking to Nandy, it makes me realise I'm too embarrassed to tell the truth. She has a way of being brutally honest about everything – not to be mean, but just because she is one of the most down-to-earth people you could ever meet.

When Nandy started at *Beautique*, I had already been there a few months. I watched her from across the office on her first day, in her low rise bootcut jeans, chain belt, baker boy cap. I didn't just want to be friends with her because she was like a cool Asian Kate Moss with a Birmingham accent; I wanted to be friends with her because she looked like she didn't care what anyone thought of her. Being around Nandy made me feel like I cared a tiny bit less too – as though little particles of Nandy's sparkling nonchalance settled on me, making me feel like a bolder version of myself.

She's an only child, and her mother Anu died when she was eighteen. As Nandy puts it, 'a fucking inconvenient age to lose a parent'. Her father was broken, and has never really mended. So, Nandy just ploughs on, swearing, laughing, holding it all together – for her father, for the memory of Anu, for her husband, Ash, and the kids and, quite often, for me too. She told me once that if she stopped for a second and thought about it all – *really* thought about it – she'd find she had thirty years of tears to catch up on, and 'nobody has time for that bollocks'.

She's the only London friend I have who comes over to Wiltshire to see me, and the only one who really cared when I left. She loyally treks across the city from Leytonstone to get the train at Paddington, armed with a bag of weed and obscure ingredients like asafoetida to make curries in my kitchen using Anu's old recipes. We talk and talk and laugh and eat. Once, not long after Father Pells died, we got really stoned and were so immersed in a David Attenborough documentary about toucans we decided to take notes.

The next day we walked all the way through the fields to Lacock and read the ramblings out loud, snorting hysterically as we stomped along in our inappropriate shoes – Nandy: cowboy boots, me: FitFlops *(#gifted)*. Amongst other incomprehensible nonsense, I'd written that 'toucans cannot chew', as if this would be an important piece of knowledge to remember, and also that 'they are NOT (underlined about five times) graceful in the sky'. I'd also put 'ungraceful' in brackets after this as though to make it extra clear. Then in Nandy's handwriting it said, 'THEY HAVE A DARK SIDE', although neither of us could remember what that was.

Then last night's mixed vegetable sambar (followed by a cheese board, obvs) came back to haunt Nandy and she had to go and shit behind a tree. I was laughing so much my cheeks hurt for days – it was the first time I'd laughed since my father's funeral five weeks before. And now I feel like I'm not being honest, and Nandy isn't here with that wonderful big sisterliness. But I'll tell her soon. I'm pretty sure she's going to be delighted for me.

Later, at home, I'm eating cheese and watching a YouTube clip I found of Gabe playing 'Shallow' from the Lady Gaga film on the piano with one of his students. He's really good. I zoom in on his hands and wonder if YouTube tells you who is looking at your videos and/or how many times. Paranoid, I switch to Instagram and there's Cassia, posting pictures of her Margot Tenenbaum outfit: 'It's time for the *Luscious* Halloween party *#GRWM* (Get Ready With Me)!' She even posted some pictures from the party itself. I scan them and can see one with me in the background, talking to Merlyn. I look completely bizarre from the side with my mask on, all slouched next to Merlyn with her wonderful posture. Thankfully, due to my costume, nobody would know it's me.

I spread some Chaumes on a cracker. It's quite a punchy one, with base notes of my mother's cat Eartha's litter tray... It's disappointing, as Say Cheese normally gets it so right. It isn't really helping my two-day hangover either. I push the tray aside and put *The Good Place* on, wondering immediately how anyone can be that tall and slim but have such big tits. Jameela Jamil is truly blessed.

My phone pings. It's Merlyn.

> Erica my dear. Any thoughts on what we talked about at the party? M

I know I am getting Chaumes on my phone but I want to respond quickly.

> Hi Merlyn. I've been thinking about it. Are Yuvana Labs legitimate? I couldn't find much about them online…

I can see that *Merlyn is typing…* Hurry up Merlyn, I need to go and wash this cat litter off my hands. Then the message appears:

> Absolutely! I've been consulting for them for a while, my dear.

> OK. And what about the procedure itself, will I have to stay in overnight?

> Heavens no. It's non-invasive. Well, only mildly invasive. And just one tiny injection to help you relax. But hardly any down time!

Well, that's better than a month in hiding, I suppose. I'm not Linda Evangelista; I have Sainsbury's to get to.

> How long will the effects last?

> It's a reset. You'll just start getting older again from your new age. You'll quite literally turn back time!

I stop typing just to take this in, and for long enough for Merlyn to message again.

> I understand you might have reservations Erica, but I'd like to offer this to you rather than the next person on the list.

Oh wow. I'm top of a list? Nice. Wonder who else is on it… Holy crap. Bet it's bloody Cassia.

> Can I ask who else you have in mind?

> Cassia Carver is next. You know her from Beautique, don't you? And then Imani Diamond, and Lily from @LuxeLooksWithLily.

My Chaumy fingers are sliding about typing as fast as I can. I'm not losing out on anything to Cassia Carver again.

> Merlyn – you know what? It's such a great opportunity. I'm in. Thank you.

> That's wonderful news, Erica!

> One thing: it's reversible right?

> It is, although as far as Yuvana Labs are concerned, who would want to turn the clock forward again once it's been turned back?

I'm not sure if I'm meant to answer that, so I don't. I can see Merlyn is typing again.

> I'll send you some details for the pre-treatment consultation in the next couple of weeks. How tremendous, Erica!

Later still, I lie in bed attempting to sleep, listening to the baby next door crying, and wondering if I need the loo enough to get up. But of course, now that I've thought about it, I'll *have* to get up. This is middle age: thirty-three per cent planning the next pee, thirty-three per cent avoiding cameras, thirty-three per cent trying to work out what terminal illness is looming based on some random pain – and the one per cent is reserved for one's own particular weirdness, because I think everyone gets a bit weird after forty-five. I, for instance, talk to the pigeons on my patio and, firmly believing them to be the same pigeon, call them all Douglas.

Maybe I'm too middle-aged for anything, even a nanobot, to restore my 'factory settings'. Maybe it won't work. But maybe it will – and frankly, what have I got to lose? Nothing's going to change. I'm going to spend my last, what have I got, twenty-five, thirty years (who knows, maybe less) slathering on neck creams that I didn't pay for that don't even work, and googling local music teachers who will run a mile when they see my saggy old, not remotely Jameela Jamil, tits. So frankly, dodgy or not, Yuvana Labs – you're my only bloody hope.

Chapter Six

There's a deli in Devizes

It's Friday, and although I'm heading over to Josie's tomorrow evening, tonight I have nothing better to do than watch Cassia Carver's weekly live vintage cocktail-making. (From a *Glowgetter* account I still have the log-ins for; I'm not a total amateur.) I've been obsessing about Cassia even more than usual recently, for some reason. Anyway, I pour myself a giant glass of Rioja and wait until about ten other people have joined her live, so I don't look too conspicuous.

Before we get to the main event (making a Snowball, as it's heading towards Christmas), we have to endure some 'tablescaping', which involves Cassia waving a red tablecloth in the air like she's trying to antagonise a passing bull, then laying out lots of #*eclectic* gold plates 'sourced from local antique markets', one of which I definitely saw in Dunelm in Swindon last weekend. She's twittering on about #*simplepleasures* while she waits for 'everyone to join her in the scullery'. I mean, what? It's not bloody *Downton Abbey*, Cassia. She's also wearing a belted brown jumper dress that would make me look like Friar Tuck. So annoying.

As making a Snowball takes about thirty seconds (you just add lemonade to Advocaat, let's be honest with ourselves here), Cassia strings it out for about twenty minutes by telling some tedious anecdote about how when she was a child she used to think Advocaat was made of avocados, which is clearly made up as no child has even heard of Advocaat and would certainly not care/have ever thought about what it's made of. She also keeps doing that irritating wink at the camera and then a kind of bobbing curtsy thing when she sticks the maraschino cherry in the top of the Snowball. I really want her to spill it. So, slightly Rioja-ed up, I start typing 'snow bollocks more like' into the live chat but then remember *Glowgetter* absolutely loves her, and doesn't particularly love me, so delete it.

I wonder if she knows about the WULT® thing? I'm guessing that as I said yes, Merlyn wouldn't have needed to tell anyone else on the list. I wonder why I was top of said list – it's not like I've got that many Instagram followers. Maybe it's just Merlyn keeping an eye out for me, like she always seems to. But I also wonder why Merlyn didn't do it herself. Mind you, she's about sixty-five, maybe it's not worth it if you're only going to come out the other side looking forty-five... pretty much pointless. I finish my Rioja and get an early night.

The following day, I have no plans other than an intensive getting ready session before I go to Josie's. I spend the morning wearing a double chin reducing peptide mask I was sent to try, (which has the appearance of a damp jockstrap that loops around your ears) while I work on an article for the *BeautyBuzz* website, which hasn't commissioned me in ages. I'd originally pitched an idea about the new 'glass skin' trend that teenagers seem to love, and the dangers of really young girls using the high-potency Korean products you need to achieve it. It was called *Please Keep Off The Glass*. Anyway, they weren't keen on my 'wait till you get to my age' stance (Seoul-based ChokChokie is their biggest sponsor) so the one they went for is about salicylic acid toners and whether they're safe to use, and I've decided to call it *Peel Or No Peel*. To say I'm pleased with that headline would be a massive understatement.

Thanks to this, which must surely mean I'm getting my mojo back when it comes to puns, and now that I've decided to go ahead with the WULT® treatment (and actually have a date for the pre-treatment consultation next week), I'm in a reasonable mood as evening arrives. I'm also trying a new contouring make-up trick for jowls, because now that there's a possibility of looking younger on the horizon (if the treatment actually works, that is), they are bugging me more than ever. It's all about using bronzer and highlighter to create shadows under your chin that aren't really there. In dim lighting, and as long as I make sure I speak to people straight on and not at an angle, it seems as though it may work. In fact, it could even be a 'contour de force'…

—

Josie's door knocker is shaped like a bumblebee and quite heavy, and I find it impossible not to slam it down really hard, making what could be considered an impolite level of noise for a Saturday night dinner guest who hasn't really brought anything of note with them. Well, I do have a body scrub for Josie and some Kiehl's for men stuff for Keith. But the bottle of Orvieto Classico I also brought is only two-thirds full. And as for the chrysanthemums, which I bought last week to give to Mother Pells as an apology for pocket dialling her, every single petal except two has dropped off on the thirty-second walk to Josie's – leaving a trail of white exclamation marks along the road.

Josie is cooking her signature chicken with potatoes and prunes for me and our friend Keith. Keith – an acerbic, moustachioed green energy consultant – lives in a converted chapel in a village a few miles outside the town, and his husband Stephen is, like Josie's wife Laure, often away. Josie and Keith call themselves 'work widows' and moan about and miss their spouses in equal measure.

Héloïse opens the door, hair shiny with head lice lotion. Okay, what do I smell of today, Héloïse? At least I don't have nits.

'You smell of poo,' she says.

Wow, no frills tonight. I smile because, after all, Josie is pretty much my only friend nearby, if you don't count my mother, which you don't. And also, my mother lives twenty minutes away, which is not nearby, in the same way that the M&S garage is not nearby.

'Fox poo,' continues Héloïse, without breaking eye contact.

'Right. That's quite specific,' I say. 'Anyway, is your mum…'

'There.' Héloïse interrupts and points to the road behind me and indeed, there is a fox shit, and indeed, it has my footprint right in the middle of it. I do that thing where you lift your feet and look at the bottom of your shoes, one after another, like you're practising the Charleston.

'Take them off.'

'Okay.' Why do I always obey her?

I walk into Josie's cottage, holding both boots, shouting, 'I'M TAKING THEM OUT THE BACK, THEY'VE GOT FOX SHIT ON THEM,' and at such a pace that I inadvertently scrape one of them on the hall wall. I spot Héloïse rolling her eyes.

—

Later, after the chicken, Josie is squatting in the back garden wearing rubber gloves, hosing my boots down. A few feet away, I stand with Keith in Josie's (far too small) 'gardening Birkenstocks', smoking some of Nandy's weed that I found in my pants drawer.

'I don't feel you're apologising quite enough, Ms Pells,' says Keith, sniggering.

'Sorry Jose. And in my defence, Keith, I did clean the hall wall…'

'It's okay, Erica.' Josie's voice is muffled as she's pulled her top up over her nose to hide the smell. 'I'd rather do it myself. To be honest they're cleaner than they were before.'

'Oh really? Great. Thanks,' I say.

'Are you both ready to go to the pub when I've finished? Evelyn from next door is coming round in ten to keep an eye on Héloïse. I just need to put the leftovers in the fridge for Laure. She's back from Geneva tomorrow. She loves the bits around the edges where the pomegranate molasses go all Marmitey on the potatoes…'

She goes back inside muttering something about Tupperware while I hand the joint to Keith.

'I got the Kiehl's face wash you like, and the hand salve,' I say, pleased I actually remembered to bring them over.

'You're an angel. My dry cuticles are indebted to you.' He eyes me closely. 'You look foxy, Erica.' He snorts with laughter at his own joke. 'Too soon?'

'Thanks darling,' I say. 'I'm trying a new make-up thing.'

'You certainly are, girly-pop! The Perch won't know what's hit it.'

He throws the end of the joint into next door's garden, and we head back inside, laughing.

In the kitchen, Héloïse, who has spoiled the candlelit vibe from dinner somewhat by putting the big light on, is setting up UNO on the table to play with Evelyn. She eyes us suspiciously, sniffing loudly, then her eyes rest on me.

'Erica, what's that on your face? Were you at Violet's party too?'

I stare at her, bemused.

'I didn't get my face painted,' she goes on, 'because I wanted Greta Thunberg and the woman said I had to stick to the list of animals.'

How strong was that weed? I have no idea what she's on about. I turn to Keith for guidance.

'You do have something on your cheeks, Erica,' says Keith, 'but I'm fairly sure it's not residual face paint from Violet's party.'

JEEZ, I know what it is. It's my bloody contouring, which is not cut out for kitchen lighting. I walk over to the mirror on the end wall and look at myself. Admittedly, it's not great, but it will be fine at The Perch, I'm sure. It's Héloïse's fault for putting on that million-watt light.

'It's my contour.' I'm conscious I sound snappy.

'There wasn't a condor on the list,' says Héloïse.

'Contour. It's a trompe l'oeil make-up trick for a sculpted jawline.' That's what it said on the YouTube video anyway. 'It looks great in low lighting.'

'There was an eagle though?' says Héloïse.

Just as I am wondering how much further down this bird of prey cul-de-sac we can go, Keith, sensing my discomfort, steers me out of the kitchen and up the hall towards the front door, shouting to Josie that we'll see her in the pub.

—

Keith and I arrive at The Perch – a big barn of a place, all flagstone floors scattered with Persian rugs and high, timber-framed ceilings. It's Saturday, so it's busy, warm and bright. I feel both at home in such a noisy, crowded place (thanks to my clubbing days) yet simultaneously not really that used to it, because I live on my own and interact mainly with the postman and a half-French child.

As Keith goes to the bar, I find a too-small-for-three table, dragging an extra chair over. I scan the bar to see if I can see Gabe, and wonder if the lighting is too much for my trompe l'oeil make-up, which I'm now, thanks to said half-French child, concerned hasn't worked. Annoying really, as the YouTube video (*Hide Sagging Jowls With This Simple Contour Trick!*) was quite an investment, at fifteen minutes long. I'm just wondering if I should go to the loo and check it in the mirror when Josie appears.

'You okay, Erica?' says Josie.

'Yes... why?'

'No reason, just checking in on you.' Josie is always checking in.

'Thanks Josie. I'm fine. I'm good.'

'Gabe's over there by the way.' Josie directs her gaze in a diagonal direction behind me, just as Keith returns from the bar and puts down his pale ale, Josie's G&T and my red wine.

'Who's over where?' he says.

'Gabe,' says Josie. 'Erica fancies him. In the corner. Looks a bit like Gerard Butler. Checked shirt.'

Keith lowers his glasses and peers over them. 'He's a Wiltshire eight. Which as we all know is a London six.'

I snort into my wine. '*Wiltshire Eight?* Sounds like a group of wrongly accused ham smugglers.'

Gabe stands up and heads towards us. Oh crap. He's approaching at an angle, he's meant to be face on. I should have just worn a giant polo neck.

Josie stands up and hugs him, then turns back to the table.

'Gabe, this is Keith, and you know Erica?'

'Hi Keith. And Erica, good to see you, you look very... well.' He has a deep voice with a very faint west country accent. What does he mean 'well'? Why did he pause? I wonder if he remembers that the last time he saw me I was retching in the doorway of FILLINGZ?

He asks a neighbouring table for a spare stool, then pulls it over and sits down next to me, while Josie and Keith are suddenly engrossed in conversation.

'Josie tells me you're into cheese.' Not the opener I was expecting, but at the same time, what could be better than a Wiltshire Eight talking to me about cheese? For a second, I almost forget the bad lighting.

'I am indeed. I get the Say Cheese subscription box.'

'Oh really? I've heard that's a good one. Have you ever had a Blue Vinny? It's made quite near here. They used to drag mouldy horse harnesses through the milk to encourage the mould to grow.'

He's quite geeky and intense, but in a good way.

'Seriously?' I say.

'Nowadays the blue is created by adding penicillin. You could say they had to "rein it in"...'

I'm confused, then realise he's making a pun. A cheese pun. Glory be.

Now he's waiting for me to react. His face is smiling, expectant, genuine.

'Ha! Very good,' I say. 'And also, kind of gross. I would like to try it though... I have a penchant for the pungent ones.' For a second, I forget to hold my chin up and do the happy meerkat thing.

'Me too.' Gabe nods approvingly. 'There's a deli in Devizes that sells it, maybe we could head over there one day, if you're not busy. Get some crackers to go with it. I like the charcoal ones, do you?'

'I do, except...' Oh god, I was going to say, 'they make your poo go black'. I really don't get out enough.

'Except...?'

'Except... they can make a cheeseboard look...'

Look what? COME ON, think of something.

'Macabre.'

Because that's not weird at all.

Gabe does a sort of half-smile, which could also possibly include a hint of concern. Then, clearly keen to move on, he pulls out his phone to google the deli. But he shows it to me too quickly, and we both watch the last search (*how much hair is normal at fifty-one?*) sit on the screen for an excruciating minute until the pub wi-fi decides to slowly bring up the deli website.

It's awkward. But there's a certain solidarity in it. We catch each other's eyes and smile, and out of the corner of my eye I can see Josie looking over and smiling too.

—

Moments like this always remind me of one person: Kofi. It seems a long time ago to me now, but at the same time like I saw him yesterday. He was the best of times, and indeed the worst of times. He was how I hoped it would all turn out, and the worst-case scenario.

We met when I was working at *Time Out* in the late Nineties as a junior editorial assistant, which meant inputting events into the relatively new website. I was living in Holborn, in a flat share with a girl called Miranda, who waitressed and played *Quake* on her PC most of the time – and a guy called, well, Guy, who played *Dungeons and Dragons*, mercifully mainly at the homes of his friends. On Sunday mornings he would make a huge fry-up, which he ate sitting on the toilet, reading the paper. He's dead now, I heard.

I was drinking a Red Stripe on a sofa one night at the Velvet Rooms when Kofi sat down next to me. He was a friend of a friend of a DJ I vaguely knew through another friend. I'd like to think I remembered what Carl Cox was playing at that moment, but to be honest, I don't remember the names of any of the songs from that era. Instead, I always say, 'the one that goes <insert random lyric about never stopping and/or giving up or having the key and/or secret>'. Either that or I unsuccessfully try to imitate the bass by going 'DOOF DOOF DOOF'. Nandy always finds this hilarious.

Kofi offered me a Marlboro Light, and lit one for himself, blowing a perfect smoke ring. I was high as a kite and loved everyone in the room, but this man entranced me.

'I was watching you dancing... I'm Kofi,' he said.

'I'm Erica. What does Kofi mean?'

'Born on a Friday.' He blew another smoke ring and licked his lips to reveal the paler interior of his mouth.

'It's Friday today,' I said.

Later, we went back to my flat and had sex for what seemed like days. Kofi would go out to the shop for supplies every so often, and we would swap the Nightmares on Wax CD for the Rae & Christian one. Sometimes I would wander into the kitchen in Kofi's t-shirt and make cups of tea using Miranda's milk, which we would drink in bed. Outside, who knew what was happening, who cared. Who cared about anything? Sleep, other people... We had each other, and our bodies seemed to fit together so perfectly.

Kofi was the first big love affair of my life. There had been a few others, but not like this. Things moved quickly. We hardly spent a night apart and it wasn't long before paying two rents didn't make sense. I moved into his flat in Camden and our lives intertwined. The flat, which Kofi shared with his friend Pete (who worked at the same homeless charity as Kofi, just off Charing Cross Road), had shiny black walls and a roof terrace. There were DJ decks in the living room and a constant stream of visitors, talking, drinking, dancing (there was a worn-out patch in the corner that served as the dancefloor). Kofi was the life and soul and I was quite happy to bask in his glow. He had one eye on me, even when he was DJing – he'd look over, mouthing 'you okay?'. He made me feel wanted, an emotion that had previously been in short supply.

After the millennium, Pete moved out, and we didn't replace him. I was earning more now that I was working at *Beautique*, and Kofi had been promoted to support worker, dropping 'assistant' from his job title. Kofi got the landlord's permission to paint the black walls of the flat yellow and sand the floors; I think he wanted to make it look more homely. The dancefloor disappeared, and he bought some of those giant round paper lampshades from the new Swedish furniture warehouse that had opened in Bristol, not too far from my parents' house. They'd met Kofi once, at a carvery lunch. Simon was there too. It didn't go well: Kofi and I had smoked a joint on the way and arrived watery-eyed, giggling, hungry as hell. Mother and Father Pells exchanged glances. But we didn't care; we were in this together. It was so good to feel like someone was on my side. Until, of course, he wasn't.

Chapter Seven

White boots, like Bond girls

I expected Yuvana Labs to look like a... lab. A large white building, possibly flat roofed, maybe in the desert. Armed guards, that sort of thing. And in my head, everyone who works there looks amazing and wears white clothes and maybe also white boots, like Bond girls. Disappointingly, although it is white, Yuvana Labs is a Georgian house in Kensington, which is rather lovely but just not what I had in mind.

It's a few days later and I'm sitting in the reception area on a blue velvet sofa wearing a puff-sleeved dress that I thought would make me look smart, but is making me feel cold as it's quite thin and summery. Thank god I wore tights. On the walls around me are several big screens showing films of women with white hair and glowing skin hugging Labradors on beaches, set to stirring classical music.

I've been waiting for about ten minutes now and am getting bored, so google *How to get green eyeshadow off sheets*. Not very easily it seems. A message from Mother Pells interrupts my research.

> Erica, Carol's funeral is next Tuesday.
> Love Mum. x

I reply with 'OK,' a sad face emoji and a couple of kisses and I'm just about to check if my body scrub article has gone live when the receptionist, who could be anywhere between fifteen and eighty and has the appearance of a glazed doughnut, stands up.

'Erica – this way,' she says.

Hoping the treatment won't make me look as peculiar as she does, I follow her into another room, also furnished with velvet sofas – as well as light fixtures that can only be described as 'oligarch' in style. On one of the sofas is a suited man who looks like Jude Law, which isn't necessarily a bad thing, and another shiny, immobile-faced woman wearing a peach jumpsuit and very high white mules.

'Welcome, Erica.' The Jude Law man stands up. He's very charming and makes the kind of eye contact – with pale blue eyes – that leaves me with the feeling that he might be trying to hypnotise me and/or read my mind. But also, the feeling that somehow, I don't mind and/or care.

I say hello but it comes out in my weird banana voice, which I then correct by clearing my throat. This in turn sounds like someone using a waste disposal unit, prompting the peach jumpsuit woman to hand me a glass of water, as if she knew this was going to happen.

I swig gratefully and sit down opposite them.

'There's no need to be nervous, Erica,' says Jude Law, whose actual name is Dr Marcus. So, he must be the 'Dr M' I found on Google. Is Marcus his first name or his surname? I would rather it was his surname as that seems more like the name of a real doctor. Dr Marcus does more of the eye contact/hypnosis thing and suddenly it doesn't matter. He could be called Dr Who and I would still be sitting here nodding away like one of those Funko Pop toys Héloïse collects.

'I know Merlyn has told you all about WULT®, and that you're in the process of completing the necessary legal paperwork,' he continues.

'Yes…'

'Which is all just a formality, of course. So, as a recap, our patented treatment, which is currently in "stealth mode" pending the launch, requires a short, mildly invasive procedure involving an implant into the hypothalamus area of the brain. The implant works by sending tiny nanobots to "restore the factory settings" of the stem cells that control the ageing process.'

He pauses and Peach Jumpsuit passes him a clipboard with some papers attached to it.

'How old are you, Erica, remind me? You must only be around forty…' He scans the clipboard.

I am secretly delighted I remembered to pluck my chin hairs this morning.

'Forty-seven actually…' It was probably just a compliment to put me at ease, but I'll take it.

'Indeed. Well, Erica, as you know, this isn't the "reduction of fine lines" or "improvement in skin texture" you might get from a high-end serum. WULT® will make you literally look twenty years younger. How do you feel about that?'

I go to say 'pleased' but feel this isn't quite enough, so switch to 'great' halfway through, resulting in 'plate'.

Peach Jumpsuit hands me more water. I shake my head.

'I mean great. Great.'

'Indeed,' says Dr Marcus again, exchanging glances with Peach Jumpsuit. 'Naturally, the effect isn't immediate – although the process starts as soon as you have the implant, the full rejuvenation takes around ten days. You'll be sending us photo updates during this time, and we'd like you to keep a "Transformation Diary" of your progress. Then, you'll come back here after two weeks for a Youth Review. Merlyn will be in touch with you about the social media promotion we're expecting in return. As you know this is a very expensive, cutting-edge treatment.'

'Of course, yes...'

'It's also worth mentioning that the effect is reversible – in other words, the implant could be removed. But we don't anticipate many requests for this, as I'm sure you can imagine.'

'No...' Or was I meant to say yes? Should I be worried about how weird these people are? Or do they think the same about me, with my unseasonal puff sleeves and not entirely convincing 'condor'?

'Indeed. Well, I think that covers everything. As soon as we're ready, one of the team will be in touch to schedule your treatment.' He stands up, and Peach Jumpsuit does the same, weirdly in sync as though they've been practising. I take this as a sign that my appointment is over.

Shit. Got. Real.

I wish Nandy was here with me to laugh at Peach Jumpsuit. But then she might persuade me this isn't a good idea. And it is a good idea. It has to be. Because the thought of just carrying on as before, with bad contour make-up, watching Cassia's *#cocktailsofinstagram* reels until my life slips through my fingers, is so sad it makes me feel sick. I want young me back. I want another chance. And maybe this is it.

On the train home, I'm in such a good mood I allow myself to fantasise about Gabe, who will no doubt rapidly go off me once he sees my face in repose when we're watching *The West Wing* and eating food from an excellent local Thai takeaway, which is what I picture people in committed relationships doing. Although we did have a great conversation in The Perch the other night, once I'd made sure he was looking at me face on and there were no angles involved. It also felt like we embarrassed ourselves equally, with me talking about macabre cheeseboards and him showing me his hair-loss-related Google searches.

He kissed me goodbye on the cheek and, at the risk of sounding like Héloïse, I noticed that he smelt of beer and Head & Shoulders. I felt a kind of fizzing feeling in my chest, which I am assuming wasn't just an early sign of fatty plaque build-up in my arteries (I've recently written an article called *Five Healthy Heart Breakfasts For Fifty Plus Women* for *Top Health* magazine). Is this what it feels like to be attracted to a real person rather than Paul Hollywood from *The Great British Bake Off*? As an example, obviously, not him specifically.

The following day, Josie sent me a message saying that Gabe had asked for my number, and was it okay to give it to him? I pretended that I hadn't seen her message until later, not wanting to appear desperate and/or needy, but then caved after a medicinal Malbec at six p.m. I replied saying 'yes' with a smiley face emoji with hearts for eyes, one that Josie uses a lot and therefore must be The Emoji of Nice People.

Gabe messaged me within about half an hour, so he clearly wasn't as worried as me about looking keen, but I like that. His message, which was charming and said all the right things about how lovely it had been to chat the night before, etc., etc., also asked me if I'd like to come with him to the deli in Devizes he'd mentioned — and maybe even call into the (newly reopened after significant renovation) Trowbridge Museum on the way back 'if we had time'. I googled said museum, which I perhaps should have heard of as it's only ten minutes away, and amongst many other exhibits it boasts a very rare complete Spinning Jenny, one of only a few in existence. Be still my beating bobbin.

I wanted to feel excited about this, as Gabe clearly was, but it all sounded a little bit middle-aged to me. However, as Mother Pells said to me recently, 'beggars can't be choosers,' and I do rather like him. Maybe once I get my treatment, we can be a much hotter and more interesting couple that people marvel at and say things about like, 'He's punching above his weight,' rather than 'Is that his mum?' We could go to a party in London together and bump into Cassia, whose husband is 'not all that' according to Nandy, and rarely features on her Instagram for what we assume to be exactly that reason.

I replied — 'sounds lovely!' — and suddenly there was a plan to meet up the next day. I pretended I 'had some work to do first thing', which was, of course, just to ensure that there was adequate time for my face to de-crumple, and we met in Devizes at eleven a.m. I took Josie's Kia Picanto, which she sometimes lets me borrow in exchange for collecting Héloïse from swimming on Wednesdays, feeling it was too early in the relationship to assume we'd share the same transport. After a coffee at the deli and a lengthy perusal of the cheese counter, Gabe bought some Royal Bassett Blue and I bought some Wiltshire Loaf, which might sound like bread but is actually a local cheese and bloody gorgeous. I have decided the same about Gabe, who today smelt slightly of wood smoke. I felt the fizzing feeling in my chest again.

'How long have you lived in Wilshire?' he asked me as we left the deli.

'I erm... a while. I came here by accident,' I said, realising immediately that this sounded both odd and like I don't like Wiltshire, which is perhaps not the right thing to say to someone who is from, and chooses to remain in, Wiltshire.

'Have you had any big...' He paused long enough for me to wonder what the hell he was going to say. '...loves in your life? Relationships, I mean.'

It was the first time we'd talked about anything more serious than whey skimming. But I find it easy to chat to him: his face is so genuine; it doesn't feel like he has any agenda. There's an openness that I want to breathe in, like when you stand on top of a big hill. Which, to be fair, I don't do that often.

I didn't know how to reply. My past boyfriends don't make much of a relationship CV. So I said, trying to be funny, 'To misquote Groucho Marx, I don't want to date anyone who would want to date someone like me.'

He laughed, thankfully, and held the deli door open for me. As I walked out, he touched the small of my back, as though to guide me, or, it almost felt like, reassurance, a wordless acknowledgement that he got what I meant.

On the way back into town, I followed Gabe's car (a really old Volvo, which he says is 'nearly a classic') and we went to see the Spinning Jenny, which was annoyingly really interesting and although I've now forgotten them, for a while I was in possession of some facts about the Industrial Revolution. Gabe bumped into someone he knew at the museum shop and introduced me as 'my good friend Erica'. I must have been successful at my contouring/careful angles because when we parted in the museum car park, he kissed me, on the lips this time, and I could hear him sigh. I rather hoped this was a positive sort of sigh and not one of disappointment at spotting one of my neck worm segments, which I am really hoping will be a thing of the past soon.

Chapter Eight

Entrusting our sister to God's mercy

I'm writing an article called *Ten Lip Masks To Treat Your Smackers*, for the beauty section of a supermarket magazine called *Fresh Living*, and as usual, I'm distracted. Why do certain words look so odd when you stare at them for a while – in this case: 'smackers'? It's not a great headline, admittedly, but magazines like this would never let me freestyle. If I had my way, it would be *Lip Lip, Hooray*! But maybe I should stop trying to make the headline funny and concentrate on the article itself, the part I'm not so good at. Cassia Carver would make light work of this... sometimes I wonder if I'm even cut out for this kind of writing, which is a depressing thought as it's been the basis of my entire career.

I google my name to see if last week's lash growth serum *Tried and Tested* feature has gone live, then roll my eyes when all the search brings up is another death announcement. At least this one is from Kansas and not Florida, for a change. I scan the page and I'm about to head to Instagram to see what Cassia's *#OOTD* is when I spot the opening line: 'With heavy yet grateful hearts, we announce the death of Erica Mary Pells, born 1926'. Heavy yet *grateful*? What, as in they're grateful she's dead? I read on. She had an amazing career, tons of children and grandchildren and devoted her retirement to philanthropy. In lieu of flowers, 'the family suggests honoring her with contributions to the Baker University Wetlands Discovery Center'. So by 'grateful', they mean lucky she was around so long. Wow. Who would say that about me?

A message from Mother Pells brings me back to earth.

> Erica, could you collect me on the way to the crematorium, I can't remember the way. Probably The Inevitable. x

> OK Mum. I'll be at yours at 11.30. x

> Thanks. Been thinking about poor Carol this morning, wonder what she'd be doing now. x

Before I can reply, another message lands, this time from Nandy.

> How's your vag?

I smile and, thinking of Gabe and the fizzy chest feeling, reply quickly.

> Unexpectedly coming back to life haha

'Erica, you look like a clown,' are Mother Pells' first words as she gets into the car.

'Erm… thanks Mum. Lovely to see you too,' I say as I manhandle Josie's Kia out of her driveway.

The atmosphere is tense on the fifteen-minute drive, and I can tell it isn't just about my blatant disregard for the twenty mph speed restriction zone near the primary school.

'You're wearing a lot of make-up, Erica. You look like one of the Kardashables.'

'Oh my god, Mum. I thought you'd want me to look nice for Carol's funeral. Out of respect.'

Mother Pells harrumphs. 'Respect for Carol went out the window when you sent that horrible message about her coming back to life. It wasn't funny in the slightest, as you seemed to think.'

Ah. The message for Nandy about my vagina. Probably not worth explaining that.

'Sorry Mum. That wasn't meant for you.'

'Who else are you texting about poor Carol? For goodness' sake, Erica. Anyway, Simen is now coming today too. At least *he'll* show some respect.'

'Sorry… Did you just say SEMEN?' I nearly veer off the road.

'Simen. S-I-M-E-N. But yes, it's pronounced "Semen". It's the Norwegian version of Simon. Didn't Simon tell you that's what he wants to be known as now? It's because he did his ethnicity DNA test. He's four per cent Scandinavian! I think it's on my side, not your dad's.' She arranges her bosom proudly with her forearm.

'So, to be clear, he's ninety-six per cent NOT Scandinavian and he's changed his name? Jesus wept.'

'Please don't talk about Jesus on the way to a funeral, Erica.'

I grit my teeth and focus on not getting snapped by a speed camera in somebody else's car.

—

I used to like the autumn, watching the trees change colour in Regent's Park and poring over *Marie Claire's 101 Ideas* to find the perfect plum-coloured jumper and brown coat for the new season. Now this time of year just says rising energy bills and flu jabs, with some vitamin D deficiency thrown in for good measure. There's also the fact that I hate it when people use the word 'brisk' to describe the temperature, and autumn sees the beginning of this season, which lasts until around April the following year.

The other reason I'm not keen on autumn is because that's when Father Pells died. They said that he would have 'a good few years in him yet' if he hadn't been exposed to those chemicals at work. Apparently, they were experimenting with ways to make aircraft invisible to radar – I didn't understand it then any more than I understand it now. But it happened, and to start with it was just skin rashes, and a fatigue he couldn't shake. After retirement didn't give him his energy back, he had more and more tests. Mother Pells retired too, earlier than planned, to look after him. He would sleep a lot, and nothing seemed to ease his itching. His face hollowed and the light behind his eyes dimmed.

Test after test, then finally a diagnosis: a rare form of cancer. They would do 'all they could', but the reality was, he'd been poisoned. People at work were talking about lawsuits – a few other members of his team had health problems too. A cloud settled over the house, and even Oli and Sam – fighting, laughing, breaking the silences – couldn't blow it away. Hospital trips became hospital stays, and Mother Pells picked at her lips until they were raw, which had always been her nervous habit. I gave her expensive lip balms that I got free from PRs, but they were never going to help. He died at home. I wasn't there, but I'd said goodbye the day before. 'Make us proud, my funny little Erry,' he'd told me.

–

It's cold and windy when we get out of the car at the crematorium and my dress keeps blowing up, despite the long coat I put over it. The car park is covered in dead leaves, transformed by the rain into what look like soggy cornflakes, which I pick my way around for fear of slipping in my heels. By contrast, Mother Pells is dressed sensibly in smart 'slacks' and a black jacket. She's tall and elegant, with a silver bob, more like Simon than me; I inherited my father's short legs and heart-shaped face.

Simon gets out of his car where he's been sitting waiting for us to arrive. He's wearing a cable-knit patterned jumper with a roll neck and looks like a member of the cast of *Fisherman's Friends*, which I haven't seen, but I thought it looked funny in the trailer. Simon, on the other hand, does not look funny at all, but quite murderous.

'Erica, is that an appropriate amount of make-up for a funeral?' he says as he walks towards us.

'Hello, Semen. Is that an appropriate amount of knitwear? Why are you dressed like you're off to trawl a fjord for salmon?'

We glare at each other until Mother Pells ushers us towards the crematorium entrance making that clicking sound with her tongue that people use when toddlers try to eat houseplants. I can tell it's mainly directed at me.

Inside, I see Carol's children, Kristin and David, who are also in their forties, in the front row. They smile at Simon (why, in that jumper?) and shoot daggers at me, as they have done ever since the rabbit incident. Move on – it would be dead by now anyway, decking or no decking.

The three of us sit a couple of rows behind them and wait in silence as the room fills up.

'Sally?' A bald man sitting in the row in front turns his head. Mother Pells smiles politely but clearly doesn't know who this is.

'Clive. Carol's cousin. We met a few times,' says the man.

'Of course,' says Mother Pells. 'Do you remember my daughter, Erica, and my son, Simen?'

She's actually introducing him as seminal fluid. This is a new low. Fortunately, at that point, the pallbearers enter with the coffin, followed by Carol's husband, Mike, and the service starts, so Clive turns to face the front.

It's a long service. After half an hour (Kristin's poem, David's reading, two hymns and a blessing) I'm bored. I manage to use the order of service, tilted at an angle, to hide the fact I'm watching Cassia Carver's Teeth Whitening Treatment Reveal (*#smilemakeover*). All her followers have been excited about this one, she's even been wearing a surgical mask on her Stories for the last week so she doesn't give away the surprise.

Someone is saying something about 'entrusting our sister to God's mercy', and I decide now is as good a time as any to press play on the reel. I'm sure I checked it's on silent mode, so what could go wrong? Taylor Swift, singing 'Are you ready for it?' – that's what could go wrong. And timed perfectly with the coffin disappearing behind the curtains too.

Scrabbling to turn it off, with Mother Pells and Simon glowering at me, it dawns on me that at least there's a new reason for Kristin and David to hate me. Bloody Cassia Carver. It's quite unnecessary to have such dramatic music for a teeth-whitening reveal, in my opinion.

—

After the service, I dodge the line-up for obvious reasons and go outside to lean on the Kia and reply to a message from Gabe asking me if I like apple chutney.

A few minutes later, Simon appears, marching across the car park towards me like he's in a long queue at the supermarket and just spotted another check-out opening.

'Hi, Semen.'

He scowls at me. 'It's SIM-en, not SEE-men.'

I pull a face that I hope expresses the fact that there's very little difference.

'I know you think everything is very funny Erica, but that's because you don't really have any responsibilities.'

'What responsibilities do you have? I mean... apart from, well, the kids. And Alannah, and I mean, your job and...' I really wish I hadn't started this list.

'And Mum, Erica. Mum. She's *our* responsibility. And she's not getting any younger. So, stop messing about with all your make-up and your memes or whatever that was in there' – he waves his hand towards the crematorium – 'and grow up. You're nearly fifty.'

Nothing winds me up more than hearing 'nearly fifty'. I roll my eyes. 'Stop telling me how to live my life, Semen.

And Mum's fine. I don't know why you keep going on about it.' I get into the Kia and slam the door, then roll down the window. 'Sod off back to your sauna.'

Chapter Nine

Tightly closed Russian dolls

It's been a couple of weeks, maybe even three, and Yuvana Labs still hasn't been in touch with me, to the point where I wonder if Glazed Doughnut tried to call me and the phone slipped out of her shiny hand. Merlyn has reassured me over the course of several emails that 'everything is under control, Erica'. She has also told me about the publicity that I'll be involved in once the treatment happens. Apparently, there's going to be a three-page sponsored article in *Luscious*, with a cover shoot (of me – holy crap), to create some intrigue.

The marketing team is also setting up a new Instagram account called *@wokeuplikethis*, for me to do *Before and Afters* and share positive stories about what Yuvana Labs are calling my 'youth journey'. Apparently, I'll be known as 'WULT® Woman' who is *Nearly fifty but looks mid-twenties!* And the good news is that I'm going to get paid for the social media stuff – considerably more than I get for writing articles about things like intermittent fasting and bladder weakness for *Balance* magazine (the one they give out free in health food shops). The slightly less good news is that I'm going to have to become an 'influencer' of sorts. At least I'll have had the treatment, so I won't need to worry about looking jowly while I'm doing all the reels and stuff. And you never know, maybe I'll get more followers than Cassia, which would be quite the turnaround and rather satisfying.

I asked Merlyn how people would know that 'WULT® Woman' wasn't just a real twenty-seven-year-old, paid to fake it to make Yuvana Labs look good. 'Don't worry my dear,' she said, 'we've thought of that – we've thought of everything.' This sounded both reassuring and slightly boastful, but apparently someone called Channing is going to be in touch with me about a 'content plan' once I'm booked in for my treatment, which looks like it will be after Christmas now at this rate.

I haven't told anyone about it yet. I'm going to surprise Josie once it's taken effect. She'll be gobsmacked but that's only because she doesn't work in the beauty world, so doesn't really get it. Nandy will get it though – she might even be envious. She must see her daughter Maya and think, *I wouldn't mind looking like that again*. Maya is twenty-one and gorgeous. And Nandy really struggles with age spots. Well, she certainly has them. As for Gabe, he's in for a treat. It would be great if the treatment coincided with Valentine's Day – what a bloody brilliant gift. Here, have your girlfriend – but twenty years younger. Beats an M&S Dine In Meal For Two, like the Spatchcock Herb Chicken and Raspberry Mousse Hearts that I got from the garage last February and ate on my own.

I'm getting ahead of myself though. I'm not sure we're even at the 'boyfriend and girlfriend' stage yet. Do middle-aged people even say that? I'm guessing we're not though, due to the fact we haven't had sex, or even come close for that matter, just the odd kiss. Which is mainly because lifting doorstops has had little to no effect on my bingo wings – and whatever those chicken skin bits are called on the inside of my thighs. Maybe just chicken thighs. Bethany, thank god your YouTube videos are free is all I can say, because they're really not doing much good.

Another thing that's been slowing Gabe and me up is that after the Trowbridge Museum trip, I've only been arranging meet-ups with him where I can be face on, as I'm still trying to hide my jowls with clever use of contour. So, the cinema is out, or any event where we are sitting next to each other in an audience. We also can't do anything that involves walking together side by side, or water – so swimming (which I wouldn't do anyway due to the chicken thighs), spa, that sort of thing. It's slightly limiting but won't be for much longer with any luck, if the treatment works.

Gabe is funny and sexy, and we don't just like some of the same things (cheese, puns); we dislike some of the same things too. It's almost uncanny. The other day, for some reason, we were talking about ice dancing, and I revealed my lifelong dislike of those tights material panels you get on the costumes (seen quite often on *Strictly Come Dancing* too). I mean, they don't even look like skin. Are they supposed to? If so, then why put Swarovski crystals on them? JEEZ. If I were a judge and someone wore one of those, I would hold up a zero on principle, and Gabe wholeheartedly agrees.

We've also discussed our least favourite noises, and I shared my number one: the sound of tightly closed Russian dolls being unscrewed. Most people I've told this to haven't really got it. But Gabe laughed so hard that he got little tears in the corners of his eyes, which, incidentally, are a kind of grey-green, like broad beans. He held my hand over the cafe table (he was directly across from me, which was a relief) and said, 'Oh good grief

Erica, you really do make me laugh.' Then he told me about a friend of his called Maxine, who's some kind of comedy producer, and said he would introduce me to talk about writing scripts or sketches or something, which all sounds great apart from the fact that nobody even likes my pun headlines, so I can't imagine they would like anything lengthier.

In the same cafe, while we were picking at the cornichons (all that remained of our cheese and charcuterie platter), Gabe told me he had been married before. I braced myself – please god no, don't let him be a widower, this isn't a rom-com. Living up to someone dead would be a bloody nightmare. I should know, I've read enough obituaries of excellent worthy people in US care homes. But thankfully it was an ill-fated and short-lived marriage to a woman called Aldona in 2002, who, it turned out, just wanted UK residency. She's gone back to Poland now. I can't say I blame her, what with all the inflation and other stuff like that.

'It was one of those decisions you make when you're younger that in retrospect isn't a particularly good one,' he said, breaking the last, almost freakishly large cornichon in two and handing one half to me.

'I'm very... painfully... familiar with this.'

He looked surprised. 'Really? Do you have a dark past? Anything I should know about?'

I thought about what happened with Kofi, and decided it was too soon to share any of that, so brushed it off to make myself sound more mysterious and less... troubled. 'Ha! No, not really... just the usual stuff. No marriages though.'

'You're too cool for that.'

I have never considered myself cool, and certainly don't believe that it's the reason I've never been married, but at that point I was quite willing to let Gabe think it.

'Well maybe not cool,' he added. Good that I was able to enjoy about eight seconds of that sensation then. 'More... quirky. I like that about you. There aren't many people I can discuss cheese mould with. You're a kindred spirit.'

Did he just say kindred spirit? I didn't want to blow it so I didn't ask him if he'd read *Anne of Green Gables* when he was young. And truthly, I'd rather he hadn't, which is probably not very modern of me. So, I just crunched on my cornichon and looked into his broad bean eyes.

—

At the start of December, I finally get the date for my treatment (5 January), along with loads more online forms to complete. I hate signing things on a screen – my signature looks like 'Colin Turd' when I have to do it with my finger instead of a pen. I hope it will still be valid if there is ever a lawsuit. Which I'm sure there won't be. I went to the loo when I was at Yuvana Labs and I'm pretty sure dodgy companies don't have Aesop handwash by their sinks.

The feeling of limbo is weird, like waiting for Netflix to load when you're too far from the wi-fi. Something good is coming, but not yet. I really want to tell someone, but I'm making do with talking about it to Merlyn for now. I'm not just excited about my new look, I'm also looking forward to the ten days when the rejuvenation happens. Every day, when I look in the mirror, I'll look younger – how amazing will that be? Actual change.

Not just that pretend change when I wake up and read an affirmation on @*dailyinspoquotes* and pray something interesting will happen. It will be as though all my anti-ageing products finally work at last.

I just have to get Christmas out of the way first, which means going to Mother Pells' house, interacting with Simon (who will be going on about Norway, or maybe even something new by then) and generally trying to navigate this Gabe thing, all while secretly counting down to what could potentially be the most 'New Year, New Me' ever. January can't come soon enough.

But for now, the Christmas preparations must begin, which today, for me, involves standing in a ridiculously long queue at the butcher's to order a turkey crown for Mother Pells. Why she can't a) order it herself, or b) get one from M&S is anyone's guess. I stand looking at all the different types of animal organs in the display cabinet and wonder how one would go about cooking an ox cheek. Imagine having a cheek so big that it could constitute a meal. My cheeks are so deflated and saggy they wouldn't even be enough for an hors d'oeuvre.

I'm glad to be summoned from my reverie, which is veering towards macabre and slightly cannibalistic, by Keith, waving a bag at me and shouting, 'Ossobuco!' I'm not a hundred per cent sure what that is, being more of a purchaser of fine ready meals than an actual cook, but call 'delicious!' in reply, and let Keith keep me company and talk me through the risotto recipe he has planned while I edge further towards the counter. He offers me a lift home and as, according to the Met Office website, it 'feels like' −5°C, I gratefully accept.

Ten minutes later, turkey crown ordered, I'm in the front seat of Keith's electric Volvo, Classic FM belting out 'Carol of the Bells', which reminds me of Carol, then Taylor Swift, and I cringe so much I squeeze the Ossobuco in my lap and hope that the risotto recipe doesn't require whatever it is to be in one piece.

'I have to make a quick stop on the way, girly-pop,' says Keith.

'Okay. Where?'

'I've got some things to drop off for the Christmas Fair.'

'The Christmas Fair?'

'Yes, the Christmas Fair. The one they have every year in this town. That everyone goes to. Except you, clearly.' He laughs. 'You should though. It's actually rather fun.'

'It doesn't sound it.'

'Mulled wine at eleven a.m.? Wilma Godwin's homemade stollen? Criminally under-priced soy candles? Honestly, what's not to love?'

This appears to be rhetorical, so I don't say anything, although it does sound quite appealing, especially the wine at eleven a.m. Keith is however side-eyeing me while he drives, as though he wants a reply.

'If you ever came out from behind your LED face mask and actually left the house you would know about these things,' he says.

'I'll have you know I've got a boyfriend. Well, maybe. Kind of.'

'The Wiltshire Eight from The Perch?'

'The very one. Shame I'm a Swindon Seven. Or a Salisbury Six.' I'm on a roll. 'Or a Froxfield…'

'I get it, Erica. And I wish you'd stop putting yourself down. But I'm delighted to hear about the ham smuggler.'

We pull up outside what appears to be a church hall. I get my phone out to read an article about the £8 SPF Tess Daly swears by, which has been burning a hole in my inbox all morning, but Keith, who's already opening the boot, yells, 'Come on Erica, chop chop! Give me a hand with these.'

I'm mildly curious as to what 'these' are, so I put the squashed Ossobuco on the dashboard before getting out and walking round to the back of the car, where I stare, bemused, at the contents of the boot. It's full of what look like tiny model buildings, each one different, and some with open roofs so you can see inside. The level of detail is incredible: a miniature newspaper and pint glasses on the bar of what must be a pub, a teapot and plate of cakes on a kitchen table, a figure of a man looking somewhat precarious on a miniature ladder.

'What the hell are these?'

'Dioramas.'

'Of what?'

'Iconic scenes from *The Archers*. That's The Bull, and that's Grey Gables, oh and Pat and Tony Archer at the Bridge Farm kitchen table. And look, that's Nigel Pargetter on the roof. Poor soul.'

'And you *made* them?'

'I did indeed duckie. I love it. I figure it's better than watching Netflix all the time. And it's not like you have me round to yours much anymore when Stephen's away. What happened to our cheeseboard soirées?'

'I've got... things to do in the evening.'

'Mainline Malbec and watch David Attenborough?'

He's laughing, but this stings a bit.

'I know, I know. I've been a hermit. I think I've lost my confidence. I'm working on getting it back though. And the Gabe thing helps.'

I'm almost tempted to explain what else might be about to help, when a man and a woman come out of the hall and greet Keith excitedly. They're in their sixties I suppose, maybe older, wearing handknits that remind me of Simon's Norwegian jumper. Keith kisses the woman on the cheek and does that hand-shake-meets-arm-slap greeting to the man.

'Erica, this is Frankie... and Douglas.' He turns back to them. 'This is my friend Erica. I'm trying to persuade her to come to her first Christmas Fair.'

They make noises that suggest disbelief that I have never been to one before, so I smile politely and start unloading the boot. I wonder how Keith knows them? I listen to their conversation for clues, but I can't really follow as there seem to be a lot of in-jokes, and Frankie has an exceptionally loud laugh.

Inside the hall, a woman in her fifties with rosacea wearing an ill-advised red fleece directs me to a table, then spots the diorama I'm carrying and squeaks 'Is Keith here?'. Grabbing a man, who could be 100 judging by his mottled complexion, they rush (as much as possible given one of them has a Zimmer frame) outside, followed by an almost spherical woman who is writing 'stollen!' in gold on a cardboard sign and could indeed be Wilma herself. I haven't seen such excitement since Charlie Dimmock came to WH Smith on the high street to sign her book about ponds.

The dioramas safely stowed in the church hall, Keith takes me back home. 'There are other people in this town apart from me and Josie you know,' he says, as though reading my thoughts. 'You should get out more. It might make you happier.'

'I'm not really at a diorama-making point in my life. Or one where I'm ready to hang out with pensioners, for that matter. I get enough of that visiting my mum.'

'They're not all pensioners! Some of them are our age. Anyway, it's your loss, girly-pop. Oldies are brilliant fun. I've always thought, if life is a party, then the people who stay till the end of the night are the ones with the best stories.'

I shrug again, hand Keith his Squashobuco, and get out of the car.

Chapter Ten

A glitch in the Matrix

I got through it – Christmas that is. For something with three months' build-up it is always quite the anti-climax, since Father Pells died anyway, and I embraced that this year. Josie and Laure took Héloïse to France, Gabe was with his dad in Uttoxeter (he didn't invite me – we're not really 'there' yet but will be once I no longer look like Jeremy Clarkson). I spent a dull afternoon at my mother's over-eating and watching the King's Speech. Not the film about the stuttering, the actual King's Speech. The film would have been more interesting.

Simon wore a Nordic jumper again but was talking more about his plans to go 'net zero' than anything particularly Scandinavian, so that was a relief – or at least a different kind of annoying. But Alannah is always fun, and it was good to see the boys, although they look like men now, which is disconcerting. Nobody asked me much, or indeed expected me to offer up much, so as soon as I could, I got Oli, who's just passed his driving test, to give me a lift home. We talked about the Middle East in the car, and I felt like I should read the news more. When we pulled up outside my house, he kissed me on the cheek and said, 'look after yourself, Auntie Erica'.

Back home, I just felt really sad that Father Pells wasn't here anymore, and kept thinking about how much he was missing out on, seeing Sam and Oli grow up. I ploughed into a bottle of Shiraz and started watching his favourite Christmas film, which was *A Wonderful Life*, but it was kind of depressing and not really very Christmassy so after about half an hour, I put on *The Good Place* instead.

—

I remember it so clearly, standing in WH Smith two days after he died, buying the local paper to see if the death announcement was in it yet, and watching everyone around me going about their business. The woman at the till with a badger stripe of grey in her hair, chatting to a teenager – she knew his mum, it seemed. A man in a felt hat with a tiny, speckled feather in it, browsing the classic car magazines. A stressed-out dad with two young children buying advent calendars, far too early. None of them know, I thought. Why don't they know? Why doesn't everyone know? How can such mundane things continue to happen? We should all stop. We should all just hold onto one another, and ask, how, how could this have happened, and why will nothing be the same again?

That's the thing about death. It's happening everywhere, all the time, but when it happens near you, the idea that the world can just carry on as normal seems bizarre. It's after the funeral that it really hits you though, Auntie Viv said. You've had all the arrangements to focus on. But then you have to 'press on'. That was the hardest part. Because it didn't feel normal at all without the one person in the family who I felt, occasionally, understood me. Mother Pells 'just got on with it' (Auntie Viv's words again), which I resented even more, especially as Simon did the same and everyone said how 'stoical' he was. How typical of my family, how respectable, how moderate. Why not make it real, make it passionate, all-consuming – like the 'heart-sickness' of a literary heroine (yes, I did English A-level). Show me proper grief, one of you. Then we can all follow. But nobody did.

So, life just slowly resumed. Father Pells was barely mentioned, although I desperately wanted to shout his name out at family gatherings, just to dispel the awkward silence that settled in the absence of his random facts, cheesy jokes and quiet snigger. It drove me insane. *Don't you all feel it too – that he's not here? Don't you think that if we talked about him, it might seem, in a very small way, like he was here? And wouldn't that be a good thing?*

But it was easier to keep quiet, and just carry on, having the same conversations about what a cold wind there was for this time of year, or when would they sort out those potholes on Forest Lane, or did you want jam on your scone, it's homemade, from Dinah next door? And all with the slow, slow ticking of the John Lewis mantelpiece clock in the background. Everything is from John Lewis. If John Lewis did death, that's the one my mum would choose. 'How would you like your demise?' 'Oh, never knowingly undersold, thanks.'

—

It's 5 January. In the morning, shaky with nerves and excitement, I walk through the freezing streets to the station, past the naked Christmas trees that line the pavements awaiting the bin men. January feels so brittle, bare, lifeless. A bit like middle age. Hopefully I won't have to worry about that anymore, or not for a while, anyway.

The train is on time, unusually, and by eleven a.m. I'm in the Yuvana Labs reception area with the blue velvet sofa.

I have to wait about ten minutes, which only serves to make me feel more nervous. It's a good kind of nervous though, not like the stressful feeling of going to the garage without my Bobbi Brown Five-Minute Face on and worrying that I'll bump into someone I know. Which is precisely the kind of thing I *won't* have to think about anymore – if this works. I can't bloody wait. That feeling of freedom that I haven't felt for so long, being able to just get up and go out, without having to wait for my face to uncrumple, to go on Zooms with my camera on, or actually go to meetings in person. Holy crap, imagine that, not worrying that everyone is looking at my jowls and judging me. I really think this is going to help my career too. I'll be able to go up to London more and stop hiding away. And my social life. Keith won't be accusing me of being a hermit when I'm out at parties in London four times a week. Or did I say that about myself? Either way, this is the life I gave up when I moved to Wiltshire and accidentally got old without noticing, and it feels like at last, I have a chance to get it back.

Finally, the receptionist calls me over. It's the same one as last time, Glazed Doughnut, but she looks at me with absolutely no recognition whatsoever. I have a feeling she does this to everyone.

'I'm here to see Dr Marcus,' I say.

'And your name is…?' She flashes a vague smile with overly white teeth.

'Pells. Erica Pells.' I'm so over-excited I snigger at how much I phrased it like 'Bond. James Bond'.

Glazed Doughnut doesn't find this as funny as I do, or indeed funny at all. She turns to her laptop, types and then stops. 'Erica?' Her voice changes and she stares at me intently. 'You must be here for your WULT® treatment.'

I nod, self-conscious at the scrutiny. I have that feeling you get when you're wearing a new lipstick that's not your usual shade – as though you're unsure what to do with your mouth, and have an urge to pout like Keira Knightley. So pout I do, and I don't think it's a very good pout because Glazed Doughnut looks at me with some concern.

'Dr Marcus is ready for you now,' she says, and walks me over to the door of the room with the oligarch lighting.

Inside, Dr Marcus is on the same sofa, in what appears to be the same clothes and is looking even more like Jude Law than before. If it wasn't for Peach Jumpsuit now wearing a yellow jumpsuit, I would have a serious case of déjà vu, and suspect a glitch in the Matrix. I wonder if it's a choice between a red and blue pill with my water today – although I feel like I've already gone down the rabbit hole.

'Welcome back.' Dr Marcus doesn't stand up this time but does do the weird hypnosis eye contact thing again. Peach Jumpsuit is also staring at me, at least I think she is. Well, she's staring at something.

'How are you feeling?' asks Dr Marcus as I sit down. 'As excited as we are?'

I nod, grinning, and he turns to Peach Jumpsuit, who doesn't look remotely excited but whispers 'Yesssssss' and writes something down on her clipboard. I hear him call her 'Portia', but to me, she will always be Peach Jumpsuit.

Dr Marcus stands up and moves towards me, bending down into the kind of curtsey lunge only someone with a personal trainer could manage. 'May I?' He reaches out to touch my face.

'Um... sure,' I say as he lifts my hair out of the way and scrutinises my skin.

'There is a marked decrease in hydration and elasticity since you were here last,' he says with that 'we're not angry we're disappointed' tone teachers use. It reminds me of a recent trip to the dentist when I was asked what I 'use to brush my teeth'. Why, what does it look like I use? An old twig and some soot?

'Yeah... sorry about that.' I put this down to sinking most of a bottle of Primitivo last night, but I don't feel the need to elaborate.

'No need to apologise! It will all be bouncing back once we give those nanobots their marching orders.'

I have a mental image of lots of little Ant Men running round my brain. It's not like the Ant Man fantasies I've had in the past, by any means.

'And your family and friends,' Dr Marcus continues. 'Are they aware of your impending transformation?'

'No... not yet. I'm just getting used to the idea myself. But, I mean, I'm not worried.' I go to cross my legs to show just how unworried I am, but manage to miss and end up stamping on the floor, making Dr Marcus and Peach Jumpsuit both flinch.

Dr Marcus fixes a smile and sits back down on the sofa in an equally effortless reverse lunge movement.

'Indeed. Well, do take your time to explain it to them carefully when you reveal your new look. This is a revolutionary treatment, as I'm sure you're aware, so we have no idea how it will be received, by the public, and of course the media.'

'Okay. But I can tell them? I mean show them. As in, see them.' I'm not being very coherent.

'Of course, of course! I'm sure they'll be thrilled for you. And these logistics will really take a back seat once you are enjoying the many other benefits.' He waves a hand as if to indicate my impending transformed appearance.

'So, if you're ready Erica, Portia will take you through for your procedure.'

Peach Jumpsuit stands up, and I do the same, accompanied by a loud clicking noise from both my knees. There's no way she didn't hear it, but she doesn't say anything and instead just directs me towards another door on the opposite side of the room.

'I'm ready,' I say.

I follow her into a changing room with dark wood lockers and piles of folded putty-coloured towels. It smells of mint and feels more 'spa' than 'hospital'. Peach Jumpsuit gives me some paper pants and a putty-coloured towelling robe, and tells me to come through the door at the end of the changing room when I'm ready.

The paper pants are loose and feel like they don't really cover my overgrown cellar in the slightest. Hands shaky and fumbling, I pull the robe tightly around me, put on the matching slippers (which I am not too nervous to hope I'll get to keep afterwards) and open the door at the end of the changing room.

I emerge into a short corridor, with Peach Jumpsuit standing glistening at the end, looking like a mannequin in a shop window, her hands in a weird pose as if holding something (she is not). Has she been there all this time? Is she a hologram? An android? She springs to life and ushers me through yet another door into a room which, reassuringly, looks more medical, with several people milling about a central treatment table wearing masks. They all greet me with nods and waves. I smile weakly at them all.

'We're not going to use a general anaesthetic today, Erica,' says one of the mask-wearers, who has a voice that could either be a high-pitched man or a low-pitched woman. 'We'd like to keep a close eye on brain activity. It's harder to do that when you're anaesthetised, so we're going to sedate you quite heavily instead. Don't worry, you won't need to get the train home, we have a driver arranged for you.'

I nod and say 'Okay,' and Peach Jumpsuit leads me behind a screen to put on a surgical gown. I wonder what the point of the robe has been, and also feel slightly curious about 'heavy sedation'. If it's anything like that time I took a Valium in Ibiza in 1997, then I'm going to be in for a treat. I get up on the table, and a cannula is suddenly in my hand. This is it. I'm actually here. It's about to happen.

The masked woman doing it asks me to tell her about my journey into London, and while I am talking, I realise my speech is slowing right down... and down... and then I am thinking random, happy thoughts. Millie Bobby Brown is smiling at me... Carol's rabbit is running free across the fields... and I am filming an Instagram reel – with a jawline as tight as a gnat's chuff, as Nandy would say.

Part Two

Chapter Eleven

Wonderful things with basketweave

I'm woken by the sound of the boiler firing up in the kitchen downstairs, accompanied by a tap-tap-tap as the radiator on my bedroom wall begins to warm. I open my eyes, wondering if the events of yesterday were in fact a *Dallas*-style dream. But as soon as I move my head, I have a sudden, very sharp pain in my nostrils, which tells me it definitely happened. It really, actually happened. Holy crap. I lie there for a few minutes, taking it all in. I feel pretty pleased with myself, actually. I did something. Something different. Exciting. Brave, even. I 'did the thing that scares me', as that bloody 60 Days To Confidence app kept telling me. I 'let go of what no longer serves me' and, I hasten to add, I didn't do any of it because of the app. In fact, I stopped doing it after about ten days and made the review up. No, I did this myself. For me. Without anyone's help. Okay, maybe Merlyn's. And Yuvana Labs. But mainly by myself.

Another pain, right between my eyes. I hadn't really expected yesterday's procedure to be carried out via my nose, but it makes sense, as it's a ready-made route in, and better, I suppose, than someone drilling a hole in my skull. Apparently 'the whole process was fully outlined' in the WULT® paperwork I (or Colin Turd) signed. Maybe I should have read it first, but who even does that? It's like accepting the terms and conditions of your new version of Microsoft Word. You just scroll and scroll until it says 'Agree'. Well, I do.

I find a cool spot on my SilkySleep (*#gifted*) pillowcase, which hasn't been quite as transformational for my frizzy hair as I hoped. Washing it occasionally would probably help. The pillow, not the hair – okay, both. My bed linen could probably do with a run through on 'colour-fast cottons' too, or even just a good shake to get the cracker crumbs off, especially if there's a vague chance Gabe might stay the night here sometime in the future. Maybe I should get some of that vagina cream Nandy was telling me about. Although, here's a thought – maybe I won't need it, as WULT® might get my overgrown cellar open to the public again. I hadn't even considered that, having focused heavily up to this point on the jowls and nematode neck situation. Maybe it will work on all of me, even the inside bits? Does that mean it might help my Frequent Urination, a 'classic' perimenopause symptom, according to that article in *Glowgetter*. Sounds more like a metal band – didn't Simon see them at Donington back in the day?

I really need some painkillers. Peach Jumpsuit said they were okay to take; I remember because I noticed how she seems to hiss every word that has an 's' at the end, like 'painkillerssssssss'. Then she asked me what I did over 'Christmasssssss'. Do you really care, Peach Jumpsuit? I muttered something about 'eating too much', partly because this is true, and partly because it avoided any actual insight into the tedium that was my festive season. I was also, at this point, removing my paper pantssssssss and didn't feel it was the time for sssssmall-talk.

The car that took me back to Wiltshire after the procedure was like one of the ones in *Succession* – blacked-out windows, low lighting and a mini fridge. I lay slumped, snoozing for most of the way along the M4, a huge bandage over my nose, which Peach Jumpsuit said would be 'fine to take off once I got home'. I wonder if she was disappointed that this sentence didn't include the letter 's'. The sedation, which had for the most part worn off, was still enough for me to feel quite spaced out, and strangely fixated on the mini fridge. What was in it? And why? Should I open it? Maybe it would set off some kind of alarm. In a daze, I sat looking at it for about half an hour, picturing it containing those test tubes you get in films with smoke or dry ice or whatever it is coming off the top.

At junction seventeen, the driver turned off the motorway to head south. Feeling the change of pace, I sat up, less drowsy, and less fixated on the fridge. I checked my phone. There was a message from Merlyn, from about two hours before.

> Erica my dear – how did it go? Excited to hear. Baci, M

I wasn't sure what to say, driving through Chippenham in the dark, bandaged up, breathing through my mouth like the person on the tube who always sits right next to me. I was glad the wait was over, a little scared, but most of all, very, very excited. I'm not sure if it was the drugs, but right then I started thinking about how often I cry. Not like big snotty sobs, although sometimes I do that after a few glasses of Gavi, watching anything with Reese

Witherspoon and Mark Ruffalo in. I just mean a tear here, a tear there, at the sheer disappointment and boredom of it all. The missed chances, the faded glory. Actually, no, there never was any glory. There was a brief spell of above averageness, and then a slide into mediocrity, possibly slightly below. No wonder I'm excited about this. Sometimes I feel like nothing exceptional has ever happened to me. Nothing good, anyway.

> Okay so far! Will report back. E

What else could I say? Until it starts working, it's just a day trip to London and a nose bandage. And yes, I did open the fridge, which contained a Tupperware box with what looked like a tuna sandwich in it. I think it was the driver's.

And now, the next day, I'm in bed cracking ibuprofen out of the packet, gulping them (and a Settlers chaser) down with the remains of an M&S Berry Smoothie that was sitting on the bedside table. I gag as I realise that it wasn't from today, or yesterday, or indeed possibly even this week. To express my disgust further, I deliver a fairly ladylike fart – more of a clicking noise than anything raspy. I definitely fart more these days. Probably best that nobody does share a bed with me. I don't remember ever farting when I was in bed with Kofi, and certainly didn't with any of the one – occasionally two or three – night stands I had at university and in the early days at *Time Out*. Being in bed with someone back in those days had mainly focused on trying to position myself in a flattering pose and/or appear to be enjoying it, and not letting go in any shape or form, for fear of making an unsexy noise, or pulling a face that was as close as possible to Minnie Driver, the only celebrity I have ever been likened to.

I haul myself into the bathroom to peer at my reflection, wondering if I can see any change yet. I can't. There are massive dark circles under my eyes, and my hair has formed a kind of roof shape, making me look like Lord Farquaad from *Shrek*, which I used to watch with Simon's boys. My nematode neck appears particularly prominent this morning, and with my face in repose, the 'marionette' lines that run from the corner of my mouth to my chin seem worse than ever. Why is it, I wonder, that the older you get, the more experience you have, and the longer you've survived, the sadder you end up looking? Growing old should make you look bloody ecstatic. But it doesn't.

I wonder if this will be the last time I will feel like this. Well, the last time for quite a while – Peach Jumpsuit told me the same as what Merlyn said on WhatsApp (and it was 'clearly outlined in the paperwork'), that when you've had the WULT® treatment, you start ageing again. So, it's literally a reset. I wonder if you can keep getting the reset? But I vaguely remember her also saying you can only have it once. Or did she say, 'usually only have it once'? I might ask though – maybe she just said that so she could hiss the word 'once'. Besides, this is all assuming it works. If it doesn't then I will go and live on a croft in Scotland. I think that would suit me, apart from the physical labour and maybe the lack of local amenities. But I'd be a Highland crone, and nobody would know how old I was, so they'd assume I was about seventy. I'd wear a tartan headscarf and do wonderful things with basketweave and maybe have some sheep. I'd probably sleep better with all that fresh air too.

I touch my nose. With the dressing gone, there is nothing to see. You wouldn't know anything had happened, apart from the pain in my head like I've leant forward on a pencil.

COME ON, hurry up and work, will you, WULT®.

—

Later, an Amazon delivery man deposits six huge parcels in my hall, sent from Yuvana Labs. Opening them takes ages as I keep running upstairs to look at myself in the mirror to see if anything has happened yet. At about four-thirty p.m., I wonder if a particularly wiry chin hair that I saw earlier looks slightly less like something you might get on pork crackling. But I could be wrong, and I'm not sure that fewer porcine chin hairs will be what I notice first. I wonder what the first sign will be though?

I go back to the parcels, pulling out endless tubes of black plastic, metal screws and packets of wires, with accompanying booklets in multiple languages. One large parcel contains a tripod – I have also unwrapped a microphone, a gigantic light (which reminds me of something you might use to guide a ship back to shore) and various other items, the purpose of which I haven't discovered yet. So, this is what influencers get up to... Although they don't call themselves that anymore, do they? It's all 'content creator', 'brand ambassador' and 'digital entrepreneur' these days.

Merlyn calls the equipment the 'WULT® Woman Kit', and she's already messaged me to see how I'm getting on with it.

> Erica – has the kit arrived? The countdown is on! Baci, M

> Yes, just trying to work it all out... E

It's going to take ages to set it all up in the spare room but it's not like I've got anything else to do — apart from wait. The weather has turned really cold, making it even less appealing to leave the house than usual. I look at the parcels, then turn to my phone instead to watch Cassia getting ready in the toilets of Colbert on Sloane Square last night (#*daytonight* #*itsvintagedarling*). Am I really going to have to come up with stuff like this? What toilets am I going to use? Not even sure if they have any in FILLINGZ.

Gabe has messaged me suggesting a coffee but I'm going to hold off now until I have the new version of me to show him. Josie has also been in touch to say they're all back from France but if I can avoid bumping into her in the street, she can wait until ten days is up too. Mother Pells sent me a 'Happy New Year' message the other day, which I replied to, and having put in the hours on Christmas Day I don't need to visit for a while, so all good there. Simon's completely ignoring me, which is standard, although I can see from his Facebook that he's tired of being Scandinavian and now appears, as predicted, to be fixated on being 'net zero'. According to his last update, this involves building a compost toilet in his garden. Alannah must be delighted, especially as it now boasts a 'urine separator'. I make a mental note not to drink or eat for at least twelve hours before my next visit — although who knows when that will be...

Chapter Twelve

Age before beauty

Yuvana Labs gave me a goodie bag to take home after the treatment. It contained a packet of Grub's Up chocolate-coated crickets, some gold under-eye gel patches – which frankly I have more of in my fridge than cheese – and an 'ionic' shower head with 'three innovative spray modes'. I've had some crappy goodie bags at beauty PR events in my time – a low point being one containing a pregnancy test and a Barack Obama mask – but seriously, you've just burrowed into my brain, give me a bottle of fizz already.

Also, inside the gold embossed, Yuvana Labs branded gift bag was an iPad, for me to use to write my 'transformation diary', as instructed by Dr Marcus. The iPad is also gold, with curly writing on the back: *Age Before Beauty*. This annoys me somewhat as it doesn't really make sense – surely that's what you say to someone older when you let them go first, to be a bit cheeky? Did they think it was meaningful? Or a pun? I could have told them a thing or two about puns if they'd asked me. JEEZ.

The iPad has been lying on my sofa since I got home from London. Each day, I have to answer the same four questions, in as much detail as possible, treating it 'like a journal' – which suits me fine, having nobody to talk to about the treatment, apart from Merlyn I suppose, but all she says is that it will be 'incredible, Erica my dear'. Each time I submit my answers, I also have to use the iPad to take a selfie, which I send at the same time. Once both are done, a giant tick appears on the screen followed by an overly close-up picture of Peach Jumpsuit, smiling in approval.

Day One

1. How are you feeling physically today?
Sore nose/head. I also have creaky ankles, especially when I get up, but this has been bothering me for a while. Other than that, generally tired, irritable and more often than not, in need of the toilet (this is not new). Also, just remembered the anxiety, dull skin, sleep issues, facial hair, brain fog, and don't get me started on my vagina. Bet you're glad you asked.

2. How are you feeling emotionally today?
I don't really know. Excited but also not sure if I should be excited. Apprehensive. Jittery. Wobbly. I think I need something to calm me down.

3. Note any changes you've observed in your physical appearance since starting the treatment.
Appearance worse today (even bigger shadows under eyes). Perhaps this is the effect of the sedation or the nose injector/probe thingy?

4. Describe any reactions or comments you've received from others about your physical transformation.
Haven't seen anyone. I may see a Deliveroo rider shortly.

Day Two

1. How are you feeling physically today?
Headache/nose ache is better although not fully gone. I've only taken two ibuprofen (four yesterday). Went to the toilet slightly less last night but I think I'm dehydrated as I had some Cava delivered by way of a celebration. I'm not going to make a fuss, but this would have been a welcome addition to the goodie bag instead of the chocolate insects. Just some feedback.

2. How are you feeling emotionally today?
Weepy. Could be the Cava. Also watched the end of *The Good Place* again and the bit when Chidi walks through the door gets me every time.

3. Note any changes you've observed in your physical appearance since starting the treatment.
I'm not sure if it's related to the treatment but when I put my bra on this morning there was less 'hoicking'. I could be wrong though, maybe my bra straps moved in the wash. Otherwise, I'd say, my skin looks okay, possibly slightly brighter than it usually does post sparkling wine.

4. Describe any reactions or comments you've received from others about your physical transformation.
Not been out again. Could have gone to the shops but opted to have a freezer dinner for financial reasons (a sausage roll garland from the M&S Festive Platters range that I forgot to take to my mother's house at Christmas). Speaking of which, can you let me know when the paperwork is coming over about the promo

activity as I'd like to send you my first invoice and I don't have a PO number.

Day Three

1. How are you feeling physically today?
Okay. Didn't need any painkillers when I woke up and only went to the toilet once in the night. Also noticed I wasn't walking like Mrs Overall for the first few minutes after I got up – you may not get this reference so I will just say google it, if you've never watched Victoria Wood, you really should.

2. How are you feeling emotionally today?
Better after my hangover yesterday. Reading back through the paperwork I realise it says you're not meant to drink for the first ten days so apologies for that, I got carried away – it's a lot to take in. This is why my first selfie was a bit odd too, so I'd probably delete that one, I was just trying something.

3. Note any changes you've observed in your physical appearance since starting the treatment.
A couple of things – firstly, the grey hairs around my temples are pretty much gone. There weren't many and it's not like I would ever wear my hair scraped back (I'd look like Miss Trunchbull) but that's a nice development. Also, I noticed a definite improvement in skin firmness when I was doing my gua sha lymphatic drainage with an energising oil this morning (I am still busy writing magazine reviews by the way, as I haven't got the paperwork through from your accounts department yet – just another nudge on that).

4. Describe any reactions or comments you've received from others about your physical transformation.

I haven't been out yet, but the postman Luke had some parcels for me and told me I looked 'snatched'. I had to google this but it means: 'Slang (of a person) very attractive, especially as a result of doing something to improve their appearance'. For context he's in his twenties and normally looks at me like I'm Prue Leith.

Day Four

1. How are you feeling physically today?

Surprisingly energetic – I've been setting up the equipment you sent over in the spare room ready to do the Instagram content. Speaking of which, is someone from the team called Channing meant to be getting in touch with me about this?

2. How are you feeling emotionally today?

I haven't cried – not even a small tear, which is very unusual. Also, more optimistic that the treatment might be working.

3. Note any changes you've observed in your physical appearance since starting the treatment.

Today I look much less tired, which is welcome. I can see that my eyelids are opening more too, not just hanging over my eyes. The crow's feet and crepiness seem improved as well and the whites of my eyes look whiter. My clothes also feel looser. I might stop wearing these maternity knickers my sister-in-law gave me. (Well, she didn't give them to me exactly – they were in a bag of clothes for the charity shop at my brother's house and I took them.)

4. Describe any reactions or comments you've received from others about your physical transformation.
I went to the local shop/garage today and the man that served me did a kind of double take. I go in there quite a lot. He may have just been surprised I wasn't buying wine.

Day Five

1. How are you feeling physically today?
Woke up with a headache and been feeling tired all day.

2. How are you feeling emotionally today?
Not in a very good mood. Halfway through the ten days and to be honest it's not exactly as 'extraordinary' as Merlyn made out. I'd been hoping to have something more to show for this by now. The giant foil balloons in the shape of '27' that have just gone up in my neighbour's window are presumably for a family birthday event they're having, but frankly I feel like they're mocking me.

3. Note any changes you've observed in your physical appearance since starting the treatment.
I suppose my skin looks pretty good today and the grey hair is gone but nothing particularly new to report, which is disappointing.

4. Describe any reactions or comments you've received from others about your physical transformation.
Haven't seen anyone. Starting to wonder what the point of this is and getting quite bored. Watching *Schitt's Creek* again to cheer myself up. (I was going to rewatch *The Last of Us* but... it doesn't matter.)

Day Six

1. How are you feeling physically today?
Pretty good so I'd like to apologise for yesterday and also the gesture I made in the selfie.

2. How are you feeling emotionally today?
Also good. I'm not going to tempt fate by saying it out loud, but it's okay to write it here as that doesn't count – I think it might be working.

3. Note any changes you've observed in your physical appearance since starting the treatment.
Huge development – the lines around my neck seem to have gone. Literally disappeared. Also, my neck seems weirdly more separate from my head, it had previously merged, but my jawline is much more noticeable now. I've tried to show this in the selfie.

4. Describe any reactions or comments you've received from others about your physical transformation.
My friend Keith FaceTimed me and I answered it without thinking (I know I'm meant to be keeping a low profile). He made a kind of growling noise when he saw me, in a positive way. It's hard to explain. He did a kind of cat paw/claw thing with his hand at the same time. I don't think I'm describing this very well.

Day Seven

1. How are you feeling physically today?
Like I've got new trainers on that have really bouncy soles. I don't have trainers on, I just mean I feel really energetic. I also slept all night for nine hours.

2. How are you feeling emotionally today?
Positive. Very positive.

3. Note any changes you've observed in your physical appearance since starting the treatment.
Today I noticed my face seems to have lifted up, and the jowls that I had are barely noticeable. In profile, you just see nose and chin – not nose, chin, a weird bit, another chin, a neck, and then a kind of extra neck. It's amazing.

4. Describe any reactions or comments you've received from others about your physical transformation.
I haven't seen anyone but my mum messaged me this morning and I remembered it's her birthday soon, so I've been thinking about seeing her (and my brother and his family), which is worrying me slightly. I feel as though, looking at myself now in the mirror, the change is really noticeable. Any advice welcome.

Day Eight

1. How are you feeling physically today?
Slept for ten hours and contemplated going for a run this morning (I didn't). Instead (sorry if this is too much information but I think it's important), I have some electrical items from Gwyneth Paltrow (not her directly, from her website Goop), which I used for the first time in ages. If you don't know what I mean let's just leave it.

2. How are you feeling emotionally today?
Giggly, almost hysterical. In a good way. (The selfie hopefully shows that, ignore the hat, just been trying on some old clothes.)

3. Note any changes you've observed in your physical appearance since starting the treatment.

I've been examining myself in the mirror this morning and today what I noticed was the flabby saggy floppiness seems to be disappearing, especially under my arms and on my thighs. The skin on my body is really smooth too, without all those goosebumps, spider veins and cellulite patches. I might wear a skirt today with no tights – just inside though as it's January.

4. Describe any reactions or comments you've received from others about your physical transformation.

I haven't seen anyone, but I messaged my boyfriend (well not really boyfriend but hopefully he will be soon) and suggested we meet up, and told him I had a surprise for him. This went down well. As will my tits I imagine, they seem to be about three inches further up my chest.

Day Nine

1. How are you feeling physically today?
Really excellent.

2. How are you feeling emotionally today?
Pretty shocked. Trying to take it all in. I think it's actually worked.

3. Note any changes you've observed in your physical appearance since starting the treatment.
My feet don't have that sort of wooden-looking ridge around the sole anymore, they're really smooth. Another thing I noticed today was that the back of my hands don't look like a relief map of the Nile Delta. The veins seem to have returned to their rightful position under the skin rather than on top of it.

4. Describe any reactions or comments you've received from others about your physical transformation.

The postman Lucas (I think I got his name wrong before) came for the first time since the other day with a parcel for me and when I opened the door, he didn't recognise me. It was slightly inconvenient as he said he needed a resident to sign for parcels, so I said I was my niece and I was staying with me (confusing I know). He let me sign for the parcels in the end. Makes me think there might be some upcoming issues with identity but I'm sure it won't be a problem. Also, a quick note to say thanks for sorting out the paperwork, I've sent my first invoice to your accounts department. I still haven't heard from Channing yet about the content plan though?

Day Ten

1. How are you feeling physically today?
I'm not going to lie, I did have some (a lot of) wine last night, but I am pretty much hangover free. I tried on all my old Nineties clothes (which fit, incredibly, so glad I kept them) and did some dancing in my living room to Ministry of Sound. Again, if you're not familiar, have a listen on Spotify, I recommend the 1997 one with Pete Tong and Boy George that has Olive's 'You're Better Off Alone' on it. Not sure the couple next door with the baby were too pleased though.

2. How are you feeling emotionally today?
Like I've met my old self again. It *is* extraordinary – I'm sorry I doubted Yuvana, and Merlyn. As I'm typing this, I'm crying a bit. But not like I used to. Happy tears – very, very happy tears.

3. Note any changes you've observed in your physical appearance since starting the treatment.
Everything. Everything has changed – my face, my body, the way I feel. I'm young again.

4. Describe any reactions or comments you've received from others about your physical transformation.
I'm getting ready to tell my friends. I think they're going to be amazed, and really delighted for me.

Chapter Thirteen

The language of young people

It's the eleventh day, and for a few seconds as I open my eyes, I have forgotten. It reminds me of the days after Father Pells died – there was always a blissful moment in the morning when he was still alive in my head. This is the opposite though. I wake up with the usual feeling of low-level despair, but then it hits me like a truck. A truck full of elation, and I scramble out of bed and race to the bathroom mirror.

I pick up a face cloth to wipe the glass, as it's smeared and dirty with speckles of toothpaste. I'm not the greatest housekeeper. As an example, several years ago, I found a tray of roast potatoes in my top oven (the small, useless one nobody ever uses except to warm plates). I only cook roast potatoes at Christmas, and when I found them I hadn't hosted anyone at Christmas for four years. That was the year everyone came here as Mother Pells didn't want to cook and Simon and Alannah were getting their extension built. The potatoes weren't mouldy, which was interesting – they looked more like something one might discover amongst the ruins of Pompeii.

The remains of some cleanser on the face cloth just smear the mirror even more so I grab a towel from the back of the door and rub at the glass. Gradually a clear patch forms, and I peer in, making it bigger until I can finally see my whole face. I've done this every morning for the last few days: staring, prodding, poking... Can it be real? No Gordon Brown jowls, no sagging, no nematode neck, no crepey lids. None of it. NONE. Only clear, bright skin – plump, glowing, and just so much more *attached* to my face. I look unrecognisable. And more to the point, I look in my mid-twenties. The wait, the ten long days, are over now. The WULT® treatment has worked. It bloody worked.

Not for the first time this week, I sink to the floor, half laughing, half crying – then stand up again, looking in the mirror, switching on the lights that go around it (the ones I usually reserve for chin hair plucking). Now out comes my magnifying mirror. It's incredible, even close up. Then I'm back on the floor, slumped against the wall. Imagine what Cassia will think. No 'Mid Youth' and 'Over 40s Style' for me. Ha! This is insane. And then the tears come again, and more laughter, and more looking in the mirror, peering down my top, feeling my bum, and laughing again and again and again.

—

A little later, Lucas the postman comes, and I pretend I'm my own niece again, which seems to work and is easier.

'Is Ms Pells away then?' he asks.

'Yes, she's working in London.' Lucas doesn't seem to really care, preferring, it seems, to converse with/look at my niece.

Later still, I have to go out, partly to buy toilet roll, and partly to collect my umbrella from Je Suis Belle. Not wishing to sound like my mother but judging by the forecast, I'm going to need it. I put on a woolly hat and sunglasses and fifteen minutes later I'm on the high street. Plan is to dive into Je Suis Belle, then grab a flat white and a cinnamon whirl from the new coffee shop, Brew & Beam, which Mother Pells says is far too 'hip-hop' (I think she means hipster).

I can see from across the road that it's full of the town's (very small) Gen Z contingent, probably pleased to have somewhere to congregate that isn't called 'Sue's' and doesn't serve instant coffee from a giant urn with a side of lardy cake. This used to be my destiny – to grow old in a town full of pensioners. Not anymore.

I pass FILLINGZ, which looks shut again, and head into Je Suis Belle, where one of the Huns who did my lash lift a few weeks ago is behind the reception desk. She is wearing a scalloped fabric hairband and foundation that is about three shades too light, giving her the appearance of an unsettlingly young Tudor princess being sent off to marry a member of European nobility.

'I'm here to pick up an umbrella that was left… It's yellow, with a wooden handle.'

The Hun eyes me. 'Are you picking it up for your mum?'

'For my mum?'

'Yes – was it your mum who was in here?'

Holy crap. She thinks I'm my own daughter. This is wild. I mutter something about my mum really liking her new lashes and the Hun acquiesces and pulls the umbrella from a box under the desk. I hurriedly thank her and leave, crossing over the road to Brew & Beam.

The door to the coffee shop, in an attempt to be old-fashioned and no doubt also 'hip-hop', has an overly loud bell, so when I open it all the Gen Zs look round. One particular young man with a mullet stares very pointedly. I join the short queue behind a girl wearing platform trainers, teamed with a pair of patterned socks and a short purple dress, with an aviator jacket over the top. She smiles at me, and, momentarily forgetting what I look like, I wonder if she's about to ask me for money.

I get my coffee and pastry and turn to leave. The girl, who's by now moved away from the counter to talk to her friend, touches my arm as I pass her.

'Check the drip,' she says, showing a tongue piercing as she speaks.

Looking down at my cup to locate said drip, I grab a napkin from the counter, but can't see the issue. Then I wonder if it's my nose doing the dripping, accustomed as I am to snottiness when coming into somewhere warm from the cold. But no. I look at the girl with a questioning face.

She laughs. 'I was talking about the 'fit, queen!'

'Ah... right.' I back out the door, slowly realising that she is talking to me in the language of young people. Because she thinks I am one. SHE THINKS I AM ONE.

I'm not sure what she means, but I'm pretty sure it's a compliment about my clothes, which is firstly very nice of her, and secondly bizarre as I threw on an ancient pair of cargo trousers (the only thing that fitted my newly firmed up body) and an oversized checked shirt.

Remember that scene in *Pretty Woman* when Julia Roberts walks down Rodeo Drive after her makeover, to the Roy Orbison song? Well, this is like that in no way, it being January in a small market town in Wiltshire, and the bag I'm swinging is a Sainsbury's carrier containing an umbrella, some toilet roll and a bottle of wine. Also, *Pretty Woman* is not a film that has aged well for many reasons.

But the point is, I feel like I need a soundtrack. Because I am walking on bloody air. NOT sunshine. Do NOT make that my soundtrack.

The afternoon is spent in a dressing gown and Turbo-Dry TressWrap turban (*#gifted*), lying on my sofa, watching YouTube videos called things like *Zendaya Reveals The Concealer You Need Right Now* and admiring my own legs, which look pretty fantastic now they no longer have the texture – and appearance – of luncheon meat. Why did I always obsess about how short they were? They were – are – gorgeous. It's surely the biggest irony of youth that we don't realise how beautiful we are until, well, we're not. I also send messages and emails to create the illusion of normality before I decide how to break this to everyone, and in what order.

When I open my laptop, I see I already have one from Simon:

> Hi Erica,
> Our brief conversation at Christmas didn't go terribly well. You appear to be under pressure at the moment, although I'm not entirely sure from what.
> Anyway, I'd like to have a serious chat with you so let me know when works. I know we're seeing you for Mum's eightieth soon but that's not really the time and the place as I'm sure you'll agree.
> Alannah says she's got some Stinking Bishop for you.
> S
> Simen Pells
> CAO (Chief Awesomeness Officer)
> Cabbidge

> **An endangered species of lichen was re-introduced to Somerset to offset the impact of this email**

What's he harping on about now? Must be short of things to do today. Simon has spent his career working for start-ups with ludicrous names, in roles with ludicrous job titles doing who knows what (probably something ludicrous). Shouldn't criticise though, he has a big house in Horfield and probably (definitely) didn't need help to buy it from our parents, who think his career is on a par with Mark Zuckerberg's – while I'm not even sure Mother Pells knows what I do.

I make a mental note to reply to him later, then message Mother Pells about her birthday party, which I haven't worked out how to deal with yet. I go with 'I could bring a starter – and I'm sure Alannah will make her legendary Aussie pavlova!'

I also message Josie and thank her for some beetroot hummus she left on my front step on day six – I didn't answer the door when she rang the bell and lay on the living room floor for a while until she went away. She replies immediately saying that they are in Oxford for a few days 'so we'll hopefully see you soon'. Then she signs off, as jolly as ever: 'Happy new year if I haven't said that already! xx'

I send Gabe a GIF of Moira Rose from *Schitt's Creek* looking really excited because a) he's rewatching it too and b) I am trying to create some vague sense of build-up for when I see him. This won't be until next week though as he's back in Uttoxeter helping his dad move into a nursing home, and I have to go to London for my first Youth Review, which sounds like it could potentially involve paper pants again. Who cares though, I will probably look brilliant in them. I'm also going to have lunch with Merlyn. And see Nandy of course.

> I'm coming to London next week, you around?

> For you, mofo – always.

> Good... need to talk. It's a biggie.

> You finally had a wank?

> Something like that. I'll message you, I think it'll be Thursday.

> Looking forward to seeing your resting bitch face.

> Just you wait.

I can't wait to see her reaction. But for now, it's just me and my bloody gorgeous young face. I eat, sleep, look at myself in the mirror, drink, finish *Schitt's Creek*, look at myself in the mirror, eat, sleep, use Gwyneth's electricals (a lot – wow, I'd forgotten how fun that could be), look at myself in the mirror, laugh, sleep, cry, and wonder what the hell is going to happen next. This is what I've wanted for so long, what I've been searching for with every serum, supplement and solution I have tried, bought or reviewed over the past decade or so. I do feel happy. It just feels like quite an intense, hysterical sort of happy, like I've won the lottery but can't tell anyone or start spending the money yet.

Change is good. Change is needed. Last time change came it took Father Pells away, but it's time for some positive change. For a change. Too many changes? So what. What's so good about the status quo? I know everyone else is quite happy with some HRT and a dry robe, but I'm not ready for that yet, I'm not done. And I've got this second chance. It *is* like a lottery win. I *am* a winner. This is my time at last, another go at life, before I shuffle off to Sue's for a slice of lardy cake.

Chapter Fourteen

A darts player in the 1980s

The snacks on offer in First Class are rather disappointing. I have always imagined it as an opulent, exclusive place, like the *Orient Express* or similar – a Dowager Duchess at the bar and waiters with white cloths on their arms serving Sidecars. What even is a Sidecar? Cassia would probably know. I'm about to google it, but get distracted by a video (*Kendall Jenner Shares Her Acne Journey*). I'm only watching videos that feature young beauty tips these days. Then the steward appears out of nowhere – he looks me up and down, asks me what I'd like (a packet of Tyrrells, thanks), where I'm heading (Paddington) and if I'm enjoying First Class (Yuvana Labs paid for it. I don't share that information, although you can tell he's wondering why I'm in the expensive seats at my 'age').

This is all very strange and is going to take a lot of getting used to: going from being the invisible woman to the *very* visible woman, almost overnight. I'd forgotten how much people notice you when you're young and female. You're fair game, public property, up for grabs... Constant stares, smiles, and of course, unwanted approaches. I seriously hope the tube isn't like it was when I worked in London twenty years ago, when a penis against your back or an 'ooops!' hand on your tit was just part of a normal morning's commute. Things have improved though, right, since the whole *#metoo* thing?

Don't get me wrong, I'm not complaining. Being invisible was rubbish. And it wasn't just about looks, but being overlooked (see what I did there?). If you weren't part of a couple, you weren't invited, or asked or considered. And in public spaces, well, forget it. Middle-aged women are background noise. Unless you're in a 'role', like being a mother, or doing your job, or you're famous or something. I suppose that's why middle-aged women go for statement jewellery and those massive glasses like Val from *Glow Up*. No thanks. Youth is currency and my balance (for once) is in the black. I'm not going to lie, I do feel a bit exposed though. I'll get used to it.

There are two other young people in the carriage – both women, both wearing long woollen coats like Phoebe Buffay in *Friends*, but with less make-up than I wore in the Nineties, or indeed two weeks ago. Thank god I don't have to bother with all that contour faff anymore. The women have given me a discreet nod of approval. It's like a secret club these days, being young – exchanged glances, knowing looks – and so many compliments on your 'fit' (outfit, I have learnt since the Brew & Beam incident – just as I have discovered that 'drip', in contrast to what it previously meant to me, is a good thing.) Were we ever this nice to each other?

The fashion part of this is as complicated as the language. For example, I've noticed a trench coat and baseball cap combo is popular, a fact I recently shared with my mother on the way to Carol's funeral, just making small talk – but she thought I said 'trench foot and baseball bat' so I didn't pursue the conversation after that.

However, that look doesn't feel very 'me', and as this trip to London is my first time 'out' since IT happened, and I've decided to dress slightly differently – to match my face to my clothes and look more like other twenty-somethings I've seen – I did a bit of research on YouTube and TikTok.

I discovered that young people don't have 'looks' or 'styles' like we used to, they have 'aesthetics'. And quite often these have the word 'Core' at the end. For example, the look... sorry, aesthetic... I'm trying today is called Picnic Core, which I chose mainly because I haven't been shopping yet and had a gingham blouse at the back of the cupboard. The alternatives were also less appealing: Fisherman Core, which I feel Simon/Semen has got covered for both of us; Y3K, which feels faintly terrifying as Y2K is still fairly recent to me, or Castle Core, which is all floaty dresses and weirdly, in one video I watched, stick-on pointy ears.

My Picnic Core aesthetic also involves carrying a giant, ideally wicker, basket (which I found in a cupboard too, I think it might be Alannah's) to give the impression I could set up a picnic spontaneously at any moment (unlikely, as it's still winter) and liberal use of blusher to suggest either sunburn and/or enthusiastic consumption of strawberries. It's a 'whole thing' apparently. And genuinely confusing considering I grew up in a time when you were either square, or a goth, or a Sloane, or a raver, and that was that. To complete the look, I've also cut my hair into a blunt fringe using Ikea kitchen scissors and a YouTube tutorial for guidance, which makes me look even more unrecognisable, if that were possible. In general though, the Gen Z fashion rule seems to be: if it's far too big, doesn't match and might have previously been worn by a darts player in the Eighties, wear it – and a random person will tell you that you have 'main character energy'. What a time to be alive.

An hour or so later, I am standing in the foyer of the *Luscious* offices in Soho. The receptionist, Liz, (who I've definitely met before) thinks I'm some straight-out-of-college wannabe fashion editor trying to barge my way in and demand an internship. This is the kind of thing that would normally bring me out in a hot flush, but I feel at an unusually normal temperature. I message Merlyn.

> In reception but Liz won't let me come up.
> E

> I'll be down in 5 my dear. Excited to see the new you! I've a table booked for lunch. M

I tell Liz that Merlyn is coming down to meet me, which she clearly doesn't believe, but at least she lets me have a seat in the reception area on one of the really uncomfortable brown leather swivel chairs with a back so low, what is even the point? I watch people coming and going, several of whom I recognise – but nobody recognises me. It's bizarre, as though I'm in one of those films where people shapeshift, like… I can't think of the names of any but there's definitely one with Brie Larson, I watched it at Simon's house with Oli a while back.

Merlyn sits opposite me in Brasserie Zédel in Piccadilly. I have walked past this place many times and always wondered what's behind the grand Art Deco façade that promises 'Bar & Cabaret'. Quite a lot, I thought, as I wandered about looking for the brasserie itself in amongst doors to the Bar Américain and Le Crazy Coqs, whatever that is or indeed, who they, are.

Merlyn can't take her eyes off me. 'I'm mesmerised, my dear... It's extraordinary.' I look at her turban and can't help thinking the same.

'I was pretty hot when I was young, wasn't I? I mean – aren't I?' I say, and order the steak haché. I am hoping for *trois pièces* from the *Chariot de Fromages* afterwards too.

'I certainly prefer it to your omelette look,' says Merlyn, raising an eyebrow and sucking her cheeks in, but with a smile. 'And Dr Marcus and the team are pleased with the results?'

'Yup,' I say, mouth crammed with bread – why is butter in French restaurants like the dairy version of crack? 'Well, my review is this afternoon, but they seem happy from all the pictures I've sent in.'

'And how are you finding it all?' Merlyn is peering at my forehead, then my jawline, my neck...

'Well, I've had to pretend to my postman that I'm my own niece, and I haven't told any of my friends and family yet...'

Merlyn stops her scrutiny and looks at me directly. 'What about Nandy?'

'I'm seeing her this evening. She's going to explode when she sees me.'

'Explode...?'

'She won't be able to believe it. She'll be so happy for me.'

Merlyn nods but doesn't say anything. I continue. 'So… I'm avoiding my family, men look at me all the time, I'm constantly thinking about sex and…'

Merlyn interrupts. 'And you love it?'

'Yeah. I love it, Merlyn.'

We burst out laughing, and Merlyn tops up our glasses with Pouilly-Fuissé.

'Also, I can drink at lunchtime and not have to go to bed at six p.m. Being young is brilliant.' I laugh again, then compose myself. 'Do you know when the social media stuff is starting? I'm waiting to hear from someone…'

'Ah yes. Channing. Don't worry, he's been on holiday. The plan is that the *Luscious* advertorial – which, by the way, we will need to shoot very soon – will have the new Instagram handle *@wokeuplikethis* at the end, instead of a by-line, and readers will rush to follow "WULT® Woman". *Luscious* is also doing a social media advertising campaign at the same time, just to drive followers.'

I have never heard Merlyn talk about things like 'handles' and 'driving followers' before.

Our food arrives: my steak haché, which is basically a posh burger, and her steak tartare, which to me looks more like the ingredients for a meal than an actual meal: mince with an egg yolk on top and a lettuce leaf next to it.

'Can we have cheese after this?' I ask.

'You can have what you like, it's on Yuvana. Remember…' She reaches over the table and holds my hand, not without taking a second to scrutinise the condition of it. 'Make the most of all this, my dear. You might as well.'

Chapter Fifteen

Step Into Your Magnificence

After lunch with Merlyn, I'm back in the Yuvana Labs reception area. Although it's only been two weeks, it feels like years – twenty years, come to think of it. It's a different receptionist today, and she looks like the personification of an Instagram reel, with dusky pink clothes, hair slicked back into a neat ponytail and the shiniest lips I have ever seen. She appears to be eating some kind of high-protein cacao-nut ball type thing while tapping away on her rose-gold MacBook Air, with pointed white fingernails. Next to the laptop is a book called *Step Into Your Magnificence*.

'I'm here to...' I say, but The Human Reel interrupts me.

'Be the best version of yourself you can possibly be?' She looks at me quizzically and sips from a gold water bottle filled with bits of cucumber. I'm trying to work out what 'Core' she is when it hits me: she's a Millennial, same as Glazed Doughnut. A few months ago, Gen Zs and Millennials all merged into one undifferentiated mass: People Younger Than Me. Now I see the difference.

'Well... yes. I mean... I'm here to see Dr Marcus. I'm Erica.'

She stares at me, a penny visibly dropping. 'Well, then you must be here for your Youth Review.'

'I am.'

'Dr Marcus will be ready shorty.'

Is she calling me 'Shorty'? Or maybe she said shortly. I'm not sure enough to say anything so just glare at her and sit on the blue sofa with my picnic basket.

—

Sitting there, I find myself thinking about Nandy and how much I want her to be okay with all this. Friends like her don't come along very often. Well, not for me. I don't know why this is exactly. Maybe I'm not good at making friends, or maybe I have too strict a door policy, or maybe I don't try hard enough anymore. I made more of an effort in the past, but I suppose the old jowly me, with confidence levels so low, kind of gave up.

That said, there was a time I tried. It was about ten years ago – Josie and Laure hadn't arrived on the street, so I hardly knew anyone, even though I'd been there for the best part of a decade. I signed up to host Bella & Tot jewellery parties, lured in by talk of being a 'stylist' and 'new season drops' (but secretly appalled at the prices of what was generally silver or gold 'finish' rather than real silver or gold). It was really to meet some of the women on the neighbouring streets – I felt sure there must be more kindred spirits out there.

I dropped invitations through doors ('be sure to over-invite!' advised the Bella & Tot Stylist Guide), chose an outfit from Reiss, got fresh Botox and bought some nibbles from Sainsbury's, in those wilderness days before the M&S Food opened at the garage. I made Sangria, although I'm not sure why, and cut up a quiche. I laid out jewellery on a load of old Amazon boxes of different heights that I covered with duvet covers, and it didn't look as bad as it sounds. And then I waited for my guests to arrive, with disposable incomes and amazing personalities in tow.

Three people came. Mrs Belcher from over the road, who I distinctly remember not inviting – for many reasons, but let's pick two for brevity: she wipes her feet for about five minutes before she goes inside her house, so I feel there are issues there, and I am also convinced that when she takes PR sample parcels in for me she syphons off a few. That woman might dress as though she works at Alan's Auto Repairs, but she always smells like one of the treatment rooms at The Connaught Spa.

Guest number two was Nicky, or Nicki, or Nikki or… oh who cares? She lived a few doors along from where Josie lives now, but thankfully has long since moved to Market Lavington. Nicky told me as soon as she arrived that she was 'well known at the school', which to me sounded like a matter for the police but to her appeared to be something to boast about. She could only stay for half an hour as her husband was 'doing bedtimes' and Flora was 'overtired'. So am I, listening to you, I thought. She ate most of the quiche and knocked over one of the Amazon boxes, ruining my display of Clip-on Teardrop Hoops.

Guest number three – Fern, a 'hedge witch' from the street parallel to mine – was the only one to alert me to the fact that my eyebrows were raised, making me look surprised, something I hadn't realised while I was getting ready. Two words: cheap Botox. Maybe that's why Nicky kept talking, thinking I was actually interested in what she was saying. Back to Fern, no, I didn't know what a hedge witch was either, but she was late because she was 'harvesting wolfsbane' and wondered if the Bella &

Tot range included amulets, so I got the general idea. In summary, by eight p.m. I was on my own drinking a bowl of Sangria. It wasn't all bad though – even though there were no purchases on the night I did get a big order online the next day, not from a name I recognised but I didn't care, it was enough to qualify me for a free Kimberly Tourmaline Necklace.

—

After about five minutes, The Human Reel gets up and leads me towards the door. As she opens it, she says, with apparently no irony whatsoever, 'You didn't come this far to only come this far.'

I can't really think how to reply so say 'Righty-ho!', which leaves me wondering who is weirder, me or her.

In the room, Dr Marcus is on the same sofa and looks identical to how he did last time. Is it like *The Great British Bake Off*, where the contestants appear to wear the same clothes all weekend, presumably for continuity? When Josie, Héloïse and I watch it together we always wonder if they have multiple sets of clothes, or if someone washes them and dries them overnight, or if they just wear them dirty. They must get quite sweaty, we all know how hot it can be in the tent. Especially when it's chocolate week, for some reason.

'Erica!' Dr Marcus jumps up theatrically as I enter the room and guides me to the blue velvet sofa, as if I somehow wouldn't be able to see it, despite it being huge and three feet away from me.

'How are you? You're certainly looking… as we'd hoped!' he says.

Peach Jumpsuit makes a hissing sound, which I think is 'Yessssssss', but sounds more like air escaping from an inflatable. She is staring at me and my picnic basket with noticeably more interest than she ever has before.

'I'm good,' I say. 'Thank you. And I mean that – thank you. This is amazing.'

For a second, it almost looks like Peach Jumpsuit is smiling, but it might just be the oligarch lighting or the way her face is stretched so tight.

Dr Marcus can hardly keep still, and after sitting down for a second, he leaps up again and squats down in front of me, in a move that I have never been able to do at any age. He stares at my face, looking at it from every possible angle, touching me lightly on the chin with a beautifully manicured finger to get me to lift my head up, then down, then to one side, then the other.

'Stupendous,' he says, after a minute or so. It reminds me of the sort of adjective generated by AI on LinkedIn. 'Congratulate Kelly Norris on Two Years at Prestige Consulting Services – Stupendous news, Kelly!'

'It's going to change my life,' I say, surprising myself at how serious I sound. 'For the better, that is. I mean, it is already. Doing that.'

Peach Jumpsuit hands me a glass of water. How does she know that I can feel my throat tightening with emotion? That wine I had with lunch is really coming back to haunt me.

'Have you told your family and friends yet?' asks Dr Marcus.

'No... I'm meeting my best friend in a couple of hours though.' I might be nearly fifty, but I still get a warm glow from calling Nandy my best friend.

'Indeed,' says Dr Marcus. I might start saying 'indeed' more, it's such a non-answer.

'And do you have any friends in Europe? You may have noted in the paperwork that the treatment won't be available in certain European territories, so we would rather keep it under the radar over there. For now, at least.'

I can't help thinking that with the internet pretty well established, it's going to be tricky to pick and choose where – and by whom – this gets talked about, especially if we're about to launch an Instagram account to promote it... But I nod anyway. I've got a fringe like Emma Watson and a jawline to match, so who cares about 'certain European territories'. Not me.

'Excellent. And now, Portia will take you through for your review.'

Peach Jumpsuit, who has been perfectly still, and holding her hands in a weird mannequin pose again, springs to life and stands up, then ushers me through the far door of the room. This time, I notice, my knees don't click when I get up.

Chapter Sixteen

Does Australia have its own dark web?

After a rather dull hour with Peach Jumpsuit taking photographs of me from every possible angle – and asking me questions that I'm sure she came up with, as practically all of them ended with an 's' – I have a couple of hours to kill, so decide to hit the shops so I can expand my 'Core' repertoire beyond Picnic.

On Regent Street, I head into Hollister, momentarily confused as to why they have a whole front section of facecloths before I realise these are in fact tops, similar to the ones I last saw on the Sugababes. Handkerchief, bandeau, bustier... it's a whole world of items I would previously have avoided like the plague, due to many things, but mainly bingo wings and the 'do I wear a bra with that or not?' question.

But the whole bra thing is no longer an issue. I have actually, several times recently, Forgotten. To. Put. One. On. I know, it's a lot to take in. But aside from my glorious jawline and line-free visage, my tits are really one of my favourite bits of the new me. They're like gorgeous bao buns, just sitting there, perky and firm and delicious. Why didn't I appreciate them when I was younger? What an idiot I was to think they were too small. They're bloody perfect. Anyway, I grab a handful of tops (and I mean handful, there is very little fabric going on here) and a pair of 'ultra-low rise' jeans and head for the changing rooms.

I expected these to be the kind of chaotic communal affair I remember from Topshop in the Nineties but instead, there are rows of cubicles with lockable doors, seats, mirrors and even a range of lighting options. Normally in this situation I would have held my own gaze in the mirror for fear of catching sight of the hideous bin bag of yoghurt that was my body. Today though, I lose track of time admiring myself to the extent that someone knocks on the door and shouts, 'You okay, sis?'

Sis? Is that the new 'bro'? Or maybe it's not, maybe it's someone who is out shopping with their sibling, and has knocked on the wrong cubicle door. This is a minefield. What do I say? Spluttering, I stop admiring my norks and pull on a lace-up-the-front white top, which to me looks faintly 'Linda Lusardi' but according to the saleswoman (I say woman, but she looked the same age as Héloïse), is 'Coquette Core'.

'Just... vibing.'

What the hell? Why did I say that? I think I must have picked it up from one of the TikToks. What does it even mean?

There's a pause. Then...

'For real.'

And then footsteps walking away.

Triumphant, both with my effortless use of Gen Z language and how brilliant my tits are, I buy all the face cloths and the jeans and head to the tube, grinning like a loon.

Nandy's terraced house always smells of warm washing on radiators and toasted cumin seeds, and is a jumbled mess of clutter belonging to Ash, her artist husband, and her two children, Rohan and Maya, who are grown up and have left home but come back frequently for Nandy's cooking – which her father often travels over from Walthamstow for too.

I am slightly thrown that I'm going straight there, given the nature of the surprise I have for her, but Nandy's shift at *Metro* was called off so she doesn't want to come into town. 'Just stay the night,' she said. 'I'll make the Tangdi kebabs you like and we can get cosy and watch *30 Rock*.'

It's freezing and already nearly dark when I get off the tube at Leytonstone to walk the ten minutes to Nandy's. I call her on the way. I'm praying that Ash won't be there, or the kids, but don't want to ask – don't know how to ask – without it being awkward.

'Can you come and meet me on Pretoria Road?'

'Is your bag heavy, old lady?'

'Kind of...'

'Okay... fine. We can get a bottle of red from Yardarm.'

A few minutes later I can see Nandy walking towards me in a massive black puffa coat and red beanie hat with her dog Pakora, a Schnauzer, trotting along next to her on a lead. She's about to walk straight past me, but I grab her sleeve, making her jump out of her skin. Nandy assumes the Ready Stance that she learnt at self-defence classes, arms up. I resist the urge to burst out laughing.

'Nandy – it's me. It's Erica!'

'Erm – no, it's not, but thanks!' She keeps her arms up, turns and continues walking, but much more quickly.

'Nandy, JEEZ... it's me!' I shout after her. She doesn't look back.

I feel like someone in a sci-fi film that has to prove they haven't been possessed by an alien, and frantically try to think of things that only she and I would know.

'I know about the time you crapped behind a tree?' I shout after her. 'You think I should masturbate more? I brought you that Diptyque candle you like but I think smells like old greenhouses? It's me. IT'S ME.'

Nandy stops and turns around slowly. Pakora's tiny tail is wagging as if he recognises me, which helps.

'Erica?' She walks towards me as if approaching a particularly frisky horse. 'What the FUCK did you do to yourself? And why are you carrying a picnic basket?'

'I know, I know. This is why I wanted you to come out and meet me. Is Ash in? The kids? Your dad?'

'No. Thank fuck. This is enough for one person to take in, we don't need to crowdfund it.'

There's a moment when we just stare at each other. And then we hug – big, long and hard. If Nandy could hear me say that she'd made a joke out of it.

—

A little later, we're on Nandy's sofa, Pakora curled up between us, *30 Rock* on the TV.

Nandy tops up my glass with red and looks at me. She's smiling but there's a weird edge to it that I'm not keen on.

'You're fucking mental. What were you thinking?'

'It can't be that much of a surprise – I've been trying to find something that would genuinely work for the last twenty years… I mean, isn't that what we're all in this for? To look younger? Isn't that what we do?' I can feel myself sounding defensive, so I lighten it up a bit. 'I was also thinking it might make my vag work again, you know…'

'Most people just get HRT, Erica.'

I laugh. She's not laughing though.

'But I mean, come on, look at my face.' I poke my cheeks, lift my chin, stroke my neck, tilt my head from side to side, grab a tit in each hand through my gingham blouse just to show how high up they are. 'You should see if you can get it too!'

'No thanks.'

She gets up and walks over to the kitchen area of the open plan ground floor and fiddles about with the kebabs.

'Don't do that now, Nandy,' I say, feeling the atmosphere in the room like a tight, pre-exam feeling in my chest. 'Come and talk to me.'

She turns around, kebab in hand, which she waves as she speaks. 'How can I talk to you when I don't know what to say? I don't get it, Erica. You don't even look like you. You look like a complete stranger. Have you thought what your family are going to say? Your weirdo brother is going to have a field day.'

'I know, I know... And we have my mum's eightieth coming up too.' I take a massive gulp of wine.

Nandy watches me and I can see she's regretting being so harsh. She's probably just miffed she wasn't picked for it.

'Look, Erica, I'm not having a go at you. This was your choice, and you're an adult, so I guess you've given it a lot of thought. I'm just getting used to it, I suppose.'

'It's okay,' I say. I wonder if she's thinking about getting it too? Although I'm not sure there will be other freebies on offer. Perhaps Merlyn could get her a discount? How brilliant would it be if we both looked younger – we could even go out on the town together (although I'm acutely aware nobody says that anymore).

I tell her about Gabe, but she still seems on edge. Maybe things between her and Ash have lost their spark... it's been a while since she had that first rush of romantic feeling and me talking about it probably reminds her of that.

There's a pause in the conversation, which isn't like us.

I try another subject change. 'Did you see that comment on Cassia's "January Empties" reel? Someone asked her if she's due for a chin wax.'

'Oh well, it's Friday tomorrow so no doubt she'll be making a Mint Julep in the scullery... that'll cheer her up,' says Nandy, who seems almost back to her old self now, thank goodness.

—

I wake up in Maya's bedroom and the first thing I see is Madonna staring down at me. How funny that Maya has the *Desperately Seeking Susan* poster on her wall. I was obsessed with that film – Madonna's jacket, the lace gloves... and the bit in the 'Into the Groove' video when she held her armpits over the hand drier. I would spend hours with a painted-on beauty spot and one of Mother Pells' old lacy bras tied round my head, pouting at myself in the bedroom mirror. It seems like yesterday, but for Maya, it's as long ago as Marilyn Monroe was to me at that age. Getting old seems to have happened in a heartbeat, and I feel like I didn't get a proper chance to enjoy being young. But I have another chance now.

Nandy's working in town so once we're up and showered, we get the Central line in together at rush hour, standing squashed against each other in the packed carriage, holding the handrails above us. Nandy looks at me and shakes her head every couple of minutes.

'Are you writing an article about it?' she asks as the train sways from side to side and the 'ugly air' (Héloïse's description) blows through from the next carriage.

'No... they're doing it. It's like a sponsored article, an advertorial thing.'

'Okay... so you won't even get paid?'

The train lurches. 'Yeah, I will. I'm doing some social media for them.'

Nandy pulls a face. ' 'Cos we all know how much you love social media...'

I don't reply, but wonder if she said that because she only has about 500 followers and just shares pictures of her patio planters. Sometimes I feel like Nandy should move with the times a bit. She doesn't even seem to like shifts on the features desks, so I don't know why she does them.

When the train gets to Oxford Circus, Nandy gets off, hugging me as much as she can in the crowd. 'Don't go changing,' she says. She has a weird watery-eyed look.

'Too late,' I call after her.

And she's gone, just a red beanie hat bobbing up and down along the platform, getting smaller and smaller until she's out of view.

Fifteen minutes later, I change at Notting Hill Gate. This stop always reminds me of when I used to go to the carnival with Kofi. I've been thinking about him a lot recently, it must be because I look like I did when we were together. I wish I could focus on the good bits, but memories of that terrible night keep flooding back instead. Me crying... the police... Kofi, unable to look at me... I shake it all away. I don't want to spoil things. This is meant to be a positive time. A new start.

Soon I'm at Paddington station on a bench, dipping bits of croissant into my flat white while I wait for the Swindon train. I check my emails on my phone. There's one from Merlyn, arranging the cover shoot for *Luscious* next week. I'm just about to watch Cassia's nauseating 'thank you' reel for reaching 150K followers, when my phone rings.

It's Simon. He sounds both surprised I answered and infuriated, possibly because I haven't replied to his email – or indeed been in touch at all since Christmas. He also appears to be stressed and somewhere outdoors, and there are strange noises in the background, like birds or one of those percussion instruments that are never seen in orchestras, only at nursery schools.

'Erica?'

'Hello, Simon.'

'Surprised you're actually answering your phone.'

'Surprised you're actually calling.'

'Well, I said I needed to speak to you.'

The strange noise gets louder and I can hear Alannah shouting, 'Simon, close it now, CLOSE IT!'

'Sorry, have you called me at a bad time, Simon?'

'It's fine. It's the quokkas.'

'The what?'

'Quokkas. They're antipodean marsupials that eat waste vegetation. We're becoming completely self-sufficient, Erica.'

He says it like he's announcing a breakthrough in the fight against cancer. I put my phone on loudspeaker so I can quickly google 'quokka'.

'It says quokkas are endangered, Simon – are you meant to keep them?'

'Well, no, not really. Well, not currently. Alannah got them on the Australian dark web.'

'Does Australia have its own dark web? Is that where you got your urine separator?' There are more shrill noises and some garbled shouting, so Simon doesn't hear me.

'They're the world's happiest animals, Erica!'

'Doesn't sound like it.'

The squeaking reaches a crescendo. I hold the phone away from my ear. 'Why are you calling me, Simon?'

'Oh yes, yes… So, I need to speak to you about Mum.'

I roll my eyes and am thankful my voice is still the same, even if the rest of me isn't. This doesn't feel like the phone call to make any announcements.

'Didn't we have this conversation at Christmas?'

'Well, I tried to, Erica, because I'm worried about her. She's struggling with the stairs. She twisted her ankle the other day coming down. I think we need to think about a plan for her quite soon.'

'Simon… she's nearly eighty. I'm sure it's nothing to worry about. And I don't think she wants to move or anything.'

'Are you suddenly an expert in geriatrics, Erica? Have you moved on from being an expert in…'

More squeaking, then a bang.

'In what, Simon?'

'In lipstick. Or rouge or something… Hold on. Shit! Right, I have to go…'

He hangs up, leaving me shaking my head feeling annoyed that I didn't have a chance to take the piss out of him for using the word 'rouge'.

Chapter Seventeen

Projecting a stealth wealth aesthetic

The Fuchsia Frenzy Strappy Lace Bodysuit I ordered from Victoria's Secret (thanks Yuvana Labs for prompt payment of my first invoice) arrived this morning and I think Gabe is going to be delighted by how little fabric was used during its production. Not from an environmental perspective, I just mean that it's very revealing. But honestly, I look bloody great in it, although I do say so myself. Thank god he hasn't seen me naked yet – he was never introduced to the bingo wings or chicken thighs, so even though my face has clearly changed, maybe he can imagine my body always looked like this...

The fly in my ointment is Nandy's rather lukewarm reaction to my new look, but I'm pretty sure that it's because she's also in the industry, so is feeling left out. *Metro* wouldn't get offered such a thing and frankly, considering her last feature was called *I'm A Fussy Eater – Can I Take A Packed Lunch To My Friend's Wedding?*, I don't think she's a contender for a trial like this. What she thinks really, really matters to me though. She's my best friend and I need her to be happy for me. Maybe she just needs time to get used to it. Josie is more polite so I'm not expecting such negativity from her.

What did *not* arrive this morning, annoyingly, were samples of the new Elemis bath range, some of which I was going to add to Mother Pells' eightieth birthday present. After saying 'I don't expect much from you, Erica, as I know you don't make a lot,' she asked me for a heated poncho from Lakeland, which is not only expensive but sounds like something you would find as a runner-up prize in a raffle at a nursing home. But if that's what she wants, then so be it. Maybe I can get one 'gifted'. I make a mental note to do a *#journorequest* for 'Birthday Presents for Elderly Relatives'. I'm still collecting freebies of course, even though I'm not writing as much – I need to focus on the WULT® social media for the time being.

Thankfully Channing, the elusive marketing/social media person, has finally got in touch to 'support me with the WULT® Woman content'. Although I look young, Channing is keen for me to remember that the target audience for my 'content' is rich middle-aged women – they're the ones Yuvana wants to sign up for the treatment. He uses the word 'content' a lot, as well as 'advertisement' and 'omnichannel'. It's all quite daunting – just because I'm not worried about my jowls anymore, doesn't mean to say I've become confident in front of a camera. The whole looking around like there's a fly in the room and/or banana voice both remain an issue.

At least I've managed to get the tripod set up in the spare room, as well as both lights, which are surely visible from Josie's house, if not outer space. Do they need to be this bright? Even though I have zero skin worries these days – apart from the unwelcome return of blackheads – it still seems a bit 'operating theatre'. As well as a giant tripod, there's also a smaller phone stand for when I'm 'out and about', but I can't really see what that would involve unless it's filming a trip to the garage during which I walk past Alan's Auto Repairs and a field with a goat in. Then there's my background. Channing sent me some instructions for creating 'a minimalist backdrop' (I'm planning to move the Peloton) with 'a statement plant' (will the dying basil on the kitchen windowsill do?) and 'bougie accessories' (pass). He told me to 'remember the rule of thirds' which is not possible as I don't know what it is in the first place.

Channing has also emailed over some 'concepts' for ways to address the issue that I mentioned to Merlyn – namely, how will people know I'm not just a woman in my mid-twenties pretending that I'm older? The first idea is *#flashbackfridays* – every Friday, I will share embarrassing photos from my youth and my followers will have to guess the year, or the story behind them. I make a mental note to go up into the attic when I'm at Mother Pells' house for her birthday party and see if I can dig any old photos out. That's if I go to the party – although at the moment, I'm planning to. I can't stay hidden from my family forever, and who knows, they might even be impressed with me for a change. Either that or Simon will bring one of his marsupials and cause a welcome distraction.

The second idea, which sounds terrifying, is a weekly *#popquiz*, involving being played snippets of Eighties and Nineties music, which I will then have to name. Optimistic, as I can barely remember what I just came into the room for, although this forgetfulness seems to have improved slightly since the treatment. And finally, there's an *#ama*, which I had to google – 'Ask Me Anything', it transpires. Channing then finished the email with *#vibesonpoint*, which is pretty much unfathomable, unless it's a joke. But I add it to my mental Gen Z language database anyway.

This morning, I'm attempting to make my background look passable for Channing with a fake Ikea plant I found in a kitchen cupboard (the basil was rejected), a pile of old *Wallpaper* magazines courtesy of Keith a while back, and an 'objet', which apparently is *not* missing a 'c' and is about 'projecting a stealth wealth aesthetic'. At least I know what an aesthetic is now, even if I'm not sure about the rest of that. I go for a sculpture called 'Elbow' that Nandy's husband Ash gave me – which I personally think looks more like a pepper grinder but what do I know – and Channing is more into this than I anticipated.

And now I'm bored, so I decide to make use of all the equipment and do a practice reel following a Clean Girl make-up tutorial I found on YouTube. I really need to update my make-up routine as I don't need all that contour anymore, but I *do* need my face to match my new Gen Z outfits. Sorry – 'fits.

Well, first up, can I just say there's nothing clean about it? I haven't put on this much make-up since the whole Cheryl Tweedy WAG look of the mid-Noughties. And also, what the hell is with the incessant finger waggling? If these Clean Girls aren't tapping the bottle of foundation with their pointy nails, they're flapping their fingers under their chins like a substandard impression of a prawn, and pursing their lips like koi carp. It's all quite fishy. Am I going to have to start doing this too? Mind you, it could be a way to distract viewers from my banana voice.

I start the tutorial with a Clean Girl bun, not to be confused with a messy bun which was what I wore –

and indeed still wear – around the house every day. No, this is more reminiscent of early J-Lo, as if your hair has been melded to your head using a glue gun. Then I'm told to fill in the gaps at the top of my forehead with mascara because apparently nobody wants an uneven hairline. Heaven forbid.

Now for the products themselves. There's quite a lot of skincare prep, making me nostalgic for the single layer of Neutrogena moisturiser under some Dream Matte Mousse, which was my go-to when I was young the first time round. Peculiarly, the woman doing the tutorial pours the products down her cheeks with a dropper – I mean who does that? Her, apparently. (Her being someone called @*thatgirlliv*.) And then the make-up itself, which purports to be 'fresh' but is in fact about ten layers of primers, concealers, highlighters, foundations, blushers and powders. Oh, and then enough setting spray to weatherproof a tent.

I've finished, and actually, I look pretty good. Shiny, but not in a Peach Jumpsuit sort of way. And then, just as I'm busy admiring my Hailey Bieberness in the ring light mirror, the doorbell rings.

Who could that be? The spare room overlooks the front door so I peer out of the window. It's Josie. Right, I'm not going to answer it, I'm not quite ready. I'm just going to let her ring the bell – she'll go away soon. I mean, not that I want her to go away per se – she is my friend, and I love our chats – it's just the timing is a bit off. But as I turn back from the window, I walk straight into the bloody tripod, trip, and then stagger into the stupid ship-to-shore light. Then I yowl. Josie probably, okay definitely, heard all that.

She did indeed. And she is now shouting through the letterbox at me, which is frankly a bit much. 'Erica, are you okay? It's me, Josie.'

I know who you are, Josie. I sign for your deliveries on a borderline daily basis.

'I've got some Frank Cooper's marmalade for you from Oxford. It's to say thanks for taking in my parcels... and for that contouring stick thing you gave me. I haven't used it yet but I'm erm... sure I will.'

You should, I think to myself as I come down the stairs. Anyway, here goes.

I open the front door.

'Hi... er... oh...' says Josie. 'I was expecting Erica. Hi. I'm her neighbour, Josie.'

'Josie, it's me,' I say. 'It's Erica.'

Josie looks at me and says, 'No.' Then she looks at me some more, and some more... I don't say anything, I just smile and wait for her to take it all in and get excited.

After a minute, she still hasn't said anything, so I break the silence and invite her into the hall. She walks in looking dazed, but still doesn't say anything.

'I had a beauty treatment at New Year, Jose. Amazing, isn't it? I look pretty young, don't I?' I tilt my head from side to side so she can get a good look, lift up my chin and give her a twirl, hands on my hips.

'Is it permanent?' She looks really pale for some reason.

'Erm... yes, if I want it to be! I mean, well, I'm still going to age, but from where I am now, which is mid-twenties. It's like a reset. Incredible, isn't it? It's nanotechnology. I'm so bloody lucky doing the job I do because I'm one of the first people to try it. I'm sure everyone will be getting it soon though...'

I trail off again because Josie hasn't said anything else and it's getting quite one-sided.

Then she puts her hand on my hall wall as though to support herself, and bursts into tears.

Chapter Eighteen

Brunch, a mani-pedi, then shopping

That went well then. JEEZ. I really didn't expect a reaction like that from Josie, who is normally so calm. After she came round, then left in tears, she has since messaged me saying that she needs time to process my 'decision' and that in the meantime she'd rather we didn't meet up – she especially doesn't want me to see Héloïse as she's 'not sure what message this sends'. Wow. I mean, this is meant to be a positive thing, and it feels like she's turning it into a problem.

It's not like I've gone on OnlyFans – I've had a scientific treatment, and a revolutionary one at that. Surely from a solely educational perspective this is a positive thing? And yes, I look younger as a result, but so what? That's not going to ruin Héloïse's life. If anything, she might even be inspired? Or empowered? I'm a woman who took control of her future. I think that's inspiring for a young girl anyway. I keep rereading Josie's message. The word 'decision' makes it sound like I did something dreadful, and I think it's a bit unfair of her. Since when is wanting to feel like yourself again such a terrible thing?

Mind you, her sign-off was more upbeat and she said Héloïse has a present for me from Oxford. Maybe, like Nandy, she just needs time. Although Nandy and I are now communicating mainly with stickers rather than words. This morning, I sent her my favourite, one of Cassia screen-grabbed from a reel where she's pulling a face like she's smelt a terrible fart. Nandy replied almost immediately with one of Merlyn looking disapproving. And that was the end of the 'conversation'. As for Keith, he tried to FaceTime me again the other day, but I declined it, slightly concerned about what Josie might have told him, and she's definitely said something because he then messaged saying 'Here if you need me, girly-pop.' I'll reply soon, and maybe meet up with him… I just can't face adding him to the list of unsupportive friends just yet.

The whole thing has put me in a bad mood so, although I'm not really a 'going for a walk' person, especially not on my own, I have an urge one morning later in the week to clear my head and actually leave the house, inspired by an article on the *Glowgetter* website – *Get Out! Five Ways Fresh Air Can Boost Your Mood* – but anyway, I decide to head over the back fields to Lacock. It's sunny – still cold, but there are signs of spring now February is here and the other day I saw a crocus. Or a snowdrop. It was some sort of flower. The point is, I feel like I need to cheer myself up. Aside from the Josie debacle, the post-treatment euphoria is definitely waning and I still haven't even seen Gabe yet, although I know he is back from Uttoxeter. Also, today's dead American Erica Pells (from Eureka, Kansas) made me feel like a particularly poor example of our name, having had a sixty-year marriage and a hospital wing named after her. I should really stop reading these obituaries.

I'm also a bit stressed out about the social media stuff. There's still time to get some practice in though: the Instagram account isn't going live until the *Luscious* article comes out, and we haven't even done the cover shoot yet. According to the 'content calendar', the first reel is called *Meet WULT® Woman*. It's an 'introduce yourself' in which I tell everyone stuff like 'my favourite chocolate in a box of Celebrations' (would rather have cheese), 'my guilty pleasure TV show' (all of them), and my 'perfect day' (it's not 'brunch, a mani-pedi, then shopping' but that's what I have to say). Channing wants me to get a few reels 'in the bank, so we've always got content ready to post' – this is important apparently, in case I'm 'ill, or travelling', which I rarely do apart from to London, but perhaps some kind of more exciting life awaits me. That would be a pleasing development.

I get ready to go out and wrap up in my puffa jacket, hat, scarf and sunglasses – if I keep the scarf halfway up my face, and the hat pulled down, the look is a little 'Elephant Man' but I suppose I'm still vaguely recognisable even though it's hard to see how young I look. After Nandy and Josie's reactions, I'm taking it slow with the big reveals, and dressed like this, I've so far said hello to my neighbour (the one with the baby) about three times, and she hasn't batted an eyelid, although that baby screams constantly so she's probably half-blind with tiredness, if that's a thing. Sounds like a thing.

After I've drained my cafetiere, checked my emails (nothing of note) and watched Cassia make that viral breakfast wrap everyone is going on about (how does she eat on camera and not look like she's a seagull regurgitating fish for her young, like I do?), I am ready to leave, Elephant Man disguise on.

The walk out of the town takes about fifteen minutes, then it's a case of following the footpath that goes down the side of the fields. Most of them are just ploughed and empty but there are a few tractors out doing things, maybe planting stuff? For someone who (kind of) lives in the country I don't really know much about farming. But then I didn't really ever intend to live here.

After about half an hour, the sun is rising a little higher in the sky. You can tell the birds like it, they're going nuts in the hedgerows, and I have seen two bumblebees so far. One flew right into my face, which was a bit traumatic. There's a smell too, kind of mossy and damp... like growingness. Or is that growth? Yes, growth. Like everything is coming out to play again after the winter. I'm glad I came on this walk.

Six fields on, I pass the tree where Nandy had a shit. It always makes me laugh. I hope she comes to visit again soon, when all this has settled down. I'm sure she will. It really is beautiful here. Walking is so tiring, though. Thankfully, I brought a water bottle with me like some kind of normal outdoorsy person, so I sit down on my bag beneath a tree (not the Nandy tree, it's several years ago, but frankly, still too soon) and have a rest and a drink. I close my eyes and listen to the birds and insects, feeling quite proud I'm doing something so mindful and actually enjoying it.

'Erica!'

I snap out of my moment of zen with a start and pull up my hat slightly, looking around. It's Gabe, about twenty feet away and walking towards me. What the hell? Of all people, in all places. He's obviously recognised my coat and hat but hasn't seen my face yet. Holy crap. This isn't how I'd planned it. Well, I hadn't really planned it at all but the first time I wanted him to see the new me definitely wouldn't be in a field, needing the loo, which I do now thanks to that ill-advised cafetiere of coffee just before I left. My big reveal was also meant to involve lingerie in some way, of the frenzied fuchsia kind, or at the very least one of my new Linda Lusardi tops. But this is what I've got to work with, so...

'Gabe!' I stand up, wobbling on the roots around the base of the tree. 'Fancy meeting you here!'

He's getting closer now and his face is changing expression to one of puzzlement.

'I know what you're thinking,' I call out. 'But it *is* me. Surprise!'

By now he's reached me. He's shaking his head and frowning as he looks at my face. He seems very, very confused.

'I can see you're shocked that I'm out on a walk...' I'm desperately trying to keep it light as his expression looks similar to Josie's the other day, and that didn't end well. At all.

'I don't get it,' he says. 'Erica? How is this possible?'

'Amazing, isn't it? I thought you'd be gobsmacked, and you are. It's a new hi-tech beauty treatment. I look twenty years younger!'

He stares at me. 'How? Why?'

I laugh. 'Why d'you think?'

'Erica, honestly, I have absolutely no idea.'

Shaking his head, he sits down on a big root at the bottom of the tree that is curved around like the back of an antique chair. He's wearing much more walk-appropriate clothes than me – those trousers with a zipped section you can remove to turn them into shorts, and a big orange jacket with lots of pockets. From the angle I'm at I can see his hair is a little thinner on the top of his head, which I hadn't noticed before. His eyes look tired, and he seems much older than me.

There's an awkward silence. I squat down and lean on one knee – easy for me these days – so I'm at the same level as him.

'If you had the chance to look younger – be younger – wouldn't you take it?' I say.

He makes eye contact with me for the first time. 'Not if everyone around me stayed the same, no, I don't think I would.'

What a strange answer – as if that makes a difference.

I attempt to lighten the mood. 'Well, on the bright side, you get a younger version of me. If you... erm... want it – me – that is.' I tilt my head just so he can get the full benefit of my chiselled profile. This is so much easier than trying to do the meerkat thing.

I reach out my hand and he takes it, then looks at it, the hand of a twenty-something, unmarked, no age spots, no veins. Then he replaces it back where it was on my knee.

'Why? Why would you do this?'

Hasn't he already asked me that? 'Because I don't want to look old and grey and saggy. It's not how I feel inside.' I know I sound a bit snappy, but this is going pretty much the opposite of how I planned.

'But there are other things to make you happy, surely. I mean, not that I think that you are – were – grey or saggy or...' He trails off, shaking his head.

'They're not enough,' I say, wondering if the 'other things' he's talking about include him.

He stops shaking his head and just stares ahead with a weird, watery-eyed look. Even though I have twenty-seven-year-old thighs, I can't keep squatting any longer so I stand up, which only serves to remind me how much I need to pee.

'Is it permanent?' he asks.

'It's more like a reset. I mean, I've started ageing again now, from where I am, if you see what I mean. But maybe once I start looking older I can get it again...' I stroke my cheek, reminding myself – and him – of its softness.

'We're like Aragorn and Arwen, a mortal and an eternal...' he says.

'Who? What are you talking about?' Not only does he look thin on top, he's talking about people I don't know. I'm starting to think I can do better than this.

'Oh, it doesn't matter.' He looks up at me. 'Erica, I really like you. You do know that, don't you?'

'Well... erm... yes, I suppose so.'

'But this isn't a game to me. I'm too old for that. I know we've been messing about with all the jokes, and the cheese and...' He trails off and picks at the bark on the tree trunk next to him. 'The point is, the "you" I like... is the "you" I met, Erica. The *real* you. Funny, cool Erica.'

Oh so *now* I'm cool.

'This *is* the real me! Just without the wear and tear.' Anger is rising in my chest. 'I'm tired of people telling me to age "gracefully". Bloody hell, what does that even mean? And why should I accept something when I have the power to change it? This isn't just about looks – it's about refusing to be invisible.'

I should write that down, it's really good.

Gabe doesn't seem that impressed though and is pulling a piece of bark apart with his fingers, not looking at me. Even from where I'm standing, I can smell the mossy dampness again, mixed with Gabe's warm, clean, Head & Shoulders scent.

'I liked the wear and tear,' he says.

'Well, I didn't.' The anger rises again, and I grab my bag from the ground next to him, then turn and stomp back towards the town, hastened by annoyance, my youthful legs and a desperate need to pee.

I don't look back.

Chapter Nineteen

Piccadilly Circus / Blackpool Illuminations

After this disappointing turn of events, I am glad to escape to London a few days later for the *Luscious* magazine shoot. I have to leave painfully early to be in Shoreditch at ten a.m. Well, painfully early for me, which appears to be the same time everyone else is commuting into the city. I don't tell Nandy I'm coming. It's the first time I've been to London without telling her since... I can't remember. I send her a sticker of Pakora though. Her dog, not an actual pakora.

I'm in First Class again (thank you kindly, Yuvana), although at this time of day, the expensive seats seem to be taken up by 'city types' as Josie would call them, who are either talking loudly on their phones about how WE'RE EXPECTING SOLID RETURNS BY Q3, RUPERT or gawping at me. I'm very, very slowly getting used to this now. Unlike Gabe, it seems, who hasn't been in touch at all since I saw him on the footpath. I wonder what the returns policy is at Victoria's Secret.

The studio is five minutes from Old Street, an airy loft with exposed beams and white walls, chosen to make the most of the limited hours of daylight in February. Walking in, all I can think is, holy crap, the world and his wife is here. 'The world and his wife?' I'm glad I didn't say that out loud. I make a mental note not to use such middle-aged expressions, especially when I'm pretending to be young, which I'm not today – everyone on the shoot knows my real age. But nobody under forty says things like 'It's like Piccadilly Circus/Blackpool Illuminations in here.' They say, 'it's lit' and I know that because Channing said it in an email and I looked it up. He also said, 'it's sick' but that was about my basil plant, so I'm fairly sure on that occasion he was referring to the brown edges on most of the leaves.

Aside from the photographer himself (a gruff Scottish man in his forties called Hugh), pretty much everyone – stylists, make-up artist (who is, to my delight, only bloody Mary bloody Greenwell – a friend of Merlyn's, of course), wardrobe assistants, an art director, and a few people from *Luscious* – coos and fusses over me. They touch my face, hair, they stare and marvel, they talk and whisper about me from every corner of the studio, they bring me coffee and pastries, and oddly some Mexican food, which for me is not a ten a.m. thing at all. Quesadillas aside, it is the most attention I've had in a long time, and to be honest, after what happened the other day with Gabe, I don't hate it. I don't hate it one little bit.

The outfit they've chosen for me is a sequined bodysuit with a roll neck, which I think looks pleasingly Taylor Swift – until I put it on behind the screen and realise that despite my wobble-free new body, I look more like a sausage about to do some burlesque. Luckily, according to one of the stylists, Chaz (who is inexplicably wearing a harness – did they think he might run away?), it will only be just visible in the shots and is simply so that I can 'serve futurism'. He also tells me he is 'obsessed with me', which feels a bit much. The *Luscious* art director then mentions that the cover headline is going to be *Back To The Young School*, which in my view is a very poor pun.

The shot they choose is me caught off guard, at the start of a laugh – Hugh deliberately made me snigger by telling me he often gets mistaken for David Tennant, which is funny because he just wouldn't, ever. The background is an icy blue, to set off the sequins, and in the photo, which I look at on the little screen on the back of Hugh's camera, my skin is gleaming, my eyes are bright and my lips are shiny. I don't look beautiful, because I'm not. (I'm not looking for compliments – I know I'm not.) But I look young, and that's the shot they want, of course.

In the last half-hour of the shoot, I see Merlyn creep in, wearing fur après-ski boots and enormous white sunglasses. She hugs Mary Greenwell as Hugh takes some final shots to go inside the magazine with the advertorial. I wave and Merlyn blows me a kiss.

And then I am done, and once I've changed out of my body suit (and toned down the make-up which is a little too 'Peach Jumpsuit' for my liking), Merlyn whisks me off for a late lunch in her car, which waits outside with her driver wherever she goes. We head south-east, not Merlyn's usual preference, but for me, it's a free lunch so what the hell.

Half an hour later, we're in a noodle bar called Professor Wok, surrounded by students who all look like Chaz the stylist. Everyone seems very 'hip-hop', as Mother Pells would say. After I pretty much inhale my beef broth, and Merlyn daintily eats some Jianbing, I tell her about Nandy and Josie – and Gabe. She doesn't really say much though, just tilts her head, nods, and says 'Erica my dear' a few times. Then she pays and guides me out of the door, murmuring that she has 'something to show me'. I can't think what it would be, but don't ask as we walk a few streets, past giant murals and shops selling plants and coffee, Merlyn picking her way along the pavement in her giant furry boots, not at home at all outside her two natural habitats of Holland Park and central London.

—

Going south of the river always makes me think of Kofi. Well, most places in London do, but I remember we went to the Millennium Dome a few times, as it was called then, to see Basement Jaxx, and Faithless, I think. We came down to Tate Modern not long after it opened too, for that weather exhibition – the one with the giant sun. We lay on the floor, not just us, lots of people did, holding hands for ages and just staring at it. We were stoned, I think.

There were still parties at the flat in Camden, although it was mainly me organising them, not Kofi. Pete's decks were gone but I'd make a playlist on my iPod and we'd connect it to the speakers and dot some tea lights around the place. The usual suspects would turn up, but not as many as the old days. One night, after a pretty wild party where there had been some Es going around, most people had left. There were five or six of us, hanging out, smoking weed, drinking beers, listening to chill-out music.

A friend of Kofi's called Owen, who I didn't know that well, had gone to sleep sitting on our sofa. He had long, curly hair in a ponytail, and a goatee beard. 'Let him sleep,' Pete said, 'he was pretty wasted earlier on.' I was pretty wasted too, and had the giggles from the weed, so I balanced an empty beer bottle on Owen's shoulder. 'Leave him,' Kofi said. But I didn't. Another bottle, one on his knee, one on his foot, one on his head, then I found other things in the room, decorating him like a Christmas tree with the fairy lights from the fireplace, laughing, thinking I was so funny. I even took a photo with a disposable camera. He didn't wake up.

I suppose it was about half an hour later when we realised that Owen was dead. Pete called 999 and Kofi took the bottles and lights off him. He didn't say anything while he did it, his face was fixed with his lips tucked in, as if he was biting down on them. I was crying so hard when the paramedics wheeled Owen out on the trolley, all covered up. When the police finally left, Kofi went to bed. It was getting light and I sat on the bathroom floor, being sick until it was just this bright yellow stuff, and my stomach made noises like a monster. How right that it should – I was a monster. Maybe I could have saved him. But look what I did instead. Just look.

After that night, the floor always seemed sticky, like an aftermath we couldn't ever clean up. The flat was tainted, and everything smelt of bile and death. After Owen's funeral, nobody came round as much, and Kofi never seemed to look at me in the same way again. We didn't want to be there anymore, and handed in our notice to the landlord. I told Kofi I was going back to Wiltshire – he just looked like he wanted to be anywhere else than with me. And that was what happened. That was the awful, awful thing, and why I went home, even though I didn't really want to.

–

Merlyn and I arrive at a huge, architect-designed development of flats, with balconies and floor-to-ceiling windows. 'My granddaughter Devon lives here,' she says, waving a fob at the door, which opens slowly.

I just nod. I haven't heard of Devon, but that's Merlyn, she doesn't hold her cards close to her chest – she keeps them in a safe at an undisclosed location. I prefer this. I'd hate to find out she has a husband from Huddersfield called Brian.

We get the lift to the top floor. I wonder why Merlyn is letting herself in, but as we walk into the duplex flat, I can tell nobody is living there, although it is fully furnished, with a huge open plan living area, a kitchen island, and engineered wood floors.

'She's in New Zealand for a year,' Merlyn says as she leads me out onto the balcony, which looks right across the London skyline. I can see the skyscrapers of the city in the distance, bathed already in the pinkish light of a late winter sunset.

I take it in for a minute then turn to look at Merlyn, trying to convey, 'What are we doing here?' in a single expression. I need to get back to Wiltshire.

'It's yours, if you want it, Erica,' she says.

'What?'

'All ready for you to move in. No rent required. I thought it might make things easier for you than hiding away in your little cottage.'

I shake my head. 'No... no, thanks. I have a home, near my family. And I have friends there. And a boyfriend.'

Merlyn pushes her giant sunglasses up onto her head. 'And how's all that going, my dear?'

Chapter Twenty

Nothing grows there anymore

Party dress appropriate for an eightieth birthday: CHECK. Clean Girl make-up: CHECK. Blue Ikea bag containing carefully wrapped presents for Mother Pells, including the Lakeland heated poncho (plus a couple of freebies for Auntie Viv and Alannah): CHECK. I am nothing if not prepared with peace offerings and distractions, and determined that this reveal will go well, or at least better than the others.

As I set off, a dusting of snow on the pavements makes me immediately regret my kitten heels, although I have it on authority (*Grace* magazine) that they are – were – the *'It' Shoes Of The Winter!* It's only a twenty-minute walk to the house, but I normally do it with either trainers or FitFlops on, carrying not very much, and today I'm beginning to feel I didn't think this through. However, there isn't really an alternative, as there are never many Ubers on a Sunday here and I'm not using the local cab company again after Josie told me what happened with Weird Steve and the wheelie bin. And I can't ask Josie if I can borrow her Kia because, well, things are still a little strained, plus I don't want to drive as I'm going to need all the Dutch courage/room temperature Chardonnay I can get my hands on when I finally show my new appearance to my family.

My phone pings, so I take a welcome break in a gateway, resting the bag of presents on a wall for a minute to read the message. It's Keith.

> When are you coming out of hiding, duckie?

> I'm not hiding...

> Well, I haven't seen you for weeks.

> Assuming you heard I have a new look?

> Josie told me, yes.

> Well, it's not going down that well.

> I heard that too.

> Who from? Josie?

> Never you mind. The point is, Erica, I'm your friend, which means I'm here for you, whatever misguided choices you might have made.

> Thanks a lot.

> That was a joke.

> I'm on my way to my mum's right now. It's a family party.

> Have they seen the new you?

> No. Anyway, have to go.

I don't need this right now. Snow is seeping into my kitten heels so I put my phone away and pick the Ikea bag up. It's really coming down now. Snow when it's nearly March is the worst kind because a) it's decidedly un-festive (remember the Beast from the East? If that had been at Christmas it would have been called something much more fun, like 'Santa's Snowstorm') and b) nobody dresses appropriately for it as everyone by this point is thinking about their Coquette Core spring wardrobe. Or maybe that's just me.

After another couple of streets, I can see Mother Pells' house in the distance: a cream-coloured detached bungalow at the far end of the cul-de-sac, backed by a field with a stream. It has an immaculate gravel drive and a trellis next to the front door that Father Pells put up when they moved in. It used to have a honeysuckle climbing up it, but nothing grows there anymore.

I slow down as I get closer, which is partly to do with my increasingly numb feet, and partly due to my concerns about the reception I'll receive. I've run over the plan in my head a few times – keep it light, make it part of the celebrations, don't let anyone get bogged down with details (i.e. being unrecognisable/looking barely older than my own nephews). They'll know it's me once I start talking and get the presents out, and after a G&T and some blinis everyone will either be really impressed (unlikely, but you never know) or be asking Simon about his wind turbine to change the subject.

But as the gravel driveway comes into view, and I can see the outline of Eartha, my mum's cat, keeping watch at one of the windows, I wonder if this is the right thing to do. Why didn't I double bag the presents? You should always double bag, Josie says. But I didn't, and now they are covered in snow and the wrapping paper is going soggy. I'm close enough now to see Auntie Viv in the front room, laughing and hugging one of the boys. Is that Sam? He's really grown. And there's Mum with a plate of something – probably those little salmon mousse bite things that are swallowed as quickly as a paracetamol. She's passing one to Uncle Tony. They're probably all wondering where I've got to...

'Hello dear! Are you lost?' I look up to see my mum's neighbour Dinah, dressed as though she works on the railways in a high visibility waterproof jacket and trousers, and carrying a large shovel. Dinah is slightly scary and refers to the local council as the 'Clowncil'. Before I can reply, she continues, 'Clear it as it falls – that's the key! You never know when you might need to get the car out to go to the hospital.'

What has she got planned, I wonder, watching her scrape the driveway, making a sound with the shovel that's like nails on a blackboard but worse, and louder.

'So, dear, are you looking for someone? That's Sally Pells' house.'

Of course, Dinah doesn't recognise me. I was forgetting for a second, preoccupied with the mushy presents.

'Um... no. I'm...'

'She's got the family over today for her eightieth. Much needed. So...' She looks up from the shovelling, brushes snow from her eyes and gives me a look that says, 'Off you pop.'

I look at her, then at the house. *Much needed?* Maybe I – at least in my current form – am not. Maybe they won't be as impressed as I'm hoping. Maybe after what happened with Father Pells, they'll be suspicious of the technology – unnecessarily of course, as it's worked its magic with no ill effects at all. And then I think about what happened with Nandy, Josie and Gabe, and wonder if they will be as shocked as them, or as judgy.

The blizzard whirls, Dinah turns back to her shovelling, and I make my decision, reversing up the cul-de-sac, slipping and sliding as I walk faster. This whole thing has been a total waste of time – I thought I had psyched myself up for it but I'm not ready to face them all.

'Bye, dear!' shouts Dinah after me.

I mutter 'bye' over my shoulder in reply.

It feels like an even longer walk the other way. After a few minutes, I stop under a tree and message Mother Pells.

> Hi Mum, sorry, not feeling well so won't make it today. Happy birthday, x

I wait for the ticks to turn blue but they don't. She hasn't seen it.

I walk on. Just a couple of streets to go. I've already slipped twice, but thankfully didn't completely fall over. I did at one point grab a fence though, which means my hand is now covered in a mix of snow and a weird green slimy stuff which I want to call algae but probably isn't.

It's a complete white-out now and I'm struggling to even walk straight. A car slows down alongside me. It's Josie, windscreen wipers going at a pace. The window winds down, tipping snow onto the road.

'Erica!'

'Oh... hi Josie.'

'Get in! You can't be out in this!'

I peer into the car and see Héloïse in the back. 'Erm... I thought... you didn't want me to...'

'Oh, just get in.' She sounds uncharacteristically impatient.

I am becoming a snowman in kitten heels so obey her, opening the door and plonking myself down in the passenger's seat, bringing a whirling cloud of snowflakes into the car with me.

Once the door is shut, it seems very quiet.

'I'll have to wait here a minute for this to pass, I can't see a thing,' says Josie.

'Okay.'

'Why do you look so different Erica?' says Héloïse from the back seat.

'I had a hi-tech beauty treatment,' I reply.

There's a pause.

'The snow is spectangular,' she says.

'That's not really a word, cherie,' says Josie, who looks tense.

'I know,' says Héloïse.

Another pause. I don't say anything, and pretend to be preoccupied with brushing snow off my coat.

'I don't think you want to be young again, Erica.'

'Don't you?' I say. Children are so annoying.

'No. I think you don't want to be old.'

I stay quiet.

'Why not?' Héloïse keeps going.

'Why not what?'

'Why don't you want to be old? I thought everyone would want to be old. Doesn't that mean you've had a long life?'

Josie, who's pretending to adjust the windscreen wipers, looks at me out of the corner of her eye.

My phone pings. It's Simon.

> Not impressed, Erica.

Oh great. Someone else who's not happy with me. Honestly, you try to do something to make a positive change in your life, and what do you get? Grief from all sides. What's the point?

'I got you this.' Héloïse is persisting. She passes a small paper bag through the seats to me. Inside is a fridge magnet with a literary quote on it. I look at it but it doesn't really make sense.

'It's from a book,' she says. 'Mum said you would like it.'

'I do, Héloïse. Thank you.'

'The bag smells of parsnips.'

I sniff the bag, which doesn't at all. 'It does a bit,' I say.

Josie turns the car engine back on and slowly drives the three streets to ours. I get out, thank her and hurry inside.

I dump the Ikea bag and kick off my shoes. What a waste of time. This was supposed to be fun. 'Make the most of it,' Merlyn said. But what is there to make the most of, exactly? Being young was better when I was… *young*. This is just stressful. I might have a jowl-free face and a neck like Billie Eilish but what's the point when everyone's annoyed about it?

Reaching into my coat pocket, I pull out my phone and tap numbly, then put it to my bright red ear.

'Merlyn? It's Erica. Have you got a minute?'

—

A week to the day later, and I'm standing on Devon's balcony, looking out over London. Below the orangey-pink glow of the sunrise, I can see the Shard, at least I think it is… and further along, is that Canary Wharf? I can't really make it out, and also have a terrible sense of direction. Who cares though – it looks bloody amazing.

It's chilly but I'm wrapped in one of Devon's expensive blankets. I sit down on a stripy deckchair with my coffee – next to me on a small table is a wine glass with the remains of some red in it. The yeasty smell reminds me of when I was a child and my parents had dinner parties with their aerospace colleagues. In the morning, I'd examine the wreckage: cigars in ashtrays, glasses with the melted remains of Scotch on the Rocks, empty Babycham bottles... How debauched it all seemed.

My wreckage is just a single wine glass and a saucer with some bits of Stilton and cracker crumbs on it. Lying next to them, a little worse for having been left outside all night, is *Luscious* magazine. On the cover, behind the big (not punny enough) headline, is me, smiling and sparkling against the blue background. I reach over, careful not to spill my coffee, and touch the image of my face. Then I turn to my phone and open Instagram. The WULT® Woman account has 12K followers already.

My phone pings.

> Hope you're feeling better. Love Mum. x

I feel a brief pang of guilt for lying about being ill. Very brief though, because well, I'm away from all that crap now. I could probably pass for twenty-five, I'm living in an amazing duplex flat in one of the coolest areas of London. I've escaped, and I'm ready to start my new life. Maybe this is how Carol's rabbit felt...

Part Three

Chapter Twenty-One

Zurich is also a European city

I know Héloïse is only a kid but I'd like to flag up here that she is wrong – I *do* want to be young again. I mean, just look at me. Just bloody look at me. I'd pinch myself if my skin wasn't just immediately going to bounce back. Standing in Devon's gigantic navy-blue bathroom, blending some blush (sorry Simon, I mean 'rouge') onto my cheeks, I randomly burst out laughing just at the sheer amazingness of it all. Why didn't I ever appreciate this when I was really in my twenties? I suppose back then, the only thing I had to compare it to was looking like a child, and when you're a child, you *want* to look older.

Don't get me wrong, I'm not totally gorgeous. Not like a model or an actress or anything like that. My face is too heart-shaped for one thing, and my chin is a bit pointy. My lips have never been that full either, and my eyebrows are quite bushy. But youth is like a filter – it takes all the things that look awful when you're nearly fifty and blurs them with a soft-focus lens. I've wished so many times I could go back and appreciate it – and now look. My wishes have come true. I'm like Aladdin, but with two fewer wishes and no lamp.

I've got my Clean Girl make-up routine down to about twenty minutes now. In the Nineties I would spend all afternoon getting ready, blow-drying my hair to within an Atomic Kitten of its life, plucking my eyebrows into Sherilyn Fenn levels of arched submission and finishing the look with so much translucent powder I looked like a pastry chef. Nowadays, it's definitely more 'take me as I am' – which is easier to get on board with when your face looks like it's been reinflated after a slow puncture that lasted twenty years. And the time I save every morning not having to pluck my chin is quite incredible. Especially those really wiry hairs that used to appear from nowhere – usually in the rear-view mirror while driving somewhere important, with no access to a hot compress and my Grip-Master Pro Tweezers (*#gifted*).

I pull on a yellow jacket that Devon left hanging in the hall and head out of the flat. It's been a couple of weeks now and I'm beginning to settle in. The place is warm, comfortable, spacious… it's like getting squatters rights on an Airbnb I can't really afford. But the thing that's missing is some friends. Some fun. That is why I came here after all… to get away from the naysayers. Oh, and so I can stop skulking about in disguise. Woolly hats and scarves only really work in the winter, and finally, spring is here.

In the lift, I look at myself in the mirrored wall and can't help but do yet another half-laugh, half-whoop, half-snort of disbelief. (And I don't even mind that this adds up to one and a half.) I'm busy poking my face, admiring my jawline and pouting when the lift doors open and two young men and a woman get in. Out of habit, I immediately adopt my well-practised middle-aged stance: no eye contact and that weird tight-lipped face that acknowledges without smiling.

'Hey girl,' says the woman.

I continue to stare straight ahead, trying to figure out what came first, Schindler's Lifts or *Schindler's List*, and assuming the woman, who has blue hair in pigtails and AirPods in her ears, is talking to someone on her phone.

She looks at her friends, shrugs and laughs.

'Oh... were you talking to me?' I say. 'I was on Planet Zog.'

The woman bursts out laughing, and the two men, one blonde, one with dreadlocks, join in.

'Erm... okay girl!' says the woman.

'I mean I was... really spaced out, man.' I hastily try to think of something more current to say, but by now the lift has reached the ground floor. The three friends walk out, leaving me cringing, but the girl looks over her shoulder and smiles. 'You're funny.'

'Thanks,' I say. At least that came out like a normal twenty-something.

Seems like my 'vibing' in the Hollister changing room was beginner's luck. How am I going to make friends when I speak like bloody Austin Powers. I really need to work on this. And worse than that – okay, maybe not worse but still quite bad – there's no M&S Food nearby, so I have to walk to Deptford and get the DLR to Greenwich, which is what I'm about to do now. It's worth it though, it's a much bigger store than the one at the garage back home in Wiltshire. They've got the full Gastropub range, and since the Yuvana payments are coming in, the sky's the limit. Well, I need to be able to carry it all back on the train, but my arms can take it now I'm bingo-wing free. Today I might even get some of those seafoody things that come in a scallop shell. If only I was sponsored by M&S Food, not Yuvana Labs with their shiny faces and endless glasses of water. Mustn't grumble though. JEEZ, even that sounds middle-aged…

Walking out of the building, I struggle to put up my umbrella. Across the road, I can see the blond boy – man – who was in the lift, looking over at me. What's he staring at? Don't Gen Z use umbrellas? This is all so much more complicated now I'm 'out in the wild'. It feels like both yesterday and a lifetime ago that I was in my twenties – and in that lifetime the way young people talk and interact seems to have changed dramatically. Like a whole new language to learn, and if I'm not fluent, I will be shown up for the fraud I am. Or maybe not… looking like I do, how could anyone ever believe that I *wasn't* young? I just have to make sure nobody connects cool young Erica who lives in south-east London with WULT® Woman. Which surely won't be a problem, because why would anyone in their twenties look at an Instagram account aimed at rich middle-aged women?

I head to the station. It's only one stop to Greenwich but the train grinds to a halt halfway and an announcement says there's a 'technical fault', so I use the opportunity to sit and think about my brilliant new life and how bloody exciting it all is, conscious of the fact that I am now one of those really annoying people that sit on their own smiling on public transport. I also decide I need to make some plans, so I get out my phone, open my Notes app and make a list.

1. Get more followers than Cassia
2. Make new cool/young friends
3. Sex (alone doesn't count)
4. Go clubbing (wonder if the Velvet Rooms is still open?)

5. Get a job?
6. Deal with my family

I finish and read it back while the train makes grinding noises. So, to point one – Cassia. This is going well so far – since the WULT® Woman Instagram account went live, timed with the *Luscious* magazine article, it already has 81.5K followers. Still a fair few to go to beat Cassia, but at this rate it won't be too long, and I can finally beat her at something for the first time since she stole the *Beautique* assistant editor role from me. The followers themselves, who appear to have usernames like *@Cotswold_Lady73* and *@Cheshire_In_Stilettos* or similar, seem really friendly, leaving comments like 'Incredible! My hubby would love me to get this!' accompanied by a fire emoji, or 'I want this treatment – when is it available to the public???' or 'You look gorg – you're very lucky, WULT® Woman!!'. Guided by Channing, I'm now in the habit of replying to them with 'Thank you so much!' and 'Link in bio to subscribe to WULT® updates!' with copious amounts of heart and star emojis.

Lucky I may be, but the videos themselves are a steep learning curve and a far cry from the thirty second *Before and After* lash lift reels I used to do on my own account. I was so nervous when I did my first live *#popquiz*. Peach Jumpsuit came on as the immobile face of Yuvana Labs and played snippets from Eighties and Nineties pop songs, which I had to name in an attempt to prove I am nearly fifty and not an imposter. I didn't know how this was going to pan out given my track record for remembering the names of songs, and the fact that Gen Zs seem to be really into the Eighties anyway, so I'm not sure it proves anything. But I didn't do too badly, apart from when they played *Vienna* by Ultravox and I shouted out 'ZURICH!'. In my defence, they hadn't got to the chorus yet and Zurich is also a European city. And I erroneously called that Patrick Swayze song 'She's Got Wind', but it didn't seem to matter and Peach Jumpsuit hissed 'Yessssssss' every time I got one right. The reel even got more likes than Cassia's 'Mango Jeans Try On', which she posted on the same day. Wonder what Cassia thought about that – if she's even spotted the WULT® Woman account yet, that is.

Channing is happy, partly thanks to the new background for filming that I've created since I moved into Devon's flat. After the initial hassle of working out how to cart all the equipment up the M4 – Merlyn mercifully got this all sorted for me – my vibes were declared thoroughly 'on point' and apparently all the better for the lack of a fake Ikea plant. Devon has a monstera the size of a small car in her living room, which I am slightly nervous about killing, and huge Banksy prints on the walls. Channing said, 'Can you even handle it?', which it turns out (after I had said 'Yes', then 'No', then 'I don't know') is a good thing, and not something that needs to be replied to. He also said that the lighting is so much better than in my 'dark little cottage' – to the point where I don't even need the ridiculous coastguard lamps.

Could it all be coming together, I wonder as the train announcer apologises yet again. I exchange eyerolls in solidarity with a young couple opposite me, but ignore the middle-aged woman with shopping bags who looks really miserable. She reminds me too much of my old self.

Next on the list is the whole making new friends thing, which may take a little longer than getting Instagram followers. I don't really see myself just going out and randomly introducing myself to Gen Zs, but maybe the people I met in the lift could be a starting point. And the blond guy was very dishy. Which, once again, is the sort of thing Mother Pells would say about Monty Don. Not dishy... hot? JEEZ, I sound so dated. Next time I run into them I'll be more prepared. I might email Channing and ask him for some pointers on the Gen Z vernacular, which probably doesn't involve using the word vernacular, I'll wager. Or 'wager' for that matter...

As for points three and four, they are all pretty much dependent on point two, so not really much to say about those for the moment, other than I cannot bloody wait, and although I have slight concerns that sex has changed as it's been so long (might ask Channing that too), I'm glad I didn't send back the Fuchsia Frenzy bodysuit, which was going to be wasted on Gabe as he's clearly into older women, like that footballer, what was his name? Each to their own. And although I did like him (Gabe, not the footballer) and we had a few things in common, I'm not interested in someone who isn't going to support me when I make a big decision like this. He seems so much older than me now too.

The train makes another grinding noise, then jolts. The announcer apologises again, so I turn back to my list. Point five – a job. Now, I know I'm going to be making money from the WULT® Woman publicity, but I don't want to be stuck at home filming content all the time. Who's going to see my ultra low-rise jeans and bao bun tits if I do that? And on a slightly less shallow note, this is a chance for a career – one that doesn't burn out like a defective firework. It's a do-over. But what could I actually do? I can't go back into magazines; they're laying off loads of people these days anyway thanks to AI and nobody buying print anymore. And besides, I know too many people in that industry and there might be some resentment. And for people who don't know me, my CV might look a bit weird. No, I need a new career, and I've been thinking more and more about advertising – being a copywriter. Adverts often have punny headlines and I think I'd be really good at that. Pretty sure advertising agencies are cool places to work too, I know that from *Mad Men*. Sexy places, with lots of hot men and people drinking hard liquor during the day, which I think with my new young metabolism I could definitely do. I managed wine at lunchtime with Merlyn not that long ago after all. I'm going to see if I can find any job vacancies. This is VERY exciting. I could even work my way up and become a creative director or something. Everyone would be really impressed.

Point six. So, Mother Pells, typically, didn't even seem that bothered that I failed to turn up for her eightieth. She sent me that perfunctory message a week after about how she hoped I was feeling better, and called the other day (after six-thirty p.m. obvs) to share some long-winded saga about Dinah's log burner, but that's been about it. I did tell her I'm in London – 'I've got a big work project on so I'm staying at Nandy's' – but she changed the subject and started telling me how she forgot her dentist appointment the other day (*The Inevitable*).

Which leads me to Simon. I saw on Facebook that, since his quokkas were seized by Interpol, he's now growing a Lion's Mane mushroom in a cardboard box that is so high-maintenance with regard to its humidity requirements that he has to come home from work at lunchtime to mist it. It's this kind of thing that makes me feel more optimistic about showing my family the 'new me' – it's no weirder than anything Simon does. I just need to get it over with – that way, he can stop assuming I'm having a mid-life crisis (and no doubt bad-mouthing me to Mother Pells) and maybe just admire me for making positive changes and being picked for such a cutting-edge experiment.

I didn't put Josie or Nandy on the list because there's not really much to say. Josie and I are exchanging the occasional message. I've told her I've had to go to London to work – she sounded almost relieved. She said she'd keep an eye on my house and also mentioned she might pop by to see Mother Pells with Héloïse. I told her if she does, not to mention the treatment – for now anyway. And as for Nandy, well, she's been pretty quiet too, but she's coming round to see me at Devon's soon. I'm sure she'll have had time to get used to it all by then. I hope so anyway. I miss her. I miss Josie too for that matter.

Finally, the train begins to move. I put my phone away, and stand up to get off, enjoying the fact that most of the men in the carriage are looking at me.

Chapter Twenty-Two

Meet hot MILFs in your area

It's May, and for some reason, Merlyn has decided to come with me for my monthly review at Yuvana Labs. We meet in Kensington at midday on the square that Yuvana overlooks, under a tree weighed down with cherry blossom. The air is warm at last, and I finally have an excuse to expose my blemish-free legs for the first time in many, many years. I'm wearing a new denim skirt and chunky trainers, with a sweatshirt and no jacket, plus a bum bag (Tourist Core), although they don't seem to be called that now. Maybe bums aren't de rigueur anymore. Who knows.

As Merlyn and I greet, and do our usual kiss on both cheeks, petals fall onto her shoulders and hair. We walk together through the glass sliding doors, towards the reception desk, which is manned by The Human Reel again today. She is writing in a pink journal with *You are more than this moment* on the front, while eating a selection of berries that are lined up in multi-coloured rows in a heart-shaped bowl. I think I prefer Glazed Doughnut.

I sit down while Merlyn, who is today channelling Katharine Hepburn in wide-legged mustard trousers and a silk blouse, talks to The Human Reel, tapping her perfect burgundy nails on the reception desk as she does so. At one point I hear The Human Reel say to Merlyn, 'I'll pass that on to him' but I can't make out anything else. After a few minutes, Peach Jumpsuit appears, in an orange jumpsuit that is thankfully just tight enough to stop her from looking like the inmate of a US penitentiary. Instead of taking me into the oligarch lighting room, she directs me ('This way, pleasssssssse') through another door, which leads into the room with the lockers and the smell of mint. Merlyn remains in reception, cherry blossom petals still in her hair, tapping away on her oversized phone. Frankly, I'm not sure why she even bothered coming along.

Then it's paper pants, robe, and photo after photo – plus the usual endless and increasingly tedious questions about how I'm feeling physically (still bloody excellent), how I'm feeling emotionally (same) and what reactions or comments I've received from others about my transformation. I gloss over the last question as I don't want to get into the issues I've been having with my friends, and instead change the subject by asking Peach Jumpsuit where Dr Marcus is. Dealing with some 'pressing matterssssssss', it transpires.

I come back out into reception and Merlyn is nowhere to be seen, which is quite annoying as I have been dreaming about the *Chariot de Fromages* at Brasserie Zédel, especially the Comté, which is apparently matured in caves. I must tell Gabe about it. JEEZ – where did that come from? Gabe is part of my old life – I need to focus on my new one now. It's all about progress. Positive change. Although, on the subject of cheese, which I will *not* be consigning to my old life, the hunt for a decent deli near Devon's flat continues. The area is very different from my hometown in Wiltshire and although that's exactly what I want, it is proving difficult when it comes to procuring good cheese. I've had to suspend my Say Cheese subscription box as they won't redirect it, and the locally available Sainsbury's Favourite Cheese Selection certainly does not represent any of my favourites at all, including as it does a Wensleydale with cranberries. What an abomination.

Later, back at Devon's, I open the front door to find a note has been pushed under it. Well, I say note – it's a torn-off section of a Domino's pizza box with a barely legible message written in what appears to be green Sharpie. After a brief moment of concern, during which I think it must be a complaint about the volume at which I played *Clubland Classix: Ultimate 90s Anthems* last night, I see it's from the young woman in the lift, who I've seen a couple of times since the Austin Powers incident, and lives two floors below. She is, it turns out, called Zoe. Or Zoo. Or '200', like some sort of rapper's name, perhaps? But I think it's Zoe.

Excitingly, she has written her phone number on the pizza box and is inviting me round to her flat tomorrow evening, so perhaps my mortifying display in the lift that day was more endearing than I imagined. This will definitely be more exciting than a Christmas Fair, Keith. Thank goodness I've already emailed Channing for some tips on speaking in the 'parlance of our times' – which, incidentally, is a quote from *The Big Lebowski*, and not something I would say. I don't think.

Now it's time to get ready for my next Instagram Live. It's the *#ama* – 'Ask Me Anything' – which Channing has been helping organise. As per his emailed instructions, I posted on the WULT® Woman Instagram account last night asking people to submit questions, and glancing through them, they look pretty much like the ones I get in the comments. 'Does it hurt?' (not really); 'Is your whole body younger, not just your face?' (yes); 'Do you regret it?' (not one bit). It's a relief that there's nothing too personal... I was slightly concerned people would ask things like 'Are you having better sex?'. I'm not sure how to answer this without bringing up Gwyneth Paltrow, and I don't think this is what she would want. We might even end up having a conscious uncoupling.

Channing has told me it's not enough just to answer the questions during an *#ama* – I have to do something else at the same time. So, I'll be talking my viewers through a new make-up tutorial, to show them the young looks they could try once they've had the treatment. I was going to do Clean Girl but I have it on authority (Channing) that this is now passé. It's all about the Mob Wife aesthetic now, apparently, which is a 'fierce trend' evoking Carmela Soprano and says, 'Hold my martini' not 'Where's my matcha?'. Sounds right up my street to be honest.

A few minutes before I go live, I remember that Cassia has done quite a lot of these *#ama* sessions on Instagram, so I scroll through her profile to get some pointers. I notice that when she is thinking about a question, she does this pouty face and puts her finger on her lips, then when she thinks of the answer she appears to be pleasantly surprised at something approaching her from the side. When I try this out, the result is more akin to having just spotted an intruder hiding behind the kitchen island. Why does Cassia always look so bloody effortless? Well, the tide is turning. I got the WULT® treatment, not you, Cassia – and soon I'll have more followers too. Well, WULT®

Woman will... So you can wipe that *#invisalignjourney* smile off your face, once and for all.

The *#ama* begins. With Devon's monstera in the background, and with me wearing a fluffy pink headband (*#gifted*) to keep my hair off my face, I start by showing the *Before and After* pics that Yuvana took and chatting through what the procedure was like. Then I begin applying the 'Mob Wife' make-up: smoky eyes, a lot of bronzer and nude lips. It's all fairly straightforward – I just have to talk through what I'm doing, show off my jawline as much as possible and wax lyrical about how WULT® transformed my life. At the same time, I have been instructed to ignore any messages in the chat that ask me if I want to buy bitcoin or 'meet horny MILFs in your area' and instead focus on the ones with heart emojis that are from the women with a quarter of a million to spare. How difficult can it be?

Not that difficult, and considerably less so when I remember that my next payment from Yuvana will be in my account tomorrow. Even better – so far, there have been no banana voice incidents and no imaginary flies in the room. I've managed to answer six questions, only ignoring two: 'Would you rather own a dragon or be a dragon?' (Sorry *@mystical_lynsey02*, but I think you took a wrong turn somewhere on the internet) and 'If women ageing naturally freaks you out this much, maybe ask yourself why?' (Calm down *@sunnydayswithsonia*, it's not exactly hurting you). Then, just as I'm spritzing on some Donatella Giusti Volcanic Power Setting Mist to complete the look, I see something that makes me accidentally squirt it right into my eye: '*@cassical* joined'. I'd recognise that username anywhere.

Chapter Twenty-Three

Love this for you

Checking my email inbox used to fill me with the same kind of dread as opening an unrecognisable Tupperware pot from the back of the fridge. One of those ones with a shadowy form inside, an aroma reminiscent of pet shops and a slightly bulging lid. These days though, work is considerably less stressful. And because money is coming in, I don't have to constantly beg features editors to write 600-word articles about, for example, hydrating eye serums (called *Not A Dry Eye In The House*) – then anxiously await an email in return saying, 'It's not one for us, but thanks!' How anyone could turn down a headline like that is a mystery to me.

This morning, the day after the *#ama*, I have seven unread emails. Of these, one is spam from a personal injury lawyer about my 'accident at work' – unlikely, considering the most dangerous thing I ever do is turn my Viva La Vulva up to level three, which is what Gwyneth suggests anyway. Another, excitingly, is a response to my email to a recruitment company telling me about a junior copywriter role at a 'multi-disciplinary' agency called Behold The Banana, who apparently want to get me in for an interview. Then there's one from Ancestry.com, telling me that they 'have a hint' I am related to Simon Pells. So do I, Ancestry.com, so do I.

As for the remaining emails, I can see one from Merlyn, one from Channing, one from Simon (eye roll), and one from an email address I don't recognise: briemyguest73@gmail.com. Probably more spam. Dragging one of Devon's blankets, and dressed in a cute little Lazy Girl aesthetic pyjama set I wouldn't have even considered pre-WULT®, I carry my coffee and laptop out onto the balcony to make the most of a gorgeous, sunny spring morning. Then I dive in.

> Erica,
> I wanted to apologise for dashing off the other day – something came up at *Luscious* that I had to attend to post-haste. I hope your Youth Review went well. Yuvana are delighted with the success of your social media promotions... WULT® Woman is becoming quite the celebrity it seems, and you are a natural! Of course, predictably, there's been some criticism of the concept from the usual 'age gracefully' brigade, but that was always going to be the case. If anything crops up that you need support in dealing with, you know where I am.
> Baci
> M

I begin writing a reply to tell Merlyn about that Sonia woman's comment and Cassia lurking on my live last night (and ask her if she knows whether Devon's blankets are machine washable) but then delete it. As she says, that was always going to be the case, and Cassia was bound to find out, and she'll definitely recognise me as we worked together when we were younger. Either that or she'll think I'm AI generated. But I'd quite like her to know I was picked for something instead of her. And it won't get back to my family before I get the chance to tell them, because they aren't even on Instagram. It's not exactly a matter for the national press either.

I move onto the next email, which is from Channing.

> Hey gurl
> OMG the #ama last night was iconic fr. And you hit the big 100K! OBSESSED.
> So… yr making friends in London? Love this for you. BTW I don't really speak in a Gen Z way so not really sure what you mean lol?!? only advice I can rlly give you is maybe hold back on those salty things you say that sound like your grandma… something about 'Too many cooks' or soup or whatever it was you said on our call last week. I mean srsly big yikes, you'll get found out and cancelled for sure.
> lysm, Chan

Broth, Channing. BROTH. As for the rest of the email, it's going to take about an hour of googling to decipher it. Maybe later… For now, let's see what my solar panel of a brother has to say.

> Dear Erica,
> Mum relayed that you are in London? Thanks for letting me know.
> I'm emailing because I found a potential retirement flat for her in Bristol. I haven't mentioned it – I think it's prudent for us to look at it first before broaching the subject. It's a ground floor, which I think would

> be perfect for her – patio doors straight out into the garden.
> Will you be able to view it with me? Timings are currently difficult as Alannah has taken the boys to Australia for six weeks and I am tied to home somewhat due to my Lion's Mane (huge therapeutic potential – not sure if you're familiar?). But hopefully we can make something work.
> Let me know.
> Simon
> Simon Pells CAO (Chief Awesomeness Officer)
> Cabbidge
> **A bat corridor was commissioned in West Sussex to offset the impact of this email**

Ugh. He's so pompous. *Prudent* – who says that? I swig my coffee and look out towards the Gherkin or the Shard or whatever it is. It looks a lot better than the budgie cage in Mrs Belcher's window, which was the view from my front window back in Wiltshire.

I open the last email, the one from briemyguest71@gmail.com.

> Erica – I hope you don't mind me emailing. I much prefer this way of communicating to messages, which I suppose is a little old-fashioned.
> We didn't part on the best terms, and you might not be keen to hear from me, but I felt I should give it one more try. I meant it when I said I like you for who you are – that includes who you are now. I miss our chats. If you're up for it, I'd love to grab a coffee and catch up sometime.
> All the best
> Gabe

It feels like someone has just realised they've missed out on the chance to have a much younger girlfriend. Too late, Gabe. Your reaction that day on the field told me all I need to know.

I delete the email, then look back out at the view.

—

As I've decided that the advertising agency who have asked me in will be very cool and *Mad Men*-esque, I have gone for a Rich Aunt Core outfit for the interview. Obviously, I had to heavily research this online, but the good news is that the look is 'old money', and it appears that's what Devon is. So, I raided the vacuum-packed clothes storage bags at the top of her wardrobe and found just what I needed: a turtle-necked cashmere jumper, which I teamed with some pinstripe wide-legged trousers that I found on the Me+Em sale rail. I've also got some giant, slightly tinted glasses, and an old brooch I found that belonged to Grandma Pells. I think it's meant to be a wounded pheasant, which is a bit grim, but it's quite abstract and looks expensive and classy, from a distance anyway.

I get to the office early. It's in East London, quite near where I did the *Luscious* shoot and easy to get to from Devon's, which bodes well for my commute. If it wasn't for the giant knitted Behold The Banana sign in the reception area, I would be unsure that I'd come to the right place, as I've never seen so few sexy men, and so many dogs outside of a veterinary surgery. To the extent that, when a young woman wearing a highly unseasonal ski hat leads me through to the interview room, I ask her if it's 'bring your dog to work' day.

'Oh,' she says, 'every day is bring your dog to work day here.'

Well, it certainly smells that way, I think to myself.

I'm led into a room and introduced to Floyd, the creative director, who is pacing behind a standing desk and wearing a t-shirt with YOU CAN GO HOME NOW on the front. Is that aimed at me? If so, I don't feel like I'm off to a great start.

Next to him, and seated on a Pilates ball, is head of copy, Ramona. She has pointy ears and is wearing a pale green floaty dress, so I'm very pleased with myself for identifying an example of Castle Core in the wild. But why is she sitting on a ball? Is she in labour?

She intercepts my look and instead of a greeting says, 'We're ergonomic.'

I'm nervous and think she means 'egocentric' for a split second, so say, 'I'm sure you're not,' in a kindly, Josie sort of way, then wish I'd said something cool and Gen Z like, erm... now I can't think of any of my newly acquired phrases, my mind has gone blank.

It doesn't matter, because Ramona ignores me and instead picks a wooden box up off the desk.

Well, this is all starting to look a bit more *Mad Men*. I don't smoke but if this box has Lucky Strikes in I might just take one so they think I'm one of them. But as Ramona leans over with the lid of the box now open, all I can see inside is what looks like... sweets?

'Would you like a gummy?' she says without any suggestion that she's joking.

'A gummy?'

'Pre-biotic.'

'Right.'

'And pro-biotic.'

'Okay.'

'And post-biotic.'

So definitely not fags then. I take one and chew it, wincing at the Haribo-esque flavour. What is it with this generation and their gummification of everything? And more to the point, when is someone going to slap me on the pinstripe arse, admire my punny headlines and offer me a scotch on the rocks, along with the job. This isn't what I envisaged at all.

Floyd asks me to sit down, and they go through my (heavily fudged) CV while I try to remember my pretend date of birth and when I allegedly went to school.

'We're sorry that Chika, our client services director, isn't here today,' says Ramona. 'Her roommate's micro pig is ill.'

I snort, forgetting myself. 'Wow, okay. Someone's in for a written warning then.'

Floyd and Ramona stare at me.

'I mean, because surely that's not true?' I splutter.

Floyd takes over: 'It *is* true, so she's allowed a mental health day. And at Behold The Banana, we don't do warnings, or disciplinaries, or anything like that. In fact, we have very few rules at all.'

I compose myself and decide to be very interested in said few rules to show what a law-abiding as well as highly creative and team-playing individual I am. 'So, what rules *do* you have?'

'We don't allow clapping at the end of announcements or presentations,' says Ramona. 'It's very triggering.'

For who? Sea lions? I don't say anything though and just nod, as if this makes sense. 'Any others?'

'We have an AF rule on our Friday nights out.'

I nod, approvingly. 'You get drunk as fuck? I've heard that about ad agencies. One of my friends was at Saatchi's in the Nineties.'

Floyd and Ramona exchange glances. 'How old is your friend?' says Ramona, bouncing quite vigorously now.

'She's the same age as…' I think quickly, '…someone in their late forties. I believe in cross-generational friendships. We can learn so much from other age groups.' This is the first thing I've said that they seem to agree with.

Floyd makes eye contact with me at last, if he can see my eyes through my tinted, Rich Aunt glasses.

'Where do you see yourself in ten years?' he asks. Holy crap, are they still wheeling that one out?

I say something impressive that I got off their website on the way here about being committed to creating effective, award-winning content for a range of challenger brands. Ramona's bouncing slows down and Floyd stops picking his nose, which he's been doing on and off ever since the interview began.

Just as I'm about to add some other nonsense I remember about how I'm 'not interested in building brands, but inventing worlds they can live in', the ski hat girl reappears, with two dogs in tow, and tells Ramona and Floyd they're late for 'frisbee'. At first, I assume this is the name of a company, and they're late for a meeting with said company, but then Floyd picks up an actual frisbee from the desk and waves it at me.

'Up for some frisbee, Erica?'

I try to think of a reply that both gets me out of playing frisbee and ensures they still like me, and plump for 'I'm actually nursing a frisbee injury, but I'll be back in training next week.'

I'm not being big-headed or anything, but I'm pretty sure I've got the job.

Chapter Twenty-Four

Imminent bad decisions

My carefully considered trip to the off-licence before going round to Zoe's flat may have been, in hindsight, ill-advised. I really wanted to get things right after a few, shall we say, 'unexpected generational differences' that revealed themselves at the job interview, so went for pretty much exactly what I would have bought when I was in my mid-twenties to take to someone's house on a Friday night. In other words, half a litre of cheap vodka, a large bottle of Coke, and a bottle of Chardonnay. I couldn't find any Bacardi Breezers, unfortunately, but I did throw in two packets of Marlboro Lights, which are ridiculously expensive these days. I'm not sure anyone really smokes anymore but always good to be prepared. However, when I arrive at Zoe's, my straining carrier bag doesn't get the rapturous welcome I thought it would.

I ring the bell and Zoe opens the door wearing combat trousers that remind me of All Saints. Not the shop, the girl band. What happened to them? 'Never Ever' was my karaoke song back in the day. And that dance – so easy. You just had to shift from foot to foot and look around you, as though you were waiting for your ticket number to be called at the deli counter. It was a gift, really. But that's not the point. I'm just glad I've put on one of my

Bershka handkerchief tops, so I feel like I look just as cool as her. Not cool, sick. Or whatever it is.

'Hey girl! It's Erica, isn't it? I'm Zoe. Haha! You know that already!' Zoe leads me down the hall – she speaks really fast and laughs a lot, not always at things that are funny. The flat is dusty, cluttered, hair ties lying on every surface. It's nothing like Devon's, despite there being only two floors between us.

As we come into the living room area, she spots my bag and tells me I can 'put my shopping on the table out of the way', which is awkward. It isn't exactly frozen peas and a Flash Bathroom spray – I was rather hoping we'd drink and/or smoke it. Then she offers me a cup of tea – also not what I was expecting. Unless she's referring to gossip? Channing told me that's what 'tea' means these days.

Zoe chatters on, introducing me to Kai and Jamal, who I recognise from the lift. They're sitting on the floor by a large coffee table and seem to be playing a board game and eating popcorn and grapes. Kai has a nose ring and blond hair that forms 'curtains' on his forehead and reminds me of the good-looking one from East 17. Jamal is less smiley and wearing a baseball cap back to front, which I decide must be ironic. Or not. Who knows?

'Erica is our new neighbour!' says Zoe.

'For real,' says Kai, looking up at me. 'What do you do, like, I mean, are you at college or...'

'No, I'm...' Why hadn't I planned this reply? 'I'm a... I work in... erm... advertising.' I haven't heard back about the Behold The Banana job yet but I'm pretty confident.

'For real.' He smiles. He has a twinkle in his eye, and yes, I'm aware that sounds like something from a *Carry*

On film. Thankfully, I resist the temptation to say 'Oooh Matron'.

Nobody asks me any more questions. But alarm bells are ringing: the scene is nothing like anything I recognise from my youth. Where are the banging house tunes? There doesn't even seem to be any music on at all, just a bubbling noise coming from the fish tank. Why does the room smell like scented candles rather than tequila and imminent bad decisions? And most importantly... what's with all the toys?

'Do you have kids?' I ask, desperate for an explanation of the Sylvanian Families figurines everywhere. It's less the elephant in the room, more the squirrels, rabbits and hedgehogs in the room.

Jamal looks up. 'Ha! No, they're Zoe's. She's into whimsy.'

I really have no idea what's going on. 'The rapper?' I ask, more for something to say than with any conviction. 'Whimsy' does sound a bit like 'Stormzy' though, surely? And I saw him on the Brits a couple of years ago so he's definitely a real person and (possibly) fashionable.

Everyone looks at me. Feeling I need to act quickly, I say the first thing I can think of about the toys, a character I remember from when I was babysitting Oli a few years ago. 'Personally, I like Postman Pat.'

Nobody says anything for a few seconds, so I carry on. 'I've got the van. And the... sorting office.'

There's a silence, then Zoe laughs, but appears more confused than amused. 'He's not very... whimsical, though, is he?'

She goes into the kitchen area to make my tea and Jamal takes a big mouthful of popcorn, crunching loudly and looking at me.

'We're just about to play.' He is thankfully changing the subject, and points to a console next to the giant TV, which could be an Xbox or a PlayStation or frankly, an air fryer, I really have no idea.

'Great!' I say, trying to shake off the sinking feeling that makes me wish I was arriving at Nandy's with a bottle of white Rioja and an antipasti platter.

'Are you a gamer, Erica?' asks Kai, folding up the board game and moving cushions and bean bags into position around the TV.

I try to think of a computer game I played in the Nineties, and can't, but then remember my flatmate Miranda. 'Yeah, I like Quake.' Please god let it still exist.

'Retro!' says Kai. 'Love that. My dad used to play Quake. It's a shooter though, right? We're cosier.'

'Yeah, same. I mean, I don't play Quake that often.'

Zoe reappears and hands me a cup of tea, which isn't gossip and actual tea, and very milky. I sip it, wondering why they're drinking tea at eight p.m. on a Friday. Maybe they're stoned? I can't smell weed though. Maybe they've had edibles? Hopefully I'll be offered some soon too. Or maybe they're hungover from last night. That makes more sense. Thursday was always a big night out for me too, back in the day. I drop down on a beanbag, silently thanking Yuvana Labs for the renewed ability to perform such an action without rolling over like a sheep in a snowstorm.

'Are you guys pretty hungover then?' I ask as Jamal hands me a controller that I will shortly have no idea how to operate.

I instantly regret the use of the word 'guys' – I sound like HR asking everyone in the office not to heat up fish in the microwave.

Jamal shakes his head. 'No… I don't drink. Nor do you much, do you Kai?' He tilts his head at me as though to look sympathetic. 'It makes him anxious.'

Kai nods sorrowfully. 'Too much self-care needed the next day; I just can't even.'

While I wait for him to finish the sentence, then realise he isn't planning to, Zoe sits down next to me. 'I sometimes have a fruit cider at my social deduction games night.' I smile in agreement, even though most of what Zoe has said means nothing to me. If only there was a Gen Z to Gen X translation app.

She seems very friendly, although I can't shake the feeling that she looks really young. Which she does, but then so do I. So we match – outwardly. It's just inwardly that it feels… odd. Maybe this is what it would be like talking to Millie Bobby Brown.

It will be fun, honestly, I tell myself. It will. I'm just finding my feet. These are just teething problems… I have to remember that I wanted change – and I have it now. It's not meant to be easy. I need to take a breath though, as I feel out of my depth, so I ask Zoe where the bathroom is and head off down the hall, past my bag of booze and fags lying on the table next to what looks like a pile of Pokémon cards.

The bathroom is also scattered with hair ties, and plants – but not big monstera-style ones like Devon's. Instead, the shelves are crammed with succulents in pots in the shape of smiling snails or characterful frogs, and from the window hang ferns in macramé holders like the ones Dinah has in her conservatory. I missed the memo about the return of macramé but then this also goes for drinking tea on a Friday night.

I'm not sure how long I can get away with staying in Zoe's bathroom without it looking like I'm having some sort of embarrassing incident. Like that woman who couldn't flush her poo away at her boyfriend's house and tried to throw it out the window, but then the poo got stuck between the double glazing, so the girl tried to climb between the two layers of glass to retrieve it and got stuck too, and in the end they had to call the fire brigade. That story really haunted me – imagine becoming famous for that. You'd really want to change your name and move away. But sitting on the loo googling 'whimsy', I wonder if it would be preferable to be rescued by the fire brigade this evening. I send Nandy a sticker of Simon holding one of his marsupials and looking really smug, and Nandy replies almost immediately with one of Cassia dressed as Margot Tenenbaum. None of this makes sense, but it's the solidarity I need.

Before I head back, I have a quick google of some of the things Zoe and her friends said. Apparently, being 'whimsical' seems to be a) popular with Gen Z and b) involve liking toys, fairy stories and seemingly, interior décor last seen in a retirement home. Okay. Next, 'cosy gaming'. This is playing 'low stress' games 'which allow players to express themselves without added mental strain'. Righty-ho. Finally, social deduction is a type of board game where you have to 'uncover each other's hidden role or team allegiance'. Sounds a bit like Instagram to me.

I wash my hands and look through Zoe's bathroom cabinets – nothing interesting, and a feeble grasp of any double cleansing routine. She's probably never even heard of Caroline Hirons, who I met once at a beauty event and is much taller than you might think.

I'm really putting off going back through now. Who can blame me? Convincing anthropomorphic animals to join a colony (the object of a popular 'cosy game' according to the internet) is not that appealing to me. I would also really like a drink, as it's Friday night. And on top of that, Zoe and her friends probably think I'm quite odd, judging by the number of mistakes I've made so far. I even said I needed to 'spend a penny' when I asked her where the bathroom was. I mean, who even says that? I do, it seems...

I'm bracing myself to return to the living room, when I hear my phone ping. It's Nandy again – and it's not another sticker.

> Thought you should know Cassia just mentioned you on her Insta.

> WHAT?

> Well not you exactly, your alter ego, Walter or whatever you call it.

> WULT® Woman! What did she say??

> Something about #positiveageing. And how you're kind of...

> Kind of what?

> Kind of not.

> Not what?

> Being positive.

> But I am positive. Positively young looking. Hahaha.

> Yeah.

> I have to go, I'm at Zoe's.

> Zoe?

> New friend in my building. She's 24!

> Have fun.

I am about to type 'Will do', but I can see Nandy isn't online anymore.

I don't stay much longer at Zoe's, as I'm keen to investigate Cassia's reel and escape from the latest game Jamal has put on, which seems to have a farming theme – just what you want on a Friday night. I stand up just as Kai announces he's 'unlocked a silo!'. Thank god I've got vodka. I grab my 'shopping' and head upstairs in the lift, making excuses about needing some 'self-care'. I'm quite pleased with that excuse and they all seem very sympathetic. Self-care takes many forms. This evening's being a very strong Bloody Mary.

While I'm looking for the Lea & Perrins in Devon's cupboards (surely everyone has Lea & Perrins?), I search Instagram with my other hand. I find *@cassical* within seconds – I look at it often enough... In her latest reel, Cassia is pretending to talk to her reflection in a mirror about how she feels about getting older. It's kind of cringey. She's telling herself how *#grateful* and *#blessed* she is that her wrinkles and lines are from smiles and laughter blah blah blah. Sure, Cassia, that's all very well, but good breeding and 'Mini Botox' will only get you to forty-five. When you start to look like someone Mother Pells would describe as having had a 'tough paper round', then you'll be having more than one vintage cocktail a week and wishing you'd got WULT® like me.

Cassia is going on and on and on. I fast forward the reel to get to the bit about me. Oh, here we go. Apparently, 'someone' (i.e. me), is 'championing' (eye roll) a treatment that 'doesn't align with her stance' (ooh fancy) on positive ageing. Seriously, Cassia – mind your own business. Although, thinking about it, of course she's going to leap on this bandwagon: she didn't get the treatment. And the pro-ageing brigade will love that Cassia is supporting their cause. I've come across them before in the comments sections of my articles, with their outdoor wear and salt and pepper hair: to them, any attempt to look younger is an act of betrayal and anti-feminist. Apparently, we should all be embracing our saggy bits as 'badges of honour'. Fine, do that. But surely I should be allowed to make a different choice. It feels like you can't win. If you do nothing, you're 'letting yourself go'. And if you do something like I did you're a bad example to womankind. Frankly, I'd rather be a bad example and have no chin hairs.

Chapter Twenty-Five

It's a rich person thing

Despite what I consider to be a less than successful evening, over the next couple of weeks I am invited back for more 'cosy' gaming sessions at Zoe's. They don't get any more exciting than the first, but at least I don't bother with a bag of booze again and/or question the fact that the living room looks like the 'character collectables' section of Toys 'R' Us.

Jamal (who I think lives in the flat too – it's hard to work out) seems quite suspicious of me. Kai is more friendly, although he does go on about self-care. Maybe it's a euphemism for masturbation? That's what men talked about a lot in the Nineties anyway. Zoe has also started coming up to sit on the balcony with me for cups of tea after her lectures. There are some upsides to this: I am drinking less alcohol, although I haven't been getting hangovers much so I'm not sure that even matters. And Zoe is really good company and interesting to talk to, so a good start when it comes to making new Gen Z friends.

I didn't get the Behold The Banana job in the end – apparently, the 'vibe was off', which is exactly the kind of in-depth and constructive advice I was hoping for. Say what you want about the drinking culture at Saatchi's, I bet they gave better interview feedback than that. I've asked the recruitment agency to keep me posted on any other advertising jobs that come up, and maybe once I've settled into being Gen Z a bit more and got the hang of the way things have changed, I'll be better equipped.

In the meantime, I'm still making money from Yuvana, even if I'm quite bored. And although I'm used to this – and not shy of a game or two of Clock Patience and a David Attenborough documentary to pass the time – some company is welcome. Zoe isn't just turning into my first proper friend in my new 'existence', she's also useful for learning Gen Z slang and helping me dial down the 'salty' expressions, as Channing calls them. Although the other day I did say, 'What's good for the goose is good for the gander.' Thankfully Zoe thought I was joking, or at least I think that's what her expression meant.

She's studying a post-graduate in ecology and society, or something like that, and seems more worried about the planet than me or indeed anyone I know, except maybe Josie and Laure, oh and Keith and Stephen. And Simon, but he's just so weird about everything it's hard to tell what really bothers him. I can see from his Facebook that his mushroom phase is now evolving into microdosing. The other day he was talking about 'harnessing the power of nature's gifts' and 'exploring the limitless possibilities of the human mind' – which all sounds like tech startup speak for tripping to me.

I replied to his email about Mother Pells and said I'd go and look at the retirement flat in Bristol with him, as it feels like an opportunity to reveal my new appearance while we are focusing on something else. And with Alannah and the boys in a different time zone, this could be good timing. For a change, he sounded quite pleased, and emailed me back saying he'd be in touch with a date.

He signed off saying something about how 'you don't find plant medicine – it finds you,' which gives the unwelcome impression that plant medicine might be lurking behind a bush in a nearby park.

Anyway, when Zoe and I stick to subjects like the climate crisis rather than, say, Postman Pat, it feels like the conversation flows. Even though it's pretty bloody depressing, I can't help but be impressed by how much Zoe cares about it. The other day she told me to imagine dressing up as a frog for Halloween and then having to tell my children what a frog was and why they don't exist anymore. There's a lot to think about here. Firstly, she doesn't know I'm forty-eight in a few weeks and children – for many reasons, not just my age – are never going to happen. Secondly, my fancy dress days are over after omelette-gate, but that's another story I can't really share. And thirdly, I think in that situation I'd just say a frog was a mythical creature because I would never want to be that much of a party pooper.

Zoe has asked a few questions about me, but I think I've handled them fairly well. The official statement is that I'm twenty-seven, work in social media marketing and I moved here from Wiltshire, so I don't really know anyone. I'm also hoping if I say I'm from Wiltshire she'll assume some of my 'unusual' phrases are just how people speak in the West Country. She's from Sevenoaks so maybe Wiltshire sounds distant and exotic to her. The other day she also told me that Kai thinks I'm 'a snack'. I buried my face in my cup of tea so I could a) not burst out laughing (I nearly choked) and b) work out what she meant. My idea of a snack is Reblochon spread on paprika crostini. I decided it was positive, however – like 'dish'? – otherwise why would she tell me? So, as I lowered my cup I decided the correct facial expression was 'pleasantly surprised'. Which I am, especially if it means the old (okay, brand new with tags on) Fuchsia Frenzy might be getting an airing sometime soon.

—

Finally, Nandy is coming to visit. I bought the scallop shell things again from the big M&S in her honour, and the first wine I've had all week. I also got some tulips to put on the kitchen island, and hoovered with Devon's insanely powerful Dyson. It sucked up about three hair ties, but I suppose if I'm running short I could just get one from Zoe's.

Nandy is meant to come at seven p.m. but arrives about half-past. 'Sorry I'm late,' she says, marching down my – Devon's – hall and into the living room. 'My dad turned up for dinner thinking it was Tuesday, and then Maya appeared with three bags of laundry, the majority of which appears to be hand wash only... Middle-aged problems, amiright?'

'I can't remember what they are,' I laugh and hug her, but catch an expression flash across her face that I don't like.

A tight feeling rises in my chest. Maybe she hasn't got used to this yet after all. I was hoping this evening would be the beginning of a positive new phase – one where Nandy was actually on my side. Which is what you want from your best friend, after all.

'Nice pad. That's a fucking monster of a monstera...' She looks around the room.

'It's called "maximalism", apparently.'

'Oh really?' She turns to the plant. 'Hi Max.'

I laugh again, trying to keep it light, but there's already an atmosphere descending that makes my hand shake as I pour us massive Picpouls in two of Devon's extremely delicate wine glasses, which, incidentally, I'm amazed I haven't smashed yet.

'These look like the wine glasses of someone who doesn't drink much wine.' Nandy is wandering about the living room picking up things and stroking the furniture. 'What does this Devon even do? And what does she look like?'

I notice her voice is so much flatter than usual.

'No idea – and no idea. It's a rich person thing. They just float about staying in each other's houses. Which is handy for me at the moment, as I still haven't told anyone back home about...' I point to my face.

'So you're still going ahead with this?' says Nandy, now installed on the sofa.

'Going ahead with? What d'you mean? I've already done it – you can see that.'

'I mean, is it permanent? This is what you look like now?'

'Yes. I told you that.'

'I know. I suppose I just thought you might have had a few weeks to think about it and come to your senses.'

'Come to my senses?' What the hell does she mean?

'Yes, Erica, come to your senses. You've had a chance to see how it feels, but surely this isn't what you really want, long term?'

'Why wouldn't it be? My god, Nandy, I thought you at least would understand.'

'Why "me at least"? Do you see me as someone that doesn't like herself? Someone who wants to change to the point where they're unrecognisable?'

'No, no… I just mean…' I gulp my wine. I don't really know what I mean, so I change tack. 'I've nearly got as many followers as Cassia now.'

Nandy looks confused at the subject change, but I keep going, hearing myself talking faster and feeling sweat beading on my top lip. 'She won't be happy. She looked ridiculous doing that "healthy gut" reel the other day, did you see it? I mean who the hell could say "I'm Stool Savvy" with a straight face? I bet she got thousands for that though. I'm hoping to be able to get some big sponsors too once I hit 200K.'

'I didn't see it,' says Nandy.

'It was a load of shit. Literally.' I laugh but it comes out quite manically. Nandy doesn't laugh, but instead starts flicking through one of Devon's coffee table books about Mykonos or latte art or something.

I top up our wines.

—

A bit later, scallop shells and bottle of Picpoul now empty, we sit in the deckchairs on the balcony smoking a joint, wrapped up in blankets like pensioners on a pier. London is twinkling all around us and car horns and sirens echo down below. After the wine, things feel slightly more relaxed.

'Do you think Cassia knows it's you?' asks Nandy, licking non-existent mornay sauce out of a scallop shell.

'Unless she thinks I'm a deep fake. But I hope so. I'm happy to flex a bit.'

'To what?'

'Flex. Show off.'

'Right…' I think Nandy is pulling a face behind the shell.

There's a silence. It's Nandy who breaks it though. 'So did you say you'd made a friend in the building?'

'Yes. Zoe. She's nice.' I'm pleased Nandy is taking an interest.

'What does she do?'

'She's a student. At Goldsmiths.'

'Same as Maya.' Nandy raises her eyebrows. 'Wonder if she knows her…'

I can tell it's not really a question, so I just smile and pull my blanket tighter around me. 'I'll go and put our paella in the microwave in a minute,' I say. 'Sorry it's not homecooked but it's M&S. I got Raspberry Royales for pudding. They slap.' I've heard Jamal say this and want to try it out.

Nandy looks incredulous at this. Perhaps she's not keen on paella. Anyway, she doesn't mention it and instead says: 'Maybe you and Zoe can come round to ours for dinner sometime. We like having Maya's friends over.'

For a second I smile at the invitation, then realise she's being snide. I don't say anything, but she keeps going. 'The three of you can tell Ash and me about the latest trends and slang words. We like to hear what all the young people are up to. Helps to keep us on our toes.'

The tight feeling rises in my chest again, so I try to lighten things up. 'Her friend Kai is into me, it seems.'

Nandy puts the scallop shell down. She seems to be taking quite a long time to reply. When she does, she has her eyes closed, which is a bit weird. 'How old is he?'

'I don't know, same age as Zoe I guess, twenty-four?'

'And, what, I'm confused… you're interested in him?' She's opened her eyes now and is looking directly at mine.

'Yes – I suppose I am.' I smile and lean in. 'He's pretty hot. Although they don't really say that these days, I've discovered.'

Nandy appears to be taking a deep breath for some reason, then talks really slowly and deliberately. 'And... sorry... just to be clear... you're planning to... what? Have sex with him?'

'Hopefully!' I relight the joint and then laugh, coughing out smoke. 'You know, for the plot.' Another Jamal expression.

'For the plot?'

'Yeah, you know, being adventurous.'

She does that weird incredulous look again. 'He's the same age as Rohan.'

I laugh again.

Nandy abruptly stands up. 'I'm going to go, Erica. Feel free to get in touch when you have found your mind again. Because you appear to have totally fucking lost it.'

Then she marches through the living room, grabbing her bag from the sofa, and before I can even haul myself up off the deckchair, I hear the front door slam.

Later, I'm lying in bed, wondering why Nandy, Josie – and Gabe for that matter – can't see I am just trying to be a better version of myself? But they can't, clearly. It's actually quite upsetting. I mean I didn't expect them to throw me a bloody party, but I thought they'd at least try to understand. But it feels more like I'm being punished. And so maybe it's time to move on and surround myself with people who do appreciate the new me. Maybe it's part of the change I so desperately wanted – want. Maybe the problem isn't mine. Maybe it's theirs. I mean, what do they know about how I felt anyway? They've settled down, got married, had kids. Our lives aren't remotely comparable.

I'm woozy from wine and weed but quickly check my emails on my phone before I crash out. There's another email from Gabe. I didn't reply to his last one so I'm not sure why he's in touch again. Opening it, I see it's just the contact details of his friend Maxine, the comedy producer, with a perfunctory note saying he'd forgotten to include them in his last email. But I don't exactly need to email her anymore, do I? I've got it made doing this social media for Yuvana Labs. But I'm not rude – so I reply, briefly, just saying thanks. Not really much else to say, is there?

While I'm online, I log into the WULT® Woman Insta account to see if I have any new likes or comments, and sure enough the pro-ageing brigade have clearly had a glass of sulphite-free rosé tonight. What's the latest? Oh, that apparently I 'make the Kardashians look understated'. I think you'll find it's 'Kardashable', I say to myself, suddenly and unexpectedly missing my mum. Another one says that 'this is what internalised misogyny looks like up close', which I might need to pop into ChatGPT to decipher. The last one I read before I throw my phone down on the bed says: 'You've had more work done than my kitchen.' That doesn't even make sense. JEEZ. It's not like I've had a splashback put in.

Chapter Twenty-Six

The periodic table of elements

By the time Channing calls me the next morning, the online pro-ageing backlash has got even more intense. He reassures me that this is all good publicity and that I 'slay', but also encourages me to upload some 'fresh, positive content'. So, I get dressed (a Cottage Core floral shorts co-ord from a recent Urban Outfitters haul, plus chunky trainers), and head to the Liberty beauty hall on Regent Street. I've hardly thought about what happened with Nandy last night with all this going on, and she hasn't been in touch, but I'm not really expecting her to be. I'm not going to message her – I think she needs to apologise first for storming off like that.

Liberty isn't that busy, but it's Wednesday at ten-thirty a.m. so not exactly peak time. Once I'm in the door, I do a quick 'panorama' film of the room, making sure I get all the best beauty counters in, tag my location and then post a Story with the caption 'At the Mothership' with a heart and a smiley face emoji. This will get them all back on my side, and @Cheshire_In_Stilettos will love it.

After the burst of energy involved in getting here, I realise I'm now absolutely starving, so I head up to Arthur's Café on the second floor with Eggs Royale in mind – partly because it's very Instagrammable, and partly because I had it before once with Merlyn and it's the best thing I've ever tasted that doesn't contain cheese.

I'm seated in a semi-circular booth on a blue velvet banquette, which reminds me of the sofas at Yuvana Labs. Which also reminds me, I've been expecting to hear from them with the date of my next Youth Review but nothing yet. Weird – they're normally so efficient.

I scroll through my phone while I wait for my eggs to see if there are any other comments on the WULT® Woman account. There aren't any particularly interesting (or funny) ones, apart from someone asking if I have that 'new face smell' – but thanks to the backlash my followers are now at 183K. That's nearly as many as *@LuxeLooksWithLily* – and more to the point… it beats Cassia Carver, a.k.a. the Job Thief, who is currently doing a live from her hair salon, wearing a t-shirt with the words 'Kitchen Disco' on it. Naturally, she has a celebrity hairdresser, Terence Tate, and they are flirting with each other in quite a nauseating manner while they discuss if Cassia should 'go with the grey'. Naturally, Sonia et al are all sucking up to her in the comments, saying things like 'Silver is the crown you've earned!' and 'Think of it as nature's glitter!'. It's putting me off my eggs.

As I'm trying to work out whether she's had her lips done again (I don't think she has), my food arrives. I dutifully snap a picture, making sure I get the tiled bar area in the background, and add it to my Stories before demolishing the eggs. I pause only briefly to reply to a message from Josie, which is just a link to a recipe for some Ottolenghi ricotta fritters. This is not really the kind of support I need, frankly, and the likelihood of me making these – and the accompanying hibiscus sugar – is beyond slim. I'm also not that keen on cheese in desserts, which

I thought she would know by now, so I just reply with a thumbs up, order a flat white, and wonder why I don't feel as elated as I thought I would that I've got more followers than Cassia now.

Walking back into the beauty hall twenty minutes later, I'm surprised to see a throng of middle-aged women, all beautifully dressed in Victoria Beckham and Erdem, with balayage toffee-coloured hair, and dare I say it, a fair few millilitres of Botox and filler between them. I'm not judging, I've had enough of it myself over the years. I push my way into the crowd – there must surely be a 'Gift with Purchase' at the Omorovicza counter? – and attempt to navigate my way across the hall. That's when I hear it.

'There she is!'

I look round to see who they're talking about.

'WULT® Woman!'

'Wulty!'

Whoops and cheers echo everywhere.

Turns out it's me they're talking about.

What.

The.

Hell.

Then I realise – of course, I tagged my location. Have these people really come along here to meet me? They certainly have, it seems, and they want to get *very* close.

'Hi, I'm @*FashionFindsWithFreya*!'...

'Can I touch your face?'...

'Where's your co-ord from?'...

'Can I get WULT® for my husband?'...

'I'm @*DoesThisLookTooOldForMe*! If I get the treatment with @*BriannaLovesToBuy*, can we get a group discount?'...

'Is WULT® a con – are you actually young?'...

'Do you ever get ID-ed?'...

'Do you still pee when you sneeze?'

By now I've got my back against the Sisley counter and the women are asking for selfies and pawing at me like I'm an avocado in the fresh produce section. I'm fairly sure I have coffee breath and smoked salmon in my teeth and I'm absolutely certain I didn't put on any deodorant, so it all feels a little too intimate. But I get paid for this – more than I've ever been paid, come to think of it – so I smile and pose for the photos and say positive things, which isn't that hard because well, I'm the same age as these women yet I look like their daughters.

A few minutes later, *@Gabi_glows* has her arm around me and is taking a photo when *@UnforgettableForties* asks if she can feel my tits. Tempting, I have to say, as they are incredibly pert and haven't had anyone's hands on them since about 2012, but I politely decline the offer. It's all getting a bit much and I look over at the doors to see how I can possibly escape.

'Thanks so much, ladies,' I say. 'But I have an appointment now, so I'm heading off. Great to meet you all. Don't forget to subscribe to email updates to be the first to hear when WULT® becomes available!'

I steer towards the exit but some of the women follow me, stroking my arms and taking more photos. JEEZ. I make it out the door onto the pavement but about fifteen of them come too. And now I am standing, unsure what to do...

A black car pulls up, just like the ones in *Succession*. The window winds down about three inches. All I can see is a massive pair of sunglasses peering over the top.

'Get in,' says Merlyn.

I open the door and flop down in the seat, sighing with relief. It takes me a second to notice there is a man sitting next to Merlyn, wearing a white tuxedo jacket with nothing underneath, showing a mass of dark chest hair.

'OMG you're so gorgeous – who gave you permission, gurl?' Finally, here is Channing, in the flesh. I've come to know him well enough to understand that 'who gave you permission' isn't a question that needs an answer.

We drive around Soho to shake off the women who were clearly trying to work out where we are heading – Channing even saw one of them hail a black cab, jump straight in and start following us. It's all very surreal.

Merlyn hands me a glass of Crémant, which she has magicked from the mini fridge. 'Erica my dear. I think what we have learnt today is that location tagging is an Instagram feature that should be used with caution.'

Merlyn pours herself a glass too, then Channing. 'I propose a toast,' she says.

Everyone holds up their glass.

'To WULT® Woman!'

—

After about half an hour, and a couple of bottles of Crémant (most of which appears to have been sunk by Channing, who is now singing Katy Perry songs out of the open window), we drive near Charing Cross Road and I ask Merlyn if I can be dropped off. There are no 'fans' to be seen and the car is hot, maybe because Channing is, apparently, a firework.

I'm glad of the breeze and wander along the street, enjoying the looks from men at my legs. Feeling nostalgic, I take a diversion on the way to the tube and pass close to where Kofi used to work.

Ahead of me, I can see some sort of commotion – a police car, and a group gathered around a man who is sitting on the pavement shouting something. As I draw closer, I can hear it's the periodic table of elements, which I just about remember from chemistry GCSE. He has an electric keyboard in his hand, and bags scattered around him, one of which contains what appears to be about six chickens (from a supermarket, not live chickens). There are a couple of street workers in branded sweatshirts, two policemen, and another man in a suit.

As I get closer, I recognise the sweatshirts – they're from the homeless charity Kofi worked for. A few more steps and I'm nearly level with the crowd. Some passers-by have even stopped to see what's going on. It seems the charity workers are trying to persuade the police not to arrest the man, who at that moment starts playing 'Angels' by Robbie Williams on the keyboard – pretty well actually, but I'm not sure it helps.

I'm level with them now. The man in the suit turns, not much, but enough for me to see his face. He's late forties, and has very short, black hair, with a sprinkling of grey both at the temples and through his beard.

Born on a Friday. It's Kofi.

Fifteen minutes later I am sitting in a bakery-meets-cafe nearby called The Next Chapter. If there's a business name that screams 'fresh start after a divorce' more than this, I'm all ears. It has glass walls and a cabinet in the middle of the room full of Danish pastries, all with slightly different fillings, lined up on baking parchment.

Opposite me is Kofi. I'm trying to hold the handle of my cup of flat white so that my shaking hand doesn't make it clatter on the saucer. Sweat is pooling in my cleavage and I wonder if it's going to make a damp patch on the front of my co-ord.

The dispute with the homeless man had been drawing to a conclusion and Kofi stepped away from his colleagues to stand with me in a shop doorway. He recognised me straight away, of course. I look pretty similar to when he last saw me (apart from the fringe) – the day Father Pells drove up to London and helped me pack box upon box into the back of his Volvo estate.

Even though it was only a quarter of an hour ago, I don't remember either of our exact words. I do remember him shaking his head, and saying, 'I might have known you'd do something crazy like this.' And now here we are, with coffees in front of us that we don't really want, staring at each other. This is a face I've thought about so much over the last twenty years that it feels bizarre having it in front of me – and even more so because it's like looking through one of those Snapchat filters that age you. As for Kofi, well, I don't know what he's thinking, but his mouth is slightly open, and I can see the pale skin inside, which was once so familiar, and now feels like something from another life, another time.

'It's so freakin strange looking at you,' he says. 'It's like the picture of Dorian Gray. Or Benjamin Button. Or...' He trails off.

I don't say anything, although it occurs to me that it can't be that strange if he didn't ever see the middle-aged version of me. I stop staring at him for a second and notice his wallet on the table, lying open to reveal a British Garden Centres Family Membership and what looks like the business card of a financial adviser. It's upside down and the font is curly but his name is either Martin Clack or Martin Crack. I find myself pondering which would be worse.

'How are your mum and dad?' Kofi asks after a moment, clearing his throat loudly.

Tears pool in my eyes, unexpectedly. 'My mum is fine. My dad... erm... he... passed. Away.'

'I'm sorry.' He looks it. Genuinely. Kofi was – maybe is – an empathetic person, I guess that's why he does the job he does. 'Your parents were...'

I wonder what he's going to say. Distant? Reserved? Workaholics?

'...always looking out for you and Simon.' He smiles, for the first time. 'You were very lucky. *Are* very lucky, I'm sure. I'm trying to do the same for my three.'

Kofi has kids. But that's not what I'm focusing on. 'What d'you mean?'

'They worked really hard to give you as much as they could, didn't they? Remember when they paid for us to go away to the Scottish Highlands for my twenty-fifth? And you said you had some pretty special family holidays when you were young.' He says 'young' in a strange way, staring at me again, the smile gone.

When I look back, I think of my parents working late, of freezer dinners, the key under the flowerpot. I remember Simon being 'in charge' of me (much to his delight), and that evening when Drunk Norman from five doors down banged on the door and Simon and I hid behind the curtains until our parents got home. But it was hours, and all I had was a sherbet fountain, which gave me a headache. Funny how someone who wasn't there can have such a warped version of what it was really like.

I finish my coffee, and watch the foam form a rim of scum around the cup, like the remains of a bubble bath. I want to go. This is awkward. But there's something else I need to say.

'I'm sorry. About what happened with Owen.'

Kofi's face turns from the frown he's had for most of our conversation, to a look of surprise. 'That was a long time ago, Erica. And you've said sorry.'

'I'm still sorry,' I say. 'Because it was... it meant... the end of us.'

'Don't think so...' He looks around him as though he's searching for evidence to the contrary.

'What d'you mean?'

'I mean, that wasn't why we broke up, was it?'

'I don't know. Wasn't it?' I sip at invisible coffee, trying to hide my confusion.

'No... I think we were drifting apart. The Owen thing just moved things along more quickly.' He reaches over the table, taking my hand. 'It wasn't your fault. Any of it. We were *all* idiots — it could have been any of us. And I was just ready for... a change. To settle down. I wasn't really feeling it anymore, d'you know what I mean?'

No, I do not know what you mean, I think. Kofi carries on.

'I met my wife not long after you went back west. She's a bit older. Natalie. She wanted to start a family. I mean, we both did.'

I'm not sure if he's trying to make me feel better, or worse, or just likes talking about his wife. I need to say something though, so go for: 'That's... lovely. What are your kids called?'

'We've got twin girls, Nia and Layla. And a boy. Owen, actually. They're quite grown up now.'

I don't say anything. I can't. I've spent nearly half my life being wrong about all this and it's taking a while to sink in.

'And you, Erica, did you settle down?'

If there is one molecule of liquid in this cup, I will find it. There isn't. I put it back down. 'No. It didn't happen for me.'

'Well, look at you. Still time, I reckon. If that's what you want, of course.' He picks up his wallet. 'I need to get off now, I'm giving Nia a lift to Glastonbury after work. I'm just a taxi service these days…'

I force a smile, ninety-five per cent still nauseous with shock, five per cent annoyed I don't have a Glastonbury ticket. Kofi stands up and checks something on his smartwatch, then, with a final look of what seems to be disbelief and/or concern – and could be either about me, or maybe a disappointingly low daily step count – waves goodbye.

And then he's gone.

Chapter Twenty-Seven

Find her before she finds you

Today's dead American Erica Pells (from Grand Junction, Colorado), passed away peacefully aged ninety-four, and 'made every day a good day'. I decide that this is an excellent omen, as it is my birthday. I am forty-eight. I do not look forty-eight, of course. I actually think I look younger than twenty-eight, but I've told a few people that's my age now so I have to stick to it. Anyway – maybe, like the Colorado Erica, I can now make every day a good day. I'm getting there – today is certainly already a marked improvement on last year's birthday.

I remember I had a raging Pinot Noir hangover after binge watching *Ted Lasso* until about two a.m. In the morning, I was trying to remove a hair on my top lip that had appeared from nowhere but was so long that if there had also been one on the other side, I could have curled both ends with wax and turned the whole thing into a rather dapper feature. I was right in the middle of this depilatory challenge when Josie came round with Héloïse carrying my favourite Ottolenghi almond cake, which would have been lovely if it wasn't for the depressing number of candles stuck in it. And at eleven a.m. I mean, who does that? They even lit all the candles before they rang the bell, so when I opened the door I *had* to blow them out, even though I still felt sick from my hangover and all the tweezing.

Today, I don't have to put up with such interruptions. And thankfully the positive-ageing drama seems to have calmed down a bit too. There are still a few comments on my posts, but Channing tells me to reply that 'WULT® will make you feel positive every day!' (link in bio to subscribe to updates etc). Which is true. He also says that negative comments are to be expected now that I have so many followers. Apparently 'Mother' says the 'haters gonna hate', and I have a funny feeling he doesn't mean his actual mother but in fact, and bizarrely, Taylor Swift.

Then there's the whole Kofi thing. I feel like I'm still trying to process seeing him again after all this time. I had a really weird dream he was lying in the street and Owen was lighting tea lights on the kerb. I was trying to wake Kofi up, shouting at him, 'Owen is here! He's alive! It's all going to be fine!' What the hell does that mean? Maybe that it *is* all going to be fine, but it's not like I can flick a switch and forget it all. I've played that horrible night over in my head so many times, and blamed myself every single one of them. The guilt has been in the background of everything I've done since. In fact, it's *why* I've done a lot of the things I've done since. Not just moving back to Wiltshire, but more than that, believing myself to be a bit of a crap person all round. JEEZ. I'm such an idiot. Maybe I'm not as crap as I thought. Thank god I've got my lovely new jawline to cheer me up.

I sit on the balcony in one of the deckchairs. They're starting to annoy me as they're hard to get out of. Although I wouldn't have been able to manage it at all before the treatment. Just as I sit down, Josie sends a perfunctory 'happy birthday' message. Then Mother Pells calls. She says she has a present for me but that I can 'get it when I visit', which she hopes will be soon. I decide to test the water, as it's my birthday, which surely means nobody can be cross with me?

'I'm looking a bit different these days, Mum. I had a fancy beauty treatment. You know I get them for free.'

'*Another* one, Erica?'

'Yes. This one was really good, though.'

'Does this mean you'll stop wearing so much make-up?'

'Actually, yes,' I say, trying not to sound irritated. 'It's cutting-edge technology. I'm one of the first people to try it.'

'You're going up in the world!'

Is 'going up in the world' some sort of comparison to Simon? I go to snap at her but stop myself, and just say 'Yes'. I haven't seen her for ages, and maybe I'm reading too much into it.

'Can you bring me some more of those lip balms when you come next?' she says.

'Okay, Mum.'

'Thank you darling. I keep losing them. *The Inevitable*, I'm sure...'

Once I've said goodbye, I move onto Cassia's Instagram feed, where she just uploaded an acai and banana overnight oats recipe reel #whatIeatinaday. Who cares what you have for breakfast, Cassia? But about two thousand people clearly do. She isn't finished though... hold on, what's she saying now... that there's 'something suspicious' about WULT® Woman... and that she can't understand why 'the person in question' always has the same background? Then she laughs and says, 'Maybe the poor woman is being held prisoner! We should find her.'

Just as I'm about to put my phone away, I check the comments on my latest WULT® Woman reel, which was a #GRWM yesterday. They all look like the usual kind of thing, asking when the treatment will be available, saying how great I look and/or how much their husband/partner will love it (take note, Gabe)... Wait. Hold on – this one's different. 'Why are you always in the same room, WULT® Woman??' I keep scrolling. There are about eight replies below this, one saying 'Blink twice if you need help!!!'. Then another: 'Why don't you ever go outside – are you being kept prisoner by Yuvana Labs??'. Bloody Cassia. What has she started?

By the time Zoe comes round for her usual cup of tea and chat after her lectures, I already have a hashtag: #whereswulty. I message Channing who tells me to 'touch grass'. I manage to ask Zoe what this means without blowing my cover and, apparently, it's 'come offline' and not as I had previously thought (and indeed hoped), smoke some weed, which I haven't done since I was last with Nandy.

Zoe sees a birthday card lying on the balcony table. It's the only one that came today and is from Merlyn and Channing, the oddest co-signers of a card one could possibly imagine. The card itself is just as odd. It has a picture of Keanu Reeves on the front with the words '*Keanu believe it's your birthday*', which presumably they think is a good pun. I'm sure more cards will come, they just take longer when they're redirected.

'Is it your birthday today?' Zoe laughs. Sometimes it's annoying that she giggles so much, sometimes I quite like how happy it sounds. Today, it's annoying. She asks if I'd like to come to the pub later – I think she feels sorry for me, which she shouldn't. I didn't think she ever went to the pub, so this is a pleasing development, as is the fact that she mentions Kai will be there. Maybe my first birthday as 'new me' will see me getting some action for the first time in... well, I'm too embarrassed to say how long, and I don't think Gabe kissing me really counts. I'm pretty sure it's not referred to as 'action' anymore, either.

–

The Mariner's Arms looks like a regular London pub. But instead of having the usual mix of ages, and the obligatory old men sitting at the bar, it's almost entirely full of young people. Maybe it's now hip – or hip-hop – to go to traditional pubs. When I was in my twenties, we only went to bars with names like 'Nebula Yard' or 'Infinity 2000', which invariably had exposed pipes on the ceiling, blue glass vases on the tables and served snacks, which were almost entirely based on sun-dried tomatoes.

Zoe and her friends have taken over an alcove with taxidermy birds and fish in cases on the walls. The table is sticky and littered with pints of either lager or cider, or – disturbingly for someone who generally only drinks wine or Aperol (and the occasional Bloody Mary) – a combination of both, with a dash of blackcurrant. I vaguely remember this drink from the Nineties but it was quite grungy, and I wasn't, so I can't remember what it's called. I'm fairly confident it's a 'Blacksnake'. I attempt to surreptitiously google it but the girl next to me with a Peppa Pig tattoo on her arm and lots of star-shaped spot patches on her face (what 'Core' is that – Shambles Core?) keeps looking at my phone. I hope she didn't see me checking the comments on my latest WULT® Woman reel, which incidentally was a *#GRWM* before I left to come out, using my new VolumeFlow Vortex Hairstyler (*#gifted*).

I'm just wondering if I can get away with asking for a wine list – and come to the conclusion that I cannot – when Kai, after trying to catch my eye ever since I arrived, offers to buy me the lager/cider/blackcurrant thing, even though he doesn't appear to be drinking himself. He's sweet, I like his nose ring, and under his curtains of hair, his eyes are a very clear blue.

I tuck into my drink and chat to Kai about when he got his nose pierced and if it hurt. I'm feeling pretty pleased with my birthday self – maybe this is my new crowd. Maybe I'm starting to fit in. It might just be the drink talking, but apart from accidentally saying 'Many hands make light work!' when we all helped the barman clear empties off the table, I feel like I'm holding my own as a bona fide Gen Z. I knew I'd get there in the end.

The conversation turns to families, and a guy wearing a woolly hat and glasses last seen on Timmy Mallett asks me why I'm not with mine on my birthday. I tell them my dad is dead, which seems to shock everyone – I hadn't considered how unusual that would be in a group of twenty-somethings, so allow myself to enjoy the sympathy for a few minutes. The Peppa Pig girl even puts her arm around me but I'm fairly sure she's just trying to get another look at my phone.

Then it gets weird. I make a couple of vague comments about how my mum is more interested in my brother than me, and Aimee, who has a zig-zag parting and pink tinted sunglasses on, mentions just as casually that she's cut her mum off completely. She's even blocked her number and email address. The woolly hat guy says he's considering doing the same with both his parents, and says he's 'following his truth'. I smile and nod to start with, just trying to fit in, saying yeah, I'm thinking of doing that too.

But then I remember what Kofi said. My parents did look out for me and Simon, in their own way. They weren't around as much as I would have liked, but maybe they were just working hard. For us. And he was right, we did have some brilliant holidays… One year we went on a Hoseasons boating trip around the Norfolk Broads, and a couple of years running we camped in the Forest of Dean. Once, when Father Pells got a bonus, we got the ferry to Holland to see the windmills and I brought *stroopwaffels* back for my classmates. I was very popular at school for at least a fortnight.

It all starts to feel a bit… wrong, agreeing with this. So, I take a big gulp of my horrible drink, and I say, quite loudly, 'No.'

Everyone stops talking.

'Your parents are just human!' I say. 'I'm sure they're trying their best. They might not always get it right, but I bet they have good intentions and love you, even if they don't show it in the right way. Hasn't it occurred to you that cutting them off instead of talking things through could be way worse than anything they've done to you?'

Holy crap, where did that come from?

I take a breath and Aimee immediately chimes in, taking off her sunglasses in an act of faux sincerity and sounding as if she's regurgitating lines from a TikTok video. 'Healing involves unravelling our narratives and embracing the raw emotions we've suppressed. Cutting ties with family members who aren't part of this healing journey demonstrates a dedication to working through our triggers, comprehending them, and achieving radical self-acceptance.'

I'm not sure what she was expecting me to say, and indeed even I am surprised by my reaction. I slam my pint glass down on the table and shout: 'Oh... GROW UP!'

And I stomp off to the loo.

—

I take my time. I'm shaking. Outbursts aren't really 'me'... Standing at the sink breathing heavily, trying to calm down, I pull out my phone to distract myself. But it only serves to stress me out even more, because the first thing I see are more of the *#whereswulty* comments on Instagram.

'She's back in her jail – where is it??'...

'I'm sure I saw the Shard through her windows'...

'Do they only let her out for exercise once a week? Cruel human experimentation!'

There is also now a meme of me wearing a red-and-white-striped top and hat like 'Where's Wally?' holding up a mascara wand as though it's a weapon, with the caption – 'Find her before she finds you'. Sometimes I really don't understand the internet.

I wash my hands – the sink has one of those heaters hanging over it for the hot tap that always serves up scalding water. There isn't any soap either, or paper towels for that matter. I look at myself in the mirror, jowl-free and fresh-faced. Even my beer eyes look glassy and pretty rather than snake-like, as they would have done pre-WULT®. The toilets might be crappy but it's all worth it for this. I'm ninety-nine per cent sure. Ninety per cent.

Okay eighty-five, but I knew it would take some getting used to.

Walking back along the corridor towards the bar, and wondering what the mood at the table will be like when I return, I bump into Kai. He doesn't appear to be looking for the loo, but rather for me. He asks me if I'm okay, but before I can answer, he asks if he can kiss me. How terribly *Bridgerton* of him – back in the day, I was lucky if I got eye contact before whoever it was pushed me up against the wall and tried to undo my bra. I'm three pints in and really need the night to improve. So I say yes.

Kai kisses me gently. I put my hand up to his face to make it more, well, assertive. But his cheek feels really soft and... how can I describe it? Oh, I know. Young. He feels young. And there is suddenly something about him that reminds me of... oh crap.

Oli. He reminds me of my nephew, Oli.

I break free from the kiss, turn and run back down the corridor into the toilets. I only just make it to the cubicle in time to throw up a lot of very purple vomit.

How sure am I now? About sixty per cent.

Chapter Twenty-Eight

A pigeon dressed as Henry VIII

Simon is late. He has many, many annoying habits but tardiness is not usually one of them. I fidget in a teal-coloured armchair which, with wooden arms and legs, is as uncomfortable as it looks. The whole room – the communal lounge area of the retirement flats in Bristol – is pretty heavy on the teal.

I check the time on my phone again. Thankfully, Alison, the woman who is supposed to be showing us the flat, is late as well. I look around, nervous about seeing Simon for the first time since the treatment. I can see that on the five or six tables spread throughout the room are jigsaw puzzles in boxes, and the one nearest to me is called 'Pigeons of Britain'. I assume this will be an array of different species of said bird, but leaning to get a better look, it appears to be drawings of pigeons dressed as British icons such as Elton John, David Bowie and Del Boy. Pretty sure my Gen Z friends wouldn't be able to identify the latter bird. Mind you, after my sharp exit from the pub the other night, I'm not sure they're exactly my friends. Although Zoe did message me saying that Aimee thought I was 'so real'. Is that good or bad? I am starting to feel like I don't get this generation at all. And yet I'm now one of them...

The other thing that's been preying on my mind is Kofi. I've even been wondering if I should tell Simon about it, but that's probably just due to a lack of options since my friends are not really there for me right now, and besides, I think we'll have enough to talk about. But I feel so stupid for letting what happened with Owen hang over me for so long, and for not even knowing that Kofi and I were about to break up anyway. Maybe I'm not as good as I thought at reading people. That quiz on the *Glowgetter* website that said I was ninety-six per cent emotionally intelligent was probably made up in about fifteen minutes by those twenty-five-year-olds I used to avoid in the magazine offices.

It's really hot in here. July has marked its arrival with a three-week heatwave, and it feels like this room wasn't designed for temperatures above eighteen degrees. I, however, am very much designed for warm weather. It's so much easier to look cool – and feel cool – when you are young. All I had to do was throw on a floral mini dress and sandals (Positano Core) this morning. The old me, clutching one of those handheld fans and with make-up sliding down my face, would have probably melted into a pool of perimenopause and SPF50 on the floor by now.

I look at my phone again. The *#whereswulty* memes are still going strong. Some people even think they've worked out where I live (they haven't) and are planning a 'rescue'. And I've now hit 200K followers, passing *@LuxeLooksWithLily* at last. Yuvana will be delighted. I must chase them up; I don't think my last payment came through…

I scroll to Cassia's account – I see she's pretty grey on top now. Her Stories show pics of her in Space NK fawning over Lisa Eldridge (although let's be fair, who wouldn't?). Then there's one of the *#whereswulty* meme, with a big sticker above it of the watching eyes emoji with the pupils moving from side to side. Someone clearly isn't happy with my follower count.

The door opens and some residents come in. They're all women, five of them, in their eighties I suppose, and deep in conversation. Suddenly one of them lets out a hoot of laughter, and the others all join in. Now they can't stop laughing, and the more each one laughs, the more the others do. One of them, wearing a sundress and a lilac shawl around her shoulders, looks like she's going to fall off her chair, which has the other women howling even more. I smile – it's contagious. They look over and smile back. I feel like I'm part of a heart-warming clip on YouTube – something about how brilliant it is to grow old with your best friends. Which *would* be brilliant but...

Oh wait, here he is. Through the door comes Simon, and (I was prepared for this) he doesn't recognise me. Just as he is about to go back out, I stand up and call out his name, and he turns. Okay. Here we go. Now I do feel hot.

'Simon. It's me.'

He looks blank.

'It's me, Erica. Look, I know I look different but bear with me... I'll explain.' I'm more prepared now for these interactions, after what happened with Josie and Nandy – and Gabe.

He slowly walks towards me, and I shake off the strange pang I felt for a second when I thought about Gabe. Probably just a reaction to what happened with Kai.

'Come and sit down,' I say, pulling out one of the uncomfortable teal chairs. Thankfully, there's still no sign of Alison (slightly unprofessional if you ask me), so it looks like we have a minute or two.

Simon, still silent, plonks himself in the chair, and I sit back down across the table from him. He looks at the 'Pigeons of Britain' jigsaw, and appears fixated on a pigeon dressed as Henry VIII. A confusing image indeed, but I would have thought that my appearance was more so.

I carry on regardless. 'Simon, listen. I've had a new hi-tech beauty treatment, in the form of an implant in my brain. It works by sending tiny nanobots to "restore the factory settings" of the stem cells that control the ageing process. So, I appear to be twenty years younger than when you last saw me.' I feel quite pleased with how clear that sounds, and even more pleased that he didn't interrupt.

He looks up from the jigsaw and stares at my face. I wait for the ridicule, judgement or annoyance or whatever it is Simon has for me today.

He continues to stare, then his mouth slowly changes shape. It's forming a... what? Is that a smile?

'That's... that's...' He reaches out his hand and pokes my shoulder, as if he is testing to see if I am real. '...Unbelievable. Absolutely unbelievable.' By now his face is a broad grin of joyous amazement.

'Okay...' I am completely thrown.

He slumps back in his chair, shaking his head and laughing. 'Nanobots. Bloody amazing nanobots. They're everywhere, aren't they? Just silently working behind the scenes, making everyone's life better!'

'Erm... are they?'

'Of course they are Erica!'

'Right...' I have no idea what's going on.

'This is wonderful for you. I'm so pleased. If I had a drink, Erica, I'd be toasting...' He holds up an imaginary glass in his hand. 'Nanotechnology!'

It's not until twenty minutes later, when Alison (who presumably thinks I am Simon's daughter, but doesn't ask) is showing us the walk-in shower in the flat ('it has a *very* low threshold'), that the penny drops.

Mushrooms.

I shoot a glance at Simon as he nods enthusiastic approval at a grab rail on the bathroom wall. To someone who doesn't know him, he appears completely normal. To me, he seems happier, more animated, less angry than usual. More... likeable, in fact.

Once the tour is finished, Simon and I go outside and sit on a bench. There are lawns with criss-cross paths and terracotta pots with plants in. It's roasting in the sun and a couple of butterflies are busy on some lavender in a pot next to our bench. I think Mother Pells would really like it here.

I can't think of a time when Simon and I have sat down together, just the two of us. But we are doing it now.

'That it would always be summer!' says Simon, leaning back and closing his eyes, the sun on his face.

'Have you been taking mushrooms?' I ask, watching him.

'What makes you think that?' he says, not looking at me.

'Something I saw on your Facebook.'

'Ah... social media. The great hive mind!' He sits up, points to a bee and laughs. 'It's psilocybin, Erica. Very small quantities, microdosing – I have it in chocolate. It's been a revelation. I'm just trying to get the amounts right. But I am indeed part of the "shroom boom", as it's called.'

'Well – it seems to be working for you, Simon. You look happier.'

'*You* don't,' he replies.

And there it is – I knew I couldn't have a whole conversation with Simon without him being irritating.

I change the subject, and we talk about Mother Pells, and the flat, and when we should bring her to see it. I tell him I haven't shown her my new appearance yet, and he says, 'it'll be fine'.

'That's easy for you to say.'

'What d'you mean?' he asks.

'I mean that she thinks everything you do is brilliant. Me, not so much. It was the same with Dad, although slightly less so. You must have noticed.'

'No, I hadn't actually. She always sounds really proud when I hear her talking about you. Showing everyone her fancy skin creams and telling everyone you're a top beauty writer.'

How weird. And there was me thinking the extent of her interest was procuring free lip balm. 'Wonder why she never says anything like that to me?'

'Different generation, Erica. They don't like people getting "too big for their boots". She never says anything particularly complimentary to me either...'

We sit in silence for a few minutes watching some birds on a feeder.

'Simon,' I say, eventually. 'Do you remember that holiday on the Norfolk Broads when we were kids? When those ducks got on top of the boat and you fed them your Ringos?'

'Yes! I haven't thought about that for years.'

We're both quiet again, then Simon says, 'They looked after us, didn't they? That's why it's time to return the favour.'

'I hadn't thought of it like that.'

'You should. They put down the deposit on your house. And remember when Mum bought all those horrible bracelets after you had that jewellery party nobody came to?'

I don't say anything. I can't.

Simon is clearly back on the Norfolk Broads though. 'Dad wasn't too happy – d'you remember when we left him on the bank that time we stopped for ice-cream?' he says. 'His face running up the path trying to catch us up... Mum dropped her choc ice she was laughing so much.'

He sniggers, and even though I have tears in my eyes, I laugh too – something I realise I haven't done in a while.

Later, I get the train back to Paddington, and then the tube to south-east London. I'm tired when I finally reach the flat. Just as I'm going in, I spot someone sitting on the ground to the right of the entrance, face buried in *World of Interiors* magazine. As I look over, the magazine lowers, and Keith appears over the top.

Seeing me, he stands up, puts the magazine under his arm and says in a businesslike fashion, 'Come on, girly-pop. Let's get you inside. We need to have a chat.'

He frogmarches me into the foyer.

I don't know where to start with this. I mean, it's nice to see Keith, but what is he doing here and why is he being so... officious? He doesn't seem in the slightest taken aback by my appearance, either.

As though reading my mind, he says: 'Before you say anything, Erica, firstly – Nandy told me where you live. Secondly, I know what you look like because I've seen your ludicrous Instagram – I'm *@Cheshire_In_Stilettos* by the way. And thirdly, I don't take kindly to having my FaceTimes declined.'

COME ON, I think to myself. That was just one time (or was it twice?) and I was at the check-out in M&S. But more to the point – Nandy? They don't even know each other.

'How do you know Nandy?' I press the lift button far more times than necessary.

'Erica, dear,' says Keith. 'Don't you think your friends talk about you?'

'But...'

The lift doors open and Zoe, Kai and the Peppa Pig tattoo girl get out, all staring at Keith. Zoe says 'Hey', but Kai just smiles vaguely, which is the most I can expect I suppose, possibly more, considering I projectile vomited after he kissed me. It's very awkward.

In the lift, Keith waves a hand in the direction of the departing Gen Zs as the door closes. 'I don't even want to know what *that* was all about...' I don't really want to tell him, either.

A couple of minutes later, we're in Devon's flat.

'Well, this is... awful,' he says, looking round and sucking air through his teeth, making a noise like he's tasting substandard wine.

It's airless so I open the doors onto the balcony. Keith eyes the deckchairs. 'I won't be sitting in one of those, duckie. They're not for middle-aged arses.'

'Why are you here, Keith?'

'Well, it's a bit like an intervention...'

'Don't interventions usually have more than one person intervening?'

'Nobody else wanted to come. Josie is too upset, and can't get childcare, and Nandy keeps calling you all sorts.'

I must look hurt because he adds: 'It's just how she's dealing with it.'

'Okay...'

'And as for that poor man...' He sits down on the ottoman and sighs. 'Erica, what on earth are you doing? We're all wondering. Your friends. Remember us?'

Simon's not 'poor', if that's who he's referring to. Just because he helps out a bit more than me with Mother Pells. JEEZ. And he *chose* to have kids...

'Erica?'

'Of course I remember you. It's just... this is something I need to do. And, well, none of you are really supporting me so...'

'So, what, you've just ditched us all and now you've got new friends?'

'No... I mean, well, not exactly. I'm trying. To make new friends that is. Not ditch you.'

'You're trying. Because, what, friends are like Instagram followers, you just "get" them?'

'No...' I sit on the sofa opposite him. What if Keith, Josie, Nandy... what if these are the people I was meant to belly laugh in a retirement flat with? Am I going to be on my own now?

'You know it's okay to change your mind about this?' says Keith. 'Nandy told me the treatment can be reversed. Nobody's going to judge you if that's what you want to do.'

My eyes fix on his face, and I take in a look of such exquisite concern that for a second I just want him to hug me and make it all better. I realise I'm probably now doing the 'Gen Z stare' that I've read about.

'Even if I wanted to... I can't go back, Keith. I have to make this work.'

'Why?'

'Look at me. Getting older was making me miserable.'

'We've talked about this before, Erica. Remember what I told you, the ones who stay till the end of the night are the ones with the best stories.'

I smile. I love Keith's wisdom about ageing, even if I don't really believe it. 'It's not just that. It's other stuff. Living here. The money.' I decide not to mention that Yuvana is late paying me.

'But this isn't your home. Isn't the woman who owns it going to want it back?'

'Yes – but by then I'll be rich – did you see how many Instagram followers I've got now?'

'That's not *you*. It's a brand.'

I flop back on the sofa. Why is he being so negative? I am honestly so fed up with all these naysayers. Why can't they just have some faith in me?

Keith gets up and brushes invisible bits off his trousers. 'We love you Erica, but Christ alive, you don't make it easy.' He heads for the door. 'I have to go now. Stephen and I have tickets for the Old Vic. I would have asked you to join us, but it's probably too middle-aged for you.'

'I have plans, thanks.' I don't. Yet.

'With the children in the lift?' he says, shaking his head.

And then he's gone.

Chapter Twenty-Nine

The day we dissected frogs

As soon as Keith leaves, I call Channing. I know what the problem is now. I just haven't found the right group of people yet. It's like fresher's week – you have to hang out with different groups before you find the one for you. At Birmingham Uni, I had a brief goth phase, trying to fit in with a girl in my halls of residence. I bought some stripy tights and a *Fields of the Nephilim* album, but it just didn't feel like me. For one thing, everyone drank Newcastle Brown Ale, which tastes like stew. I also briefly tried to fit in with a rugby crowd – someone from my school who had come to Birmingham like me had a cousin on the Welsh team, so I joined her in the pub to watch some matches. All the girls were wearing rugby shirts and velvet Alice bands, and were called things like Hattie and Cornelia. When I said I wasn't going to Henley Regatta they gave my seat to someone called Lettice and I had to go and stand at the bar.

Channing is very excited to hear from me, and even more excited that I want to go out with him. 'I thought you'd never ask, gurl,' he says, laughing heartily when I ask him if he's doing anything tonight. It's Friday! He's going to a pansexual night called 'Ya Basic' at a place in Dalston which apparently plays 'Nineties Nasties'. There's a lot here that I don't fully understand but it sounds more fun than drinking Snakebite (I googled it in the end) and talking about radical self-acceptance, so I'm in. Although I'm not sure what 'Core' to wear, and I'm guessing that Urban Outfitters is not considered edgy by Michaela Mammary, who is DJing this evening.

—

An hour and a half later, we're in a bar around the corner from the club and I feel like I need a soundtrack again. This is nothing like the scene in *Pretty Woman* though – it's more along the lines of one of those montages in films like *The Hangover*, when everyone is doing shots in slow motion to Bruno Mars or similar. And despite Channing's friend Baron eyeing my skirt and asking me who I 'came as', I'm having an excellent time. Let's put it this way, Keith, it's not the Old Vic.

As well as Baron – who is very small and wearing a peacock blue silk shirt tied in a knot in the middle of his hairy chest – there's Angel, who is sporting a codpiece and a pair of red fishnet tights that encompass their whole body, and Riley, who's in knee-length white socks and something similar to a school uniform. There's also Milo, and the more prosaically named Melanie (who looks a bit like Miley Cyrus), and Carter (or maybe Carton but I'm erring on the side of normality) – all dressed like they're from an upbeat version of a dystopian future. Or, less generously, as though they were given thirty seconds to grab something to wear at a church jumble sale, then had to put make-up on without a mirror. It's weird and wonderful and feels like everyone and anyone is welcome. I'm pretty sure I like it.

Nobody's drinking the same thing: caipirinhas are flying about, pints of Guinness, prosecco, martinis, and yes, I'm getting a little plastered. Channing is keeping an eye on me though – the others don't know my 'secret' and he's being very discreet, apart for announcing to the table after a round of flaming sambucas that 'Erica and I know something you don't' and dissolving into hysterical giggles. But everyone's too drunk to ask questions or care that much, which is fine by me.

Later, we stagger to the club. On the way, I look at my phone and notice that *#whereswulty* is trending. Channing and I are walking arm in arm, so I hold it up and show him.

'Don't get me started on Yuvana, gurl,' he slurs.

'What d'you mean?'

'Didn't you know? They laid me off.'

I'm too drunk to process this.

We go into the club, which consists of two or three adjoining rooms in a basement and is full of people who look like Channing's friends, only more so. It's loud and busy and people are dancing and snogging and drinking.

Finally – some fun. I throw myself into it, dancing for the first time in twenty years, if you don't count Josie's wedding, which I don't. Someone shouts 'HAVIN' IT' at me in a fake Manchester accent, which I take to mean that I look like a raver. Who cares though? I'm dancing with drag queens, men in harnesses like that guy Chaz at the *Luscious* shoot, girls in lingerie… to anything from club classics to Right Said Fred or Whigfield. So that's what they meant by 'Nineties Nasties'. It's brilliant.

An hour later and it's all feeling a lot less brilliant. The sambuca is wearing off, so I take a break and lean against the bar with Channing, Melanie and Carter/Carton. I can't really hear what they're saying, and everyone just seems to be shouting about how they're obsessed with him/her/them/her top/that song/this drink. I find myself staring out across the room, feeling a weird sense of déjà vu. It's like that cheap, oaky chardonnay – when you drink it, you can already taste the impending hangover. And right now, that's exactly how I feel – as though I've been here before, as though I already know how this night will end, and how I'll feel the next day. I might be able to cope better physically, but it's not really about that. There are no surprises for me here anymore. Why did I think I hadn't done enough of all this – when perhaps I've done exactly the right amount? Maybe I just want to drink good wine, eat Ottolenghi food, belly laugh at jokes – and be home in bed watching *The Good Place* by eleven p.m. Maybe, despite how I look, I'm too old for this.

I get a water from the barman and gulp it down. I know this sounds middle-aged, and I'm glad you can't smoke indoors anymore – but I think it's worth considering what it actually hid, in terms of ambience. And by ambience, I mean aroma. And by aroma, I mean stench. This place smells like a cross between the biology labs at school on the day we dissected frogs, and an unpasteurised chèvre log. As I begin to sober up, I also notice that everyone is glued to their phones, taking selfies and standing totally still, filming the crowd. It doesn't feel quite as 'in the moment' as the clubbing I remember. And speaking of moments, this is the one for me to find the exit. They're playing the 'Macarena', which isn't nasty, it's just plain crap.

I don't say goodbye to anyone – I can't even find them. It's a balmy night so I decide to walk home, which takes me about an hour and a half, but I need to clear my head. Crossing Tower Bridge, I stop and lean on the railings. London is stretched out along the river – I can see the Walkie-Talkie, the Shard, the Gherkin (why do I always muddle them up?), much closer than I can from Devon's. It's not the city I remember from when I lived here before, but then I'm not the person I was then either. I'm wondering if I've become someone who prefers medium-sizing it to larging it. Someone who is very happy to meet up at a deli in Devizes. And at the same time, someone who also thinks that this is absolutely fine.

By the time I get back to Devon's, I've pretty much sobered up, thanks to a bag of chips and a Lucozade en route. I let myself in and head out to the balcony to drink a cup of tea. It's noisy up here at this time, and Keith was right, the deckchairs are bloody uncomfortable, middle-aged arse or not. Channing messages 'Where r u gurl??'. I'm sure he'll be fine without me, so I don't reply. Then I remember what he told me about Yuvana – I wonder who will replace him. I'll need to ask Merlyn. And while I'm at it, I can ask her what is going on with my payments...

It starts to spot with rain and I can hear thunder in the distance, so I head inside and shut the balcony doors. I'm just putting my cup in the sink when there's a faint knocking sound. I go through to the hall and there it is again, and then a whisper. 'Erica! Are you up?'

It's Zoe. What the hell? It must be three in the morning.

I open the door. Zoe is standing in a pink unicorn onesie, holding one of the Saturday newspapers, a tabloid.

'Jamal just went to the garage. He's got insomnia,' she says.

For a second I wonder how Jamal's insomnia could possibly be a good reason to knock on my door at this time.

'He saw this.' She holds the newspaper up, and I read the front-page headline.

> WE FOUND HER!
> BEAUTY JOURNALIST ERICA PELLS,
> 48, UNMASKED AS 'WULT WOMAN'
> LIVING A SECRET 'YOUNG' LIFE IN
> SOUTH LONDON

Underneath, next to a picture of 'new me' (the meme of me dressed as 'Where's Wally?') and a picture of 'old me' (an unflattering and particularly jowly screengrab of the lash lift reel I did last year) it says:

> Shocking Revelation: Pells' Deception of
> Gen Z Friends Revealed Amid Hi-Tech
> Treatment Controversy.

Oddly, my first thought is that there were so many opportunities for a pun here, and yet none were taken.

'This is you, isn't it?' says Zoe. 'Is this why you use those weird expressions and watch wildlife programmes? And have old people round to visit – the Asian woman and that guy hanging around outside yesterday in the ugly shirt?'

I'm offended on Keith's behalf by this description of him. I thought his shirt was unusual, yes, but rather stylish. Also – 'old people'? Is that how she sees us? Or sees *them*, I suppose... And then it starts to sink in. This is a lot worse than Cassia's 150K followers knowing: this is a public 'outing', presumably at the hands of Cassia. Which is not only completely messed up – I mean, how could anyone be that jealous? (Or is it envious? I can never remember.) But more importantly, it means the news could reach Mother Pells before I have a chance to tell her myself. Holy crap. Why did I leave it so long to go and see her? She doesn't read this particular newspaper but someone in the town will. I can't let her find out like this – it's not fair on her.

Zoe is waiting for a response, but I've got more pressing things on my mind. I need to get some sleep – and then I need to get to Wiltshire.

Chapter Thirty

Time changes everything

It's six a.m. and a thunderstorm has woken me, with rain hammering on the balcony like a scene from an Eighties soft rock video. If I had a fire escape, there'd be a saxophonist on it, possibly wearing a bandana. The storm reminds me of when Simon and I were kids – long hot summers, sleeping under just sheets, and Mother Pells letting us go outside when the weather 'broke' to cool off. We would run about the garden in our pants, laughing in the rain. Then she would bring out beach towels – a Showaddywaddy one and a green tie-dye one – calling, 'Come in now, you rain-dancing rascals!'), and she'd wrap us up, one in each of her arms. It felt safe, like Gabe's hand did on the small of my back.

But in this storm, I am alone. I lie, trying to doze off again, although the rain is too loud and my brain is whirring round and around. I need to get up soon anyway. The plan is to catch an early train to Swindon and taxi from there. It's expensive, and as Yuvana still hasn't paid me I'll have to put it on a credit card, but anything to get to Mother Pells before she bumps into someone who's read the news.

Two hours later, I'm at Paddington. I get a flat white and a croissant, dipping the latter in the former, glad of the caffeine and carbs after last night's sambuca, but even more glad I stopped drinking when I did. Channing has already sent me a picture of him and Melanie joining in a 'Ruff Mudster Challenge' at London Fields – clearly uninvited and still wearing last night's clothes – which only serves to confirm that I made the right decision.

As I am passing Upper Crust, a man in the queue wearing a plastic rain poncho says, 'Hey, aren't you that old woman with the robot face?' While this is an imaginative interpretation of the news story, I'm really not in the mood for uninvited questions from strangers, so I just keep on walking across the concourse towards platform four.

The train to Swindon is less than an hour – on a good day. Today is not a good day. According to an announcement, the heavy rain overnight has caused a landslide onto the tracks, and at Didcot Parkway we all have to get off and transfer to a shuttle bus. I am squashed in next to a middle-aged woman wearing much more practical clothes than me, who is reading the Highway Code.

I'm getting really worried that I won't make it to Mother Pells in time. I am also angry with Cassia (I mean, who else would have sold the story?) and wish I had Nandy to talk to about it, or even just send a sticker to, but I don't dare – she was so annoyed with me last time I saw her, and after what happened with Kai, I can now see why. There's also the money thing, and what all this is going to mean for the work with Yuvana. I'll need to call Merlyn. I let out a little sigh and the woman next to me looks round sympathetically, then offers me a Tracker bar from her bag. 'They were the UK's first cereal bar,' she tells me. I say, 'Righty-ho,' which I'm worried is becoming my new catchphrase.

The bus smells of Pakora that time he rolled in a dead seal on the beach in Suffolk. It's taking ages via an 'alternative route' because there's flooding at Shrivenham, and the winding roads mean I keep getting either thrown into the aisle, or against the UK's first cereal bar woman. I get my phone out, and ignoring all the missed calls from god knows who about the newspaper article, I message Simon to tell him I'm going to see Mother Pells, waiting for the ticks to turn blue. They don't. What can he be doing? Misting his Lion's Mane (not a euphemism)?

At about ten a.m., we arrive at Swindon bus station, which is not, in case anyone was wondering, an Area of Outstanding Natural Beauty. After about twenty minutes – most of which is spent queuing for the toilet behind a woman having a loud video call about what I think/hope is cooking related as she keeps shouting things like 'plunge them into icy water!' and 'skim off the fatty liquid!' – I find a taxi and I'm on my way.

It's funny how long it takes your brain to process things when you don't want to. At first, I think the lights flashing outside Mother Pells' house are to do with Dinah. Some sort of outdoor decorations? She's always one for a display at Christmas so maybe she's put something together for summer? Or maybe it's a party. Maybe it's…

It's an ambulance.

The taxi driver is muttering something about how it's the third ambulance he's seen this morning and how that's 'not a good omen'. They're not bloody magpies, I think, but say nothing and instead focus on paying the £60 fare without vomiting with worry, both at the fact that my card is likely to be declined, and at what I am about to face. Thankfully, the payment goes through. I get out of the taxi and walk towards the ambulance and the people gathered beside it.

Now I am closer I can see that one of them is Josie, talking to two paramedics. She is holding an umbrella and has her arm around a child, who is wrapped in a blanket. It takes me a moment to realise it's Héloïse as her hair is short. They all turn around as I approach.

'Erica? I didn't expect...' Josie's face is serious.

'What's happened?'

'Your mum's in the ambulance.' She looks guarded, but it's Josie, so she can never not be kind. 'The stream at the back of her house burst its banks and she slipped in. Héloïse and I found her. We were dropping off some scones Héloïse made. Thank goodness...'

She pulls Héloïse closer to her. 'It was Héloïse that helped her.'

'Go and see your mum, love,' says one of the paramedics in a thick west country accent, who must be wondering how she can possibly be my mum. 'We're just about to take her to the Great Western.'

I climb in the back of the ambulance. It's more like a room than I thought it would be, with drawers and compartments full of equipment on the walls. Mother Pells is lying on a trolley wrapped in a red blanket, with an oxygen mask strapped to her face and a dressing on her head. Another paramedic is sitting with her, writing notes on a clipboard.

'Mum, it's me. Are you okay?' I bend down and take her hand.

I can see her eyes just above the mask staring at me and darting from side to side. She looks so frail, like a little bird. I want to wrap my arms around her, like she did to me and Simon in the storm. But her hand pulls away from mine, and her head shakes. She's making a noise but it's muffled. Could it be crying?

'Mum, it's Erica.' My voice comes out croaky. I go to take her hand again but she won't let me.

'She's getting a bit upset, love,' says the paramedic. 'I don't think she recognises you. Maybe better to just...' He looks towards the door of the ambulance.

'But... I...'

She's shaking her head and moaning. The paramedic strokes her arm, then looks at me impatiently, so I turn and climb back out of the ambulance.

There is suddenly something large and sharp in my throat, and it feels like I can't swallow, or speak, or even breathe.

—

Ten minutes later, I'm in Josie's car. We're dropping Héloïse off at home with Laure, then Josie is taking me to the hospital. She's put me in the back to keep an eye on Héloïse, who is next to me, shivering. Under the blanket wrapped around her, she's only wearing a t-shirt and I can just make out the design, which seems to be either a raccoon dressed as a person or a person dressed as a raccoon. I pull her close to me so she can get some of the warmth of my body.

'Thank you for helping my mum,' I say. 'You're very brave.'

Héloïse nods and leans in, fitting her head into the space between my armpit and my right tit, which seems to have been perfectly designed for this. I am comforting her. I didn't know I could comfort people.

'You got your hair cut,' I say.

'I'm a "superhairo". I gave it to the people to make a wig for the children.'

'She donated it to a kids' cancer charity,' says Josie from the front seat. 'Less likely to get nits too, which is a bonus.'

We pull up outside Josie's house and Josie takes Héloïse inside. While she's gone, I get in the front and phone Simon. He's not answering – and he hasn't seen my message. I can't call Alannah or either of the boys as they're all still in Australia and it's the middle of the night. They wouldn't be able to do anything from there anyway. By now, there are also sixty-three missed calls, two voice notes (who even does these?), eight voicemails and a new message from Merlyn:

> Erica – we must reconvene post-haste.
> Baci, M

It takes just over half an hour to get to the hospital in Swindon. Josie doesn't say much on the way, apart from telling me she's been watering the tubs on my patio and how Keith said our chat didn't go that well yesterday. Yesterday? Was that really only yesterday? Why does it seem as though everything has speeded up? I want to say to her that… I don't know. That I miss her? But I'm not sure if that's what she would want to hear. I feel like I have pushed people too far away from me, Nandy included. The only messages I get now are from a pansexual twenty-four-year-old who hasn't been to bed yet. I haven't even been able to tell anyone what happened with Kofi, and what he told me about Owen, which is burning a hole in my brain, if that's a thing.

At the hospital, Josie drops me off. I'm not convinced it's a good idea to go in and see Mother Pells, after what happened in the ambulance. But if Simon isn't here, I have to. She can't be on her own. She can't think nobody is here for her. There's a Costa inside the hospital entrance so first I get a flat white and sit down so I can call Simon again. There's a pregnant woman beside me wearing slippers and drinking hot chocolate. On the seat next to her, I can see the newspaper with the story about me on the cover, but she doesn't pick it up – she seems to be too busy stroking her belly and grimacing. Near the counter stands an elderly man on his phone. I can hear him say, 'No change at all, Linda, but maybe that's a good thing,' then he wipes his eyes on the sleeve of his cardigan.

Simon still isn't answering but then I see 'Semen is typing'. I changed his contact name last year and I'm not going to pretend it doesn't still make me laugh. Although not today.

> Rica yes

Simon? Are you OK? Mum is in hospital. I've just arrived. Where are you?

> God

> Can you get to Swindon? I think my appearance is upsetting her and one of us needs to be here.

> It's not good Eric 8

Is he drunk? It's not even midday.

> What's going on Simon?

> I ddntt get the dose right rite write... Which one is it?

The mushrooms. Of course. The one time I actually bloody need him, he's... useless.

> It's fine. I'll deal with it. I'll be in touch and let you know how she is.

Twenty minutes later, I walk into the ward. There's a woman at the nurses' station picking the mini Milky Ways out of a box of Celebrations. She gives me a weird look, perhaps wondering how I can be the daughter of someone who is eighty, and tells me Mother Pells is 'stable', but has to get a scan of her brain because of a head injury. She also tells me she has her own room, which is good. I think. Or maybe it's not. Then she says something about my visit being welcome as she 'couldn't get hold of the next of kin', which will of course be Simon, and something about how she'll be 'glad to have family here'.

'Welcome'? But maybe I – at least in my current form – am not. I walk down the long corridor towards her room and take a breath outside. Can I go in? Should I go in? What if she doesn't recognise me again? What if she gets upset? If I don't though, she will think neither me nor Simon have come. Oh crap. What have I done? I feel this unfamiliar, new protectiveness of her, and I am torn between wanting to be there for her, and the fear of making things worse. So I reverse up the corridor, pausing only at the nurses' station to write down Auntie Viv's number on a piece of paper, and hand it to the Milky Way woman. And then I leave.

—

I need to be nearby, even if I can't go and see her, so I go back to my 'dark little cottage' and let myself in. There are some takeaway menus and other letters that have been put neatly on the hall table by Josie, the only person who has keys. It feels safe, and quiet, and not that dark at all. Maybe a house *can* be a home without a cat, Auntie Viv.

Thanks to Zoe, tea has become my go-to drink in times of crisis, instead of wine. There's a fresh pint of milk in the fridge, which Josie must have put there, just in case. She's so bloody thoughtful. The fridge looks clean too, which it certainly wasn't when I left – I'm pretty sure there was some Gruyère of questionable age in the salad drawer. I spot she's also put the fridge magnet Héloïse got me on the door. It says, *Time changes everything except something within us which is always surprised by change.* I stare at it, trying to work out what it means. I think I get it now.

The rain has stopped now so, opening the French doors, I move a kitchen chair into the sunny spot, sipping my tea and trying to calm down. But I can't stop thinking about Mother Pells pushing me away. About us not being there for her. About how hard I've been on her over the years. And how I only now realise, late in the day as usual, that we all love, and grieve, in different ways. I can't bear it. As soon as the tears stop, they come again, and again, and I have to abandon my tea. My chest keeps rising and falling in panting noises, like a dog when it's dreaming. It's funny, isn't it – I used to worry about becoming someone Father Pells wouldn't recognise. Maybe I should have focused on the person that's still here.

Part Four

Chapter Thirty-One

Erica Pells ate my hamster

There's a new dead American Erica Pells – in Ava, Missouri this time. She loved pickleball and spoon carving, and it takes me a minute or so to realise that she wasn't in a retirement home, but a hospice and is – was – a couple of years younger than me. It's really bloody sad actually. She had three kids, all quite young by the looks of it from the photo. 'We are heartbroken but take comfort that she is at peace now.' I imagine that getting old would have been the preferred choice for this Erica Pells. I'm definitely going to stop reading these obituaries.

The reason I am googling my name is not to find articles *by* me, because I haven't written any recently, apart from a luxury lip balm *Tried and Tested* for *Glowgetter*, but that was just to get some samples for Mother Pells. No, I was googling so I could find articles *about* me. And there are quite a lot of them. They are a mix, from highbrow: *The Ethics Of Eternal Youth: A Deep Dive Into The WULT® Woman Controversy*; to medium brow: *Age Fright: Who Exactly Are Yuvana Labs, The Nanotech Company Behind The WULT® Woman Scandal?* (nice pun); to low brow: *WULT® Woman Puts On A Leggy Display At Swindon Station – Exclusive Pics Inside!* Oh – and no brow at all: *Erica Pells Ate My Hamster*.

But I don't want to be in the news, or famous, I never did. I've seen – okay, read – what they write about the likes of Jennifer Aniston (or should I say 'poor, sad Jen'). Probably more than I should have done, to be fair. The fame I thought I craved was simply to have more followers than Cassia, which now feels faintly absurd. Cassia, incidentally, has posted a reel about me – *WULT® Woman: the truth about Erica Pells*. It's had about three thousand views, but I haven't watched it yet, I can't bring myself to. I did however watch her reel from Friday, which was her weekly vintage cocktail – an 'Ivanhoe' prepared in the 'parlour' (*#mindfuldrinking*). She's really grey now by the looks of it. It actually quite suits her, especially with her new chunky-framed glasses.

I have also noticed that the WULT® Woman Instagram has been suspended. I wasn't planning to post anything on it, considering all the news stories, and the fact they haven't paid me – but still, it's yet another worrying development. I called Merlyn last night and left her a voicemail explaining what's happened with Mother Pells. She's clearly seen the news otherwise she wouldn't have messaged me about 'reconvening' yesterday. I really would like to talk to her – now Channing has gone I don't have another contact at Yuvana, apart from the 'enquiries@' email for making appointments and more recently, chasing payments.

I am still in Wiltshire. I haven't left the house, and have just been Delierooing food on my ailing credit card, and drinking tea. Oh, and calling the hospital. And crying. JEEZ, there's been a lot of that. It's a lonely business too: Josie doesn't come round with hugs and Ottolenghi offerings in Tupperware, Keith doesn't FaceTime me, Nandy doesn't appear with weed and spices. And I can't call them, or message them because, well, I suppose I'm too scared of what they'll say to me. I'm not Public Enemy Number One, but I'm definitely either three or four. All I've had is a message from Channing saying Michaela Mammary is DJing at 'Big Girl's Blouse' in New Cross on Thursday, and do I want to come? At least I'm popular with someone. But no, Channing, I do not.

I managed to speak to Mother Pells this morning when I called the hospital. She sounded shaky and confused, and my heart ached that nobody was there with her. She didn't say much and doesn't seem to remember what happened in the ambulance, thankfully. The nurse told me she is 'still very poorly' but also said that 'her sister-in-law' (Auntie Viv) has been in, which is a relief, and at least someone. I'm hoping Simon will be able to visit soon too as judging by his messages, he is returning to earth. Which just leaves me.

Me. Erica. WULT® Woman. Whoever I am. I'm not sure. I don't feel like the person I was when I was last here. I was hopeful then – hopeful that this would be what I wanted, what I needed. But now it feels like all it's done is push everyone away. Or maybe I've done that myself. I didn't mean to. I just thought if I could look young again, that everything would change for the better. That I wouldn't be so miserable about getting old, that I wouldn't be wondering 'what if', because I could do it all again, and do it properly. Have a star that ascends this time, like Cassia's did.

But now I'm wondering if I have spent my whole life thinking that it will be the next thing that will definitely make me happy. If I could just get my hands on that light-reflecting concealer, or that keratin blow dry, or that new plasma thing that targets multiple concerns simultaneously... Maybe WULT® isn't any different from all the things that came before, all the lotions and potions and treatments packaged up as hopes and dreams. And maybe what would really make me happy isn't actually dermatologist approved and tested on over thirty-four women, but right in front of me.

In the afternoon, I do some laundry and cleaning, which I didn't seem to manage before I left six months ago. I suppose I was in a blur of adrenalin and moderately priced Italian wine. I also clear some weeds from in between the paving slabs on the patio (with a fork, let's not get carried away), and scrub them (with an exfoliating body brush, *#gifted*). I don't know why. I feel like I need distractions. Like I'm waiting for something. For news from the hospital. For Josie to come round (she won't). For all these things – and yet none of them. Because what I am really waiting for is my brain to tell me what my heart already knows.

–

The next morning, Simon calls me early, thanking me for 'holding the fort' and apologising for what happened with his micro – or not so micro as it turned out – dosing. As both thrilling and unusual it is for Simon to be apologising to me, I can't pretend to him that I did anything. I was on my way to see Mother Pells anyway, and when I did try to help, it went horribly wrong. So it's really Auntie Viv who is holding the fort, and if she has a low opinion of me (which I'm pretty sure she does), it will be even lower after this. Simon will probably be okay – he'll make up some highly plausible excuse for his absence that doesn't involve hallucinogens and everyone will believe him because he's never been crap before, like I have. Many, many times.

'At least you were there,' says Simon. 'More than I was.'
'I might as well have not been.'

'Erry, don't beat yourself up.' He hasn't called me Erry in a long time. 'She's going to be in hospital for a little while, from what Auntie Viv said. I'm going in this morning. You can visit her when she's a bit more lucid, and explain it all then. I'll tell the nurses to keep the newspapers away from her in the meantime.'

Explain it all... Where to even start? It's quite a different story now. I'm not sure I know how to tell it. Not even sure if I want to. And maybe I don't have to, either...

―

By ten a.m., I've made my decision, and I'm on the train back to London, after two nights of sleeping in my old bed – during which my insomnia was caused by my brain whirring, and not the baby next door, who seems to have grown out of the yelling phase. I am wearing a huge pair of sunglasses that I found in amongst the boxes of products in the spare room, and a bucket hat that makes me look like I'm on my way to a rave in a Gloucestershire field in 1989, but was the only one I could find. What 'Core' is this? I don't care.

At Paddington, I take the Circle line. I'm not going to Devon's. Not for now. On the escalator, despite my excellent disguise, I notice a few people looking at me, and someone takes a photo with their phone. A man wearing a sleeveless t-shirt says something to me which includes the words 'slutty' and what sounds like 'show us your fringe' although I am guessing it is not my fringe he wishes to see. I'm not sure if his request is related to my newfound fame/infamy, or just because that's what some men do.

I was deluded enough to think, before WULT®, that the reason strange men had stopped catcalling and/or generally saying gross things to me was because of the #*metoo* movement. Turns out it was my age that silenced them, and the whole practice of objectifying women in public is still very much alive and well. Suffice to say the novelty of becoming visible again wore off within about a week of my transformation. 'Oh, do fuck off,' I say to the man. The woman on the escalator next to me, who looks like she's about fifty, whispers, 'Well done you', and I smile proudly. Although I don't look like a 'Wise Woman', as Cassia calls it, I momentarily let myself enjoy the fearlessness that middle age gives us.

It's just three stops to High Street Kensington, and soon, I'm back on the square. The storms of the last few days have passed, and the cherry blossom has given way to deep green leaves that rustle in the breeze. Walking towards the Yuvana building, I think for a second that I must have got lost – entirely possible with my sense of direction. The white pillars are familiar, but I can't see the glass entrance, just a closed black outer door. What the hell? Maybe they aren't open yet? But it's nearly midday...

Climbing the steps, a horrible tight feeling is now growing in my chest. I step back down, looking around to double-check that I'm at the correct door. Number 11... that's definitely right. I go up again, this time trying the big brass door handle, gently, then yanking it hard. Harder. JEEZ. It won't open.

I knock.

'Portia!' I yell.

Silence.

'Dr Marcus!'

Silence.

'It's Erica, Erica Pells! I've changed my mind. I want the treatment reversed!'

But nobody is coming. Because nobody is there.

Chapter Thirty-Two

A run-in with a Mint Magnum

For someone who (kind of) shares a name with a wizard, Merlyn is being surprisingly difficult to summon. It's as if she lives in a parallel universe that looks like a cross between *Ab Fab* and *The Man From U.N.C.L.E.*, and whose residents sip Crémant all day in limousines and use the word 'extraordinary' a lot. I would quite like to live in this parallel universe. But I don't. And my universe, by contrast, is a bit of a shit show.

After having a monumental meltdown on the steps of Yuvana Labs in Kensington, and trying unsuccessfully to summon said wizard, I realised that I don't have many people left to call in my hour of need. I mean, the usual suspects, Nandy and Josie, are out, obvs. As is Keith. I toyed with Channing for about ten seconds but knew he would just tell me I was 'serving him realness, queen' and this isn't an episode of *Queer Eye* (although it's worth noting that Karamo Brown would be a huge help in the current crisis). There's also Alannah, but she's still in Australia. And Simon, I suppose, who has been considerably less annoying of late, but I can't work out if that's because of the mushrooms or because he's genuinely less annoying.

I began walking back to the tube station, snivelling gently, but almost immediately slip on a Mint Magnum wrapper that was cleverly camouflaged by some leaves. I fell, as Father Pells used to say, 'A over T', and slammed down onto both my knees, and my hands, which I stuck out to save myself. I remember when Simon and I were kids and found out that 'A over T' meant 'Arse over Tit'. We were suitably shocked by this revelation, but it was back when we thought 'The F Word' was 'Fart', so no wonder.

Help was at hand, however. A large grey car pulled over as I sprawled in a hands and knees position, and a very pretty woman in her seventies got out to help, sitting me in her front seat and picking gravel off my knees and palms using a packet of Wet Ones that she got out of the glove compartment. The woman then insisted on giving me a lift to the tube station. I felt really silly next to her, young and tearful and wounded, and she seemed so mature and confident and stylish. I said nothing though, other than 'thank you'.

And now here I am, half an hour later, in the foyer of the *Luscious* offices in Soho. Liz, the receptionist, recognises me this time, one of the few perks of being in practically every UK newspaper. And thankfully, Merlyn is in the building, which I decide is unusual, based on absolutely no evidence at all.

Liz gives me directions to Merlyn's office, talking very slowly. I'm sure it's because she wants an excuse to stare at me for as long as she can – my face, and probably also my bucket hat, which admittedly looks odd teamed with a Boden cardigan from my former, middle-aged wardrobe but could possibly pass for 'Normcore'. I resist the temptation to shout 'it's not all it's cracked up to be' at her and head up in the lift to the third floor. If I wasn't freaking out about Yuvana Labs, and if I didn't have very sore hands and knees, I would feel more excited at the prospect of seeing Merlyn's office.

On the third floor, I walk through the open plan area, following Liz's instructions. The last time I was here, for the Halloween party last year, the desks were all pushed to the sides and the place was littered with rattan pumpkins and lit by those horrible Alfred Hitchcock bird ceiling lights, which I still have unsettling dreams about. Today, it is unrecognisable, with rows of twenty-five-year-olds typing away at their computers. These are the ones I used to fear, and envy. I blend in now, but I'm not sure I want to... possibly a massive generalisation but I bet they all consider the 'Macarena' a good song, collect Furbies and don't care about their parents.

Merlyn's office door is open, so I walk in to find her sitting at a large desk, cluttered with piles of magazines and product samples. There's a rolodex and an 'in tray' – I didn't think either of these things still existed, but I suppose I've worked on either my sofa or my living room floor for so long I wouldn't know much about desk accessories. Behind her, half obscuring the view of the Windmill Theatre – and making me jump until I realise it's not an actual person – is a life-size cardboard cut-out of Timothy Dalton, signed with the words: 'Reporting for duty – Tim' and a kiss.

Merlyn is wearing a voluminous green kaftan with gold embroidery and a matching silk scarf tied round her hair. She's engrossed in a conversation on her mobile but looks up at me, then points to the chair opposite her. I sit down and listen in but the only word I can make out is 'flotilla'. Waiting for her to finish, I examine my injuries and feel like Timothy Dalton is watching, and possibly judging, me.

'Erica, my dear.' Merlyn puts her phone down on the desk and pulls in her chair as though she's now giving me her full attention. 'What a to-do!'

That's one way of putting it.

'Honestly, Merlyn, I don't even know where to start with this. First of all, I'm guessing it was Cassia who sold the story? But that's the least of my worries right now.' I get a tissue out of my bag and press it on some fresh bleeding on my knee.

'Mamma mia, what happened to you?' I'm not sure if she's changing the subject or if she has only just noticed that I look like I crawled here from Wiltshire. And even though I know she's speaking Italian, I now have the ABBA song firmly planted in my head.

'I had a run-in with a Mint Magnum – I won't bore you with the details. But more importantly, what the hell is going on with Yuvana Labs? They haven't paid me and I went to their office or lab or whatever you call it this morning...'

Merlyn looks surprised. 'Why did you go there? Because of the payments?'

'No... well partly, but more because I want to reverse the treatment.'

I expect Merlyn to look shocked and/or disappointed and start trying to talk me out of it, but she doesn't. Instead, she pulls this weird face which looks almost like a smile, and doesn't say anything.

I carry on, trying to get more of a reaction. 'I want to do it as soon as possible, so I don't have to ever show my mum this again.' I wave my hand up to indicate my face, but as I'm holding the bloodstained tissue it appears slightly threatening. 'And of course in the hope of getting my friends back.'

There's that weird smile again.

'Anyway, Merlyn – I didn't get very far.'

'Why, my dear?'

'Because it's closed. Gone. Nobody's there.'

Now she doesn't look quite as smiley, and picks up her phone, tapping away.

While she's doing this, I try to find a patch of tissue not soaked by blood. Merlyn leans over the desk and hands me a floral silk handkerchief she has pulled from nowhere, like a magician. Or indeed, a wizard.

—

There was one other person I could have called from the square in Kensington. He has been sitting in my heart – actually, not my heart, that's too soppy. He's been sitting in my mind – or standing, it's up to him. Or lying down even. Really, as long as he's comfortable. I've been trying to work it out in my head, but I just don't know how. That goes for most things at the moment, but this one is a real doozy, as I believe the Americans say.

Here goes… when Gabe was underwhelmed by my transformation, I think my pride was hurt. The way he acted made me feel like I'd made a bad decision. Which, in retrospect, I probably had, but that's not the point here. When he told me he liked the 'wear and tear', I was frustrated – or at least, that's how I felt in the moment. But seriously – what a thing to say. What a bloody *amazing* thing to say. It stirred up something inside me, but I brushed it off as annoyance because the idea that someone could like the ageing version of me, warts – or nematode neck – and all, was baffling. It made me feel vulnerable, I suppose. Like I'd have to start accepting myself, and believe that I was worth being appreciated, or even loved. And I'm not sure that's something I could – can – do.

Gabe thinks I'm funny. He must have done to put me in touch with that Maxine woman, the comedy producer or whatever she is. I can't do anything about that now I suppose, if I'm not in touch with Gabe. I do miss writing though. Not the actual beauty journalism – that's a real skill, and one I don't think I've ever had, which is why I never rose through the ranks. No, I mean the funny bits, which were few and far between, and mainly unappreciated by my editors, but I loved coming up with them.

I digress. Gabe wanted to spend time with me. But I struggle to believe that someone could genuinely want to be around me because they enjoy my company. It's as though WULT® is armour, protecting me from having to rely on other things about myself... like my personality. Because I might be funny now and again, but I can also be a bit crap. Just ask my family. Or my friends. Or my work colleagues. So, I appear to have thrown the baby out with the bathwater – the baby being Gabe, and the bathwater being well, everything else I suppose. And Zoe, you can have that weird expression for free.

Chapter Thirty-Three

The Hidden Locket

After I told Merlyn that I couldn't get into Yuvana, she made a very brief phone call, the only part of which I managed to catch was what sounded like 'that man'. Then she whisked me out of the *Luscious* offices in a flurry of green silk, waving theatrically to Liz as we passed the reception desk.

Now, in the car, she hands me, not a glass of Crémant, but a first aid kit from one of the side pockets in the doors, so at least I can patch up my knees. We head west towards Mayfair, passing Hyde Park. After feeling faintly disappointed we aren't going to Brasserie Zédel as I haven't had any decent cheese for ages, I wonder for a moment if we are going to Merlyn's house, the whereabouts of which I am not exactly sure, but once we reach Hammersmith I know we have definitely gone too far.

'Merlyn,' I say, just as the car is inexplicably going round a roundabout what appears to be twice, or possibly three times, so I am leaning at a ridiculous angle. 'Where are we going?'

'To Portia Crump's, my dear,' she says, smiling beatifically.

Portia Crump. That's Peach Jumpsuit's name, it turns out. I knew she was called Portia but always imagined her surname would be something like Vanderbilt-Silk. I wonder what her house is like. I don't wonder for long though, as soon we are in Richmond and I can tell this is our destination as the driver is going slowly down the side streets as though looking at house numbers.

'She'll be able to sort this out, won't she?' I say to Merlyn.

She turns to me for the first time and reaches for my hand, but then sees it's covered in plasters and changes her mind. 'Why of course, Erica.'

We pull up outside a red-brick terraced house with a very pointy gable and bay windows. As usual, the driver comes round to open the door. Merlyn puts on a pair of huge sunglasses and gets out, looking totally out of place on this suburban street.

Peach Jumpsuit's house has a path covered in mosaic tiles and a small front garden with raised flower beds, a bench and terracotta pots full of begonias. I know they are begonias because Josie gave me some for my patio tubs. This garden looks like something out of a magazine though, while mine looks like the back entrance to a village pub.

Merlyn doesn't ring the bell but instead uses the giant silver ring on her index finger to tap very loudly on the stained-glass section of the green front door. I stand behind her like I used to when Mother Pells went round to speak to Martin's mum about him pulling my hair.

After about a minute, Peach Jumpsuit opens the door. She looks both the same and entirely different, expressionless as ever, but wearing, rather than a peach jumpsuit, or any jumpsuit for that matter, what can only be described as 'slacks', the sort one might order from a catalogue, which would come in a choice of 'Rust' and 'Arctic' and have a 'pull-on stretch waist for ease and comfort'. Hers are definitely 'Arctic', while on her feet she is wearing peach-coloured fluffy slippers with a velcro fastening. Two cats, one grey, one whose markings give the impression of wearing a fur tuxedo, weave around her ankles. This isn't how I envisaged her off-duty look, but at least she is sticking to her usual colour palette.

She doesn't look as surprised to see us as I thought she would.

'Erica,' she says. 'I haven't seen you since you became… famousssssss.'

I say hello and look past her into the hall where I can see a patterned carpet and a barometer on the wall. It's not exactly the minimalist white interior I was expecting.

'Hello, Portia,' says Merlyn.

'Hello, Merlyn,' says Peach Jumpsuit. 'You'd better come inside.'

—

Ten minutes later, Merlyn and I are sitting on the sofa in Peach Jumpsuit's living room, which has, like the hall, a patterned carpet, and a three-piece suite in a completely different purple floral pattern. At the window are net curtains, with voluminous velvet curtains over the top, tied back with cords. In the corner, on a high-backed armchair, is a copy of a magazine, lying open on a page with a short story called *The Hidden Locket*.

I am staring at her thimble collection (not a euphemism – there is one on the mantelpiece in a specially designed mahogany display unit) when Peach Jumpsuit brings through a Battenberg cake, a teapot and some cups and saucers on a tray and puts it on the coffee table in front of us.

'So, where's Marcus?' Merlyn says, confirming my long-standing suspicion that Marcus is not his surname, and therefore he does not sound like a real doctor. 'He's not answering my emails. And I was somewhat fobbed off when I came in with Erica for her Youth Review.'

Peach Jumpsuit cuts a slice of the disconcertingly bright yellow Battenberg and places it delicately on a small china plate with a cake fork, handing it to Merlyn, who waves it away. Peach Jumpsuit is undeterred, and offers it to me instead. But I'm having serious doubts about the true reason for our visit – what if it's not just about simply opening Yuvana Labs to reverse my treatment, but something more ominous? – and my appetite has disappeared. I shake my head.

'I honestly don't know,' says Peach Jumpsuit. 'He's been missing for a few weeks now. A couple of months even. We've been trying to keep things ticking over, but we had to let Channing and Alexia go, as well as some of the tech staff. That's why we closed up the lab and office.'

Alexia – that must be Glazed Doughnut, or maybe The Human Reel.

'We think it's because of his former partner,' she continues. 'The one he co-created WULT® with, who doesn't agree with Yuvana using the technology, and is suing Marcus, by all accounts.'

Peach Jumpsuit goes on. 'WULT®'s nanotechnology wasn't originally created for cosmetic reasonsssssssss. It was a lifesaving treatment for people with a rare genetic disorder. The age-reversal was a surprising side-effect, but Dr Marcus saw the potential to make some money from it – and that's when he split from his partner, who wanted to develop it for medical purposes only.'

I think about Josie's and Nandy's reactions. And Gabe's. Looking back now, I don't blame them. It's pretty gross, the whole thing, really. And it just got a whole lot grosser knowing that it was originally designed to help people. JEEZ. The sooner I can get my jowls back the better, and yes, I am aware of the ridiculous irony of this statement.

But what if I can't? I've never even considered this. 'Is Dr Marcus the only one who can do the WULT® treatment?' My voice is all croaky again.

'Yes, Erica, I'm afraid so,' says Peach Jumpsuit.

'I guess you're saying "afraid so" because he's also the only one who can reverse it?'

She nods and hands me a cup of tea, which reminds me of the colour of a particularly beefy gravy, especially after drinking the pale, milky tea made by Zoe. I suppose I should be glad she's not handing me endless glasses of water like she did at Yuvana Labs.

I can feel hot tears pricking my eyes. 'We need to find him then. I need to go and see my mum, and look like my old self when I do.'

Merlyn murmurs reassuring words and makes a show of squeezing my hand in spite of clearly not wanting to touch it.

Half an hour later, with some concerningly vague plans in place to track down Dr Marcus, we stand up to leave.

As I pass the barometer in the hall, the penny drops. I look at Peach Jumpsuit, who is holding the tuxedo cat, and say, 'If you don't mind me asking, Portia, how old are you?'

'I'm seventy-six, Erica.'

I must be staring at her open-mouthed because she says, 'Dr Marcus used me as a bit of a guinea pig, I suppose.'

I don't know what to say, then this comes out: 'Are you happy?'

She lets out a little laugh, which is unusual for someone normally so expressionless, and buries her nose in the fur on the back of the cat's neck, nuzzling it. 'If I am, it's not because of this,' she says, waving a hand at her face.

Chapter Thirty-Four

Our reptilian-mammalian overlords

It's been nearly a week. Merlyn and Peach Jumpsuit are trying to find out where Dr Marcus is, with no success so far, and the whole thing is really worrying me. I feel as though I have made, not just a mistake, but a catastrophic error of judgement. What if they can't find him? What am I going to do? How can I go and see Mother Pells again looking like this? And not just that, Merlyn has already told me Devon is coming back in September, so even though I'm now back in her flat, it's not going to be for much longer. I don't have any money since Yuvana stopped paying me and the Instagram was suspended, so I can't afford to rent somewhere else in London and I doubt Merlyn has a list of empty properties up her sleeve for me to live in rent-free.

The alternative, of course, is going back to Wiltshire. But how can I, having burnt so many bridges down there? I suppose I'll have to approach my old editors for some work again, but will they even commission me to write about menopausal insomnia and vaginal dryness when I look like this? JEEZ. Maybe I'll have to pitch to younger titles like *Sin* or *Bravura* but from what I hear, magazines aren't even that popular with Gen Z. It's all about social media – and I'm pretty sure my influencer days are over.

I did send an email to Gabe's friend Maxine, because I couldn't stop thinking about how cool it would be to write some funny lines that weren't about hair conditioners. But having messed things up with Gabe I'm not really expecting a response. She's probably heard what an idiot I am.

One small mercy is that the #whereswulty media furore seems to have died down, helped in part by vegan Instagrammer and wellness podcaster Polly of *@pollyonlyeatsplants* fame being papped at Greggs in Hemel Hempstead buying a Steak Bake. She might have got away with it and claimed it was for someone else if she hadn't wolfed down a sausage roll chaser while she was paying. The press is having a field day, although I've yet to see any of the available pun opportunities taken. Surely something about the 'steaks' being high would be a shoo-in? Regardless, it means that I am old news, which is a relief – although probably also reflective of my standing amongst my friends and family too. I'm quite the ray of sunshine, aren't I?

And speaking of family, it turns out that Simon has not been microdosing since the not-so-micro incident that prevented him from going to see Mother Pells. Which is surprising, as he is being quite pleasant to me so I assumed he must still be under the influence of psychedelics. He's got a new obsession though, called the sharing economy, which I know about because I read an article in *Grace* magazine about a woman who rents out her designer dresses and handbags. I'm pretty sure nobody would be interested in my Brie-stained Zara offerings, but it seems like a good idea. According to Facebook, Simon has so far rented out his A4 laminator (for home, school and office use) to someone called Suzanne, and his attic to a man named Jason – although I have concerns about what Jason is actually storing up there, and why.

Simon is now visiting Mother Pells every day, and explaining my absence with work-related excuses, at least until I can get the treatment reversed. Or should I say, *if* I can get the treatment reversed. All I can think about is finally getting to see her – I don't even care if all she wants to talk about is the potholes on Forest Lane. It also looks like when she gets out of hospital she might be moving straight into the flat we went to view (as long as they let her bring Eartha the cat). Simon has been organising this along with a carer to come in twice a day because her head injury has left her with dizziness and balance problems and they're not sure if these will improve at her age.

Josie has sent me a couple of short messages asking about Mother Pells, and Channing has finally realised I don't want to go clubbing with him again so has gone quiet. The only other messages I get, apart from hospital updates from Simon, are on the 'Find Dr Marcus' group chat that Peach Jumpsuit set up, the latest of which said, 'Nothing to report today.' This was from Merlyn – Peach Jumpsuit seems to mainly post really dated GIFs, the most recent being one of Dwight from *The Office* looking for something unspecified in a car park.

So now, I just wait. And I eat (not very good cheese from Sainsbury's). And I rewatch *The Good Place*. And I try not to bump into Zoe and her friends (specifically Kai) in the lift. And I avoid looking at myself in the mirror. This clear, bright complexion, this skin that bounces back immediately, this tight-as-a-gnats-chuff jawline – I don't associate it with anything good anymore. But this is my existence. I might have to get back into the wine soon, as I'm feeling quite miserable, and neither Peach Jumpsuit's

GIFs nor the Wensleydale with cranberries are helping in the slightest.

Sitting on the balcony one afternoon, I watch two crows, or maybe rooks – they're black birds of some sort. Maybe they're blackbirds? Anyway, they are either fighting or mating. Maybe not mating, that's earlier in the year, I seem to remember from a David Attenborough documentary. How do they mate? Do birds have penises? I might google that. But more importantly, are black birds some kind of bad omen? It reminds me of the taxi driver in Wiltshire and I realise I never listened to all the messages I got that day. I wonder if they're still in my phone? Picking it up to check, it appears they are.

–

Voice note:
'Hey gurl it's Chan.' <sound of 'Achy Breaky Heart' in the background> 'We've ended up at a house party in Walthamstow and OMG there's someone from *Married At First Sight Australia* here. OBSESSED. Anyway, big yikes someone just showed me the newspaper article about you – what the hell? Hope you're okay gurl. Love youuuuuuu.'

Voice note:
'Hi Erica, it's Zoe. I just wanted to say I'm sorry for turning up at your door last night, or should I say this morning. I was just a bit shocked when I saw the newspaper. I... <long pause> ...I'm not really sure why I'm phoning. I suppose I'm trying to get my head around the fact you're the same age as my mum. I just wanted to say, I'm not angry with you. I mean, I'm not happy that you tricked me, it's just, I'm sure you

had your reasons. The news stories don't seem fair. I think you're a nice person. I've enjoyed our conversations. Um… Call me if I can help. Okay. Bye.'

You have eight new voicemail messages:

First new message:
'Hi, message for Erica Pells. This is Tony, producer on *Rise & Shine*, we'd love to get you on the sofa this week with Howard and Wendy. Would Thursday morning, around eight-thirty a.m. work? The team will take care of everything, including wardrobe – we've got some great figure-enhancing dresses and court shoes and we can get your hair done too. Carol Vorderman might be on at the same time, which I'm sure will be exciting for you. Let us know if that works, and we can discuss.'

Next new message:
'<coughing> This is Mark. <weird noise possibly a burp> Hey, just saw your pictures online. Love to meet up in person… <scruffling, groaning> Or maybe you have a webcam? Do you have a webcam? <more groaning>'

Next new message:
'Erica, it's Alannah. Have you heard from Simon? Been trying to get in touch with him all day but he's not responding. It's eleven p.m. here now so heading to bed – if you speak to him can you tell him to call me tomorrow? Thanks.'

Next new message:
'Message for Erica Pells. This is Professor Graham Crosland. I've been analysing the Yuvana Labs logo, and I'm of the belief that it contains coded messages.

If you hold it at an angle and squint slightly, you can make out a pyramid, which is a clear nod to our reptilian-mammalian overlords. I'd like to discuss this with you, as well as Beyoncé's involvement: she's pulling the strings here of course. Let's chat further – in person is probably best as I suspect our communications are being monitored.'

Next new message:
'This is Brent from Grillers in the Mist. Your card payment didn't go through on Wednesday night on your order for... hold on... <scruffling> Gouda Grill artisanal sandwich with a side of dirty fries. Can you call back and make the payment, thanks.'

Next new message:
<hangs up>

Next new message:
'Hello Ms Pells. This is Francesca, one of the research team from Future Flow. We're producing a documentary series that explores the intricate frameworks of intersectional feminism, focusing on the multi-layered and concurrent forms of systemic oppression. We're particularly interested in featuring you as a case study of the problematic aspects of modern beauty standards and their detrimental societal impacts. Please give me a call at your convenience. Thank you.'

Next new message:
'Girly-pop, it's Keith. I just wanted to say sorry about pitching up yesterday unannounced. Just want you to know your friends miss you. On my way back to Wiltshire now. The play wasn't that brilliant to be honest. Hope you had a better night. Think about what I said.'

Chapter Thirty-Five

Three Corpse Revivers later

It's been a week now. I've only got dressed twice, preferring to wear Devon's *Teletubbies* onesie that I found in the back of her wardrobe. To be honest I thought better of her, although I'm not sure why, as we've never met. At around six p.m., I'm contemplating going over my overdraft limit to Deliveroo a bottle of Gavi and some Pringles, just to see me through the end of *The Good Place*, when the buzzer goes.

'Erica?' says a woman's voice through the intercom.

'Yes?'

'It's Cassia, sweetie. Can I come up?'

What the hell? I assume this must be an apology. It didn't need to be in person though. My first thought is the *Teletubbies* onesie but I suppose the last time we spoke I had an omelette stuck to my face so this could even be an improvement. I let her in without saying anything.

While she's in the lift – or possibly on the stairs knowing Cassia (*#everydayfitness*) – I lean on the hall wall. I can't really be bothered with this. I don't care whether she's sorry or not, and if she's come for any other reason, like to have a go at me for not being positive enough about ageing or something, then I don't have the emotional energy. I wish Nandy was here. She'd know what to say.

And then I see Cassia coming along the corridor, with greying hair in a ponytail, glasses, a hoodie and jeans. She looks like any other middle-aged woman as she walks past me into the flat.

I guide her into the living room area with a wave of my hand. She doesn't comment on my onesie, or anything else for that matter, but sits down on the ottoman, handbag on her knee. 'Sorry to turn up unannounced, Erica.'

I nod. I'm not saying it's okay because it's not. 'What the hell do you want, Cassia? You can't just march in here like this.'

'I want to help.'

'Help?' I sit down on the couch opposite her. 'I haven't really been getting that from you, what with starting the whole *#whereswulty* thing and revealing my identity to the press? And your reel the other day telling everyone what a terrible person I am?'

'What makes you think it was me that told the press? And did you even watch my reel the other day?'

'Well, no, but...'

'Oh Erica.' She shakes her head and looks around the room for the first time. 'You really don't think things through, do you?'

I don't know what she means specifically, and it comes across as quite patronising, but in general, I agree. So, I nod, then realise shaking my head is the correct answer, so do that instead.

'I didn't go to the press. Merlyn did. And my reel was all about the pressures women face trying to look young, and how I get why you had the treatment. I mean, I also said I hoped you'd reverse it, but I was on your side. I *am* on your side. So is she.'

'WHAT? Why would Merlyn go to the press? And what have you got to do with any of this anyway? The whole thing is really none of your business.' I suddenly feel like I'm a pawn in a game of chess that I can't even play (which I genuinely can't – I did watch *The Queen's Gambit* though and loved the costumes).

Cassia doesn't reply but gets up and walks over to the kitchen area. 'If you're not going to offer me a drink, sweetie, I'll make one,' she says, opening Devon's cupboards until she finds the one with alcohol in.

I hear her clattering about, and I'm about to tell her to get out of the kitchen – and indeed the flat – when I realise how much I need a drink. And to find out what's going on, for that matter.

Cassia walks back over and hands me a cocktail glass with a pale yellow-orange liquid in. 'Just the thing for you – a Corpse Reviver.'

I overlook the veiled insult and take a sip. It's strong and delicious. Then I think about Merlyn, and how she didn't look disappointed in her office that day when I told her about wanting to reverse WULT®.

'Did Merlyn *want* me to get the treatment reversed?'

'Of course,' says Cassia.

'Why "of course"? What the hell? I don't get it – she was the one who suggested it to me in the first place?'

'True, yes, she also wanted you to *have* the WULT® treatment, but not for the reasons you might think.'

'What would be the other reason for having it, apart from the obvious one?'

'She wanted you to have it, and enjoy it – then...'

'Then what?'

Cassia sighs, as if bracing herself to deliver the words. 'Then... regret it.'

'Again – what?'

'Regret it. Realise it's not what you want at all. Not long-term, anyway. She thought if you – someone clever and relatable – went through the whole process and then decided you didn't want it, people might pay attention. It would do a lot more than a damning review in *Glowgetter*.'

I take another sip of my drink. 'I still don't get it.' I really, really don't.

'When Yuvana offered the trial, Merlyn and I were horrified at the concept, but we decided not to say anything, as we were also part of the selection process. We knew the best way to shut the whole thing down would be from the inside out. Anyway, all the usual names came up – the big influencers like me, Imani and Lily from *@LuxeLooksWithLily*. But Merlyn and I thought, actually, we could do some good with this. Not just hand it over for someone to make themselves even more famous. So we thought of you – someone who would ask questions, I suppose. Well, she thought of you. She always does, it seems.'

'I still don't get it.'

'Erica, you're so funny, so clever, but always so desperate to look younger. Merlyn and I talked about it a lot. I love being older – so does she. Even when I was getting trolled I was proud to be a Wise Woman. Wise Women don't give a crap!'

She pauses and I can see she looks almost tearful. 'We got quite emotional when we first saw you transformed on Instagram, really hoping it would make you rethink your whole obsession with youth… Break the spell, I suppose.' She trails off.

I feel a rising anger. How dare they? I'm not their pet project. I don't need fixing. Although this does explain why I was picked over the heavyweight influencers. I never could work that out.

'That was a risky thing to do,' I say. 'I mean... how did you and Merlyn know I would even want to reverse the treatment?'

'We didn't. And at the end of the day, it was up to you. Nobody forced you into it. But we had faith in you.' She winks like she does on her reels and takes a gulp of her cocktail. 'My reels and the press thing were just to move it all along a bit more quickly, what with Devon coming back.'

I drain my drink, put the glass on the coffee table and stand up, looking around the room as if the answers are hanging from the walls. It's a lot to take in. Merlyn has always looked after me, but this is next level, life changing, fairy godmother stuff. The ball I'm going to... or trying to go to at least, could be a happier life. And that would be quite the party – if I can get there, that is.

Now the tears come – and come, and come, and drip down onto my onesie. I make a big snorting snivelling noise. 'JEEZ, Cassia. What am I supposed to do now? This has really backfired. I need to go and visit my mum, she's ill in hospital and doesn't recognise me like this. It's not just that either. My friendships are in tatters, and to top it all, Dr Marcus has gone missing, so I don't even know if they are going to be able to reverse it. What if I'm stuck like this?'

'I know, I know. I'm sorry, sweetie. This is why I came over, to see how you are. And see if I can help.' She stands up and puts her hands on my arms, as though holding me up. It's a bit weird. I haven't been this close to her in a long time. I look at her face. She's really different to how she seems in her reels, much more... human, I suppose. I suddenly don't hate her as much as I thought.

'Cassia,' I say, feeling like this is the moment to finally get it off my chest. 'I was really hurt when you got the assistant editor job at *Beautique*. I wanted it so much. But I know how you got it, about the whole Egon thing. It's okay.'

'The whole Egon thing?'

'Yeah, Egon, from the board. I mean, your dad was friends with him, right?'

'Erm... yes. But that's not why I got the promotion.'

'What?'

'I got it because of the "pro-ageing" issue I mocked up for the interview.'

I must be staring open-mouthed because she goes on. 'It had Joanna Lumley on the cover, and the headline "Grand Old Age". I was really pleased with it. What did you do for yours?'

I think about my stick-on eye serum sample and 'Young Ho!' headline and cringe so much about my obsession with youth that I almost shudder.

'Oh... it doesn't matter now.' I sniff and try a smile, glad of her half-hug. I'm getting bored of asking myself how I could have been such an idiot. So I change the subject. 'Did you say you were trolled?'

'Oh yes, relentlessly. For my hairy chin, my grey hair, turkey neck, you name it. So I thought, you know what, I'm just going to go completely grey, wear specs, stop getting my lips done – embrace it all. It's better than the alternative.' She releases her grip on me and walks back over to the kitchen.

I think about poor Erica Pells from Ava, Missouri, and nod, picking up my drink and draining the last of it. It's making my cheeks pink.

'D'you want another?' says Cassia, already pouring things into the cocktail shaker.

'I thought you were only allowed one. You know, *hashtag mindfuldrinking*?'

'Don't believe everything you see on social media.'

This is what Father Pells would have called 'a turn up for the books'.

—

Three Corpse Revivers later and Cassia and I are sitting in the deckchairs on the balcony.

'It's so noisy here,' says Cassia as a siren blares in the street below.

'I know. I actually hate it now. But I can't go back home. I'm stuck.'

'There's always hope, Erica. Come on. We're Wise Women. Let's go and make a plan.' She pulls herself up, staggers, then turns round and holds out her hands, pulling me up too.

Back inside, we get out my laptop, which we can't open to start with and dissolve into laughter. I mean, we're drunk – but let's be clear, I'm not suddenly best mates with Cassia. Nobody was holding out for that plot twist. Her incessant use of the word 'sweetie' really grates as does the fact that she talks about being 'decadent', which I'm fairly sure nobody who is actually decadent says.

'Give it here,' says Cassia. 'I'm an influencer. I know how to work Google.'

More laughing, and replenished Corpse Revivers, and Cassia is suddenly concentrating hard on reading something on a website.

'I think the problem here, sweetie, is that you have been looking for the wrong person.'

'What d'you mean? It's Dr Marcus we need. Or Marcus, should I say.'

'Yes, but if he's hiding, we're never going to find him. However, d'you know who is *not* hiding?'

'No – who?'

'Professor Brandt. Dr Marcus's former partner. She'll know how to reverse WULT®. In fact I think she had more of a hand in its creation than that phoney doctor did.'

I thought Professor Brandt was a man. Which doesn't reflect that well on me… But that's probably why I've never been able to find out much about her online.

'What's her name?'

'Rosamund.' She points at the screen. 'That's her.'

I peer at the laptop, swaying slightly, and can see a woman in her fifties, with a half-smile and neat, shoulder-length salt-and-pepper hair, wearing medical scrubs. 'Oh well done. So where is she?'

'Geneva. She works for Médecins Sans Limites now. We need to get to her.'

I might be full of vintage cocktail, but the name Médecins Sans Limites rings a very loud bell. Then I remember – Laure. That's who Laure works for. Maybe there is a chance after all.

Chapter Thirty-Six

A Jenga game that's nearly over

I feel like I need one last soundtrack. Something that goes with a slow-motion 'squad' scene, walking in a row through the airport or getting on a plane, like in *Bridesmaids*. And right now, that's exactly where I find myself – marching through Heathrow with the least likely 'squad' you can imagine. There's me, in my now standard Gen X meets Gen Z ensemble, then next to me is Merlyn, who today channels Bianca Jagger in a white, wide-legged trouser suit and her usual huge sunglasses. On the other side of her is Cassia, in full influencer mode wearing And Other Stories jeans, Anthropologie top, vintage Hermès bag (all *#gifted*), then Peach Jumpsuit, who is wearing, somewhat reassuringly, a peach jumpsuit. Last, but certainly not least, is Laure, who always looks as if she is going on a hike in adverse weather conditions. You couldn't make it up, as Auntie Viv always says.

It's precisely four days since Cassia turned up at Devon's, and a lot has happened since. The following day, at nine a.m., which I felt was the earliest acceptable time to phone someone, especially someone who you are on rather strained terms with, I called Josie. I have Laure's number, but it didn't feel right to go straight to her. Josie was quiet at first, then when I told her the story, and explained how I want to get the treatment reversed, I could hear her defrosting.

'Erica, I'm so happy you want to do this.'

'Wanting is one thing – it's whether I can or not that's the problem now.'

'Yes, I see. And I'm sorry.'

'What for?'

'For being angry with you.'

'It's okay, I get it. You didn't think this was a good example for Héloïse and I can see why now.'

'It wasn't just that, Erica. I was hurt… It was like you didn't want to be the person who means so much to me.'

I took a sharp breath and tried not to let her hear my voice was shaky. 'I'm sorry too Josie. I didn't just do this to be vain, you know. I think I felt sad about the past. I wanted to go back and see if I could do it better.' It was weird how just saying that made it so much clearer.

I heard her sigh. 'I've got bits of my past I'm sad about too. Everyone does. The only way to feel better about them is by doing things better in the present.'

I felt like if I tried to speak I would cry.

Josie told me to hold on and went to get Laure, but I could tell she'd briefed her in that time, because when Laure came on the phone a couple of minutes later, all she said was 'I will see what I can do' in her French accent.

After that, I called Merlyn, who assured me it had all been 'as ever, with the very best intentions at heart'. I didn't have the energy to argue with her, all I could think about was whether Laure was going to get us to Professor Brandt, and if this shit show was going to be over soon so I could go and see Mother Pells. I told Merlyn that her plan had worked, and that I couldn't wait to get back to my saggy old self. I also made her promise to take me to

Brasserie Zédel when this is all over and give me a free pass at the *Chariot des Fromages.*

The next day, a message popped up from Laure in the group chat formerly known as 'Find Marcus' (now hilariously renamed 'Make Erica Old Again' complete with a picture of the US flag). Cassia and Laure have been added to the chat alongside Merlyn, Peach Jumpsuit and me. She managed to get a 'short meeting' with Professor Brandt, but it must be in Geneva and in two days – absolutely no flexibility, which makes Professor Brandt sound quite terrifying.

So Merlyn got us all business class flights, and I put some cross-fingers emojis in the group chat. Then, feeling more confident that there might be a way back, I sent Mother Pells a video message that I made using a filter called 'Time Warp', which makes you look older (Cassia's idea). It wasn't until after I sent it that I noticed it probably made me look too old, and that the filter added a Zimmer frame to the background, but hopefully she didn't notice. It was only a few seconds long, saying, 'See you soon! Lots of love!' And then I just hoped that this would be the way forward, or should I say, the way back.

―

And now here we are, on our way to Geneva, and I am still hoping. Because Professor Brandt might know how to reverse the treatment, but that doesn't mean to say she will want to, and the connection via Laure seems tenuous to say the least – according to Josie, she's a lot higher up and they don't even work in the same department of what appears to be a huge organisation.

The flight lasts an hour and a half. We all sit in our little business class pods, not saying much to each other. Peach

Jumpsuit is listening to an audiobook and I hear Cassia twittering about how decadent it all is while taking photos for her Stories. Laure is muttering about how it's not really a five-person job, which I think is directed at Cassia. I'm pretty sure Merlyn, who is wearing a silk eye mask and compression socks (which I feel are possibly unnecessary on a ninety-minute flight) let her tag along because it was her idea to find Professor Brandt. She also told me in the loos of the first-class lounge at Heathrow that Cassia 'can be quite persuasive'. Sure, if you're flogging healthy gut supplements, I thought to myself, but didn't say anything.

It's the first time I've been on a plane in about four years, the last time being on a press trip to a spa in Austria with Nandy. It wasn't as fun as it sounds – we had to stand at the end of a tiled tunnel stark naked and be pummelled with a fireman's hose in the name of thalassotherapy. I felt like I was being deloused before a lengthy prison sentence. But any excitement about flying is overshadowed by nervousness. I sit thinking about the last few months and try to remember the enthusiasm I had for my new appearance when I first got the treatment. It feels like a distant memory. The stewardess offers me 'anything I want' but I resist the temptation to have some Swiss courage. Maybe I can do that on the way back later, either to celebrate or drown my sorrows.

At the airport, a car takes us to the Médecins Sans Limites office, which is only a few minutes away, down surprisingly leafy roads considering we are in a city. Nobody says much, apart from Cassia who says that the limousine is 'to die for' and Peach Jumpsuit who whispers 'Yessssssss' in reply. The building is probably close to how I imagined Yuvana Labs would look when I first went last year, a stunning architectural design with glass and wood in a tower of different interlocking levels, like a Jenga game that's nearly over. We pull up outside and Laure says, 'I will do the talking please.' Then we all get out.

Fifteen minutes later, after waiting in a huge open plan area filled with plants, we are led to Professor Brandt's light-filled corner office. She is sitting at a wooden desk, reading something intently, and doesn't look up when we all file in. Her assistant, a red-headed woman wearing a linen shirt dress, closes the door, and as there aren't enough seats for all of us, we stand in a row. Professor Brandt has glasses on and appears identical to her photo online, but instead of scrubs is wearing a khaki-coloured blouse with a tie neck. She still doesn't look up, but holds up a finger and says, 'Twenty minutes only,' in a strong European accent that could be German or Austrian, I can't tell.

We stand in silence, then she slowly lifts her head, lowers her glasses and looks over them at us. 'What's this, the Spice Girls reunion?'

Not exactly what I expected.

Then she looks at me. 'And you're Baby Spice?'

'Erm... yes.' I never thought I'd be replying to that question in the affirmative, but I know what she means.

'I think I read about you in one of your terrible British newspapers.'

'Well... I...'

She takes off her glasses and puts them down on the desk, stands up and walks round the other side of it, then perches on the corner. She appears to be very tall, so this just means she is now at eye level with us.

Laure jumps in. 'We really appreciate your time today, Rosamund. Erica has ended up in an unfortunate situation, but as Dr Marcus — I mean Marcus — has disappeared, we don't have any way of reversing the treatment.

This is why we need your help. You're the only other person who knows how to do it. And undo it.'

'Damn right I am,' says Professor Brandt. I'm starting to like her. 'And it's my lawsuit that's made him disappear, so I'm more than aware of the situation.'

It's feeling faintly promising. She certainly seems to be on our side when it comes to a dislike of Dr Marcus.

'The nanotechnology was never meant to be used for things like this,' she continues, waving her hand at me, to indicate that I am 'this'. 'How old are you?'

'I'm forty-eight,' I say, realising how ridiculous that sounds.

'What a waste of technology that was meant to do some good.' She shakes her head and stares out of the window. I feel like we're moving off topic, so despite Laure's instructions, I wade in.

'So can you help us… me?'

'I'd like to, but I'm working on a time-critical project providing urgent medical assistance to refugees in Syria. And unlike you, they have real problems.'

I can feel everyone wince. Merlyn speaks for the first time. 'In Erica's defence, she has learnt a lot from this experience and…'

Professor Brandt cuts her off: '*Danke*, Scary Spice. I don't need the backstory. My sole interest in Yuvana Labs is legal – retrieving my patents and ensuring this technology serves those truly in need.' She glances at her watch, which is as Swiss as you can imagine. 'Sorry I couldn't be of more use to you.'

It's feeling a lot less promising.

I look round at everyone and Laure shrugs, Cassia looks like she's about to burst into tears, Merlyn looks irked at being called Scary Spice and it's hard to tell what Peach Jumpsuit's expression is, but that's par for the course.

Professor Brandt's assistant appears magically, opening the office door and then standing with one arm outstretched, as if she is cabin crew demonstrating emergency exits. I get that horrible pre-exam feeling in my chest. This can't be happening – it's my only chance, unless Dr Marcus returns, which is looking less and less likely.

One by one, we file out of the room, shoulders hunched, faces resigned. There's nothing more to say. Merlyn goes first, then Cassia, then Laure, who mutters, 'Thanks for your time, Rosamund,' and then Peach Jumpsuit, who is in front of me. As she draws level with the door Professor Brandt touches her on the shoulder. She turns, and Professor Brandt looks at her, puzzled.

'Mrs Crump?'

'That's right, Rosamund. I didn't think you remembered me.'

'You were Dr Marcus's housekeeper weren't you? Back in the Nineties, when we were first working together?'

'Yesssssssss.'

'I was only in my twenties,' says Professor Brandt. 'That was a long time ago...' She smiles for the first time. 'I remember once I had a bad cold and was feeling homesick. You made me *Kartoffelsuppe*, do you recall? The potato soup my mother used to give me.'

'I do recall.' Peach Jumpsuit smiles. Everyone else has gathered just outside the door to listen in.

We all look at Professor Brandt, who is silent, but clearly thinking hard. I can definitely hear my heart beating.

'Okay,' she says, at last.

We don't know what she means yet so we don't say anything. Then she turns to me.

'I'll help you, Baby Spice. Consider it a favour returned. But on one condition. The "Woke Up Like This" *scheisse* is put to bed once and for all. The technology has huge potential, and it was never my intention for it to be used for this... mockery of nature.'

This must be a little awkward for Portia, whose skin is tighter than cling film around a Camembert. But who cares – she's saying yes.

Cassia leans in the door and speaks for the first time. 'You're a wise woman!' I knew she would say something cringey. Thankfully, Professor Brandt ignores her.

'And one final thing. I will need access to Yuvana Labs – Mrs Crump, will you be able to arrange this?'

'Of course. We don't have a lab team now though...'

'Well then – I will need all of you to help,' says Professor Brandt, with such a headmistress air about her that we all just quietly nod, and I am sure that the three of us who haven't yet been assigned a Spice Girl silently wonder which one they are.

Chapter Thirty-Seven

Thank god for potato soup

I am not a member of many group chats. I always find the names of them disappointingly pun-free, and to be fair, I don't get invited to join them very often anyway. I was a member of our street group chat in Wiltshire, which was imaginatively called 'Street Group Chat', but an admin (Mrs Belcher, it is my firm belief) removed me after I accidently posted a sticker of Paul Hollywood, with the caption 'Show me your baps', which was meant for Nandy. And I was also a member of one for a Wiltshire book group that I joined as one of my efforts to be more sociable but then left it when I realised I don't read much other than *Grace* magazine, and lately, not even that. I may address this if and when I get home – Josie is always lending me books saying things like, 'You'll love this, it's about a plucky Irish girl during the war who...' and then I switch off. That said, I have started reading some blogs about comedy writing since I emailed Maxine, although she hasn't replied so I'm not really sure what the point is. They are interesting though.

The 'Make Erica Old Again' group chat has my full attention, and I am constantly checking to see if there is any news from Laure on Professor Brandt's impending visit to London. I have to keep reminding myself that just because she has agreed to help, it doesn't guarantee she will be able to, especially given that her laboratory staff will be a fashion magazine non-executive editor, a beauty influencer, a seventy-six-year-old former housekeeper and... actually I'm not sure what Laure's job title is but I'm pretty confident it's not to do with nasal probes. Oh and also Josie, who has joined the group chat and said she will come along and help, even if it's just to stand guard. Because according to Peach Jumpsuit, Yuvana has been asked to vacate the premises, which means technically we shouldn't be going in at all, and the landlords occupy the same building, so we have to be careful they don't spot us.

At Devon's, I distract myself by cleaning and packing up. Whatever happens, I will have to move out, as it's nearly the end of August. I've lived here for six months and never even used the oven, so there is no tray of roast potatoes to discover, just some fairly average cheese in the fridge and, weirdly, a pizza takeaway menu in the freezer, which makes me smile as the restaurant is called Another One Bites The Crust. And then I think about Gabe. I wonder, if the reversal works, if he will want to see me again. It's probably too late. The day Josie drove me to the hospital, she said that he was 'keeping busy', which was a weird way of putting it, but possibly means he's now seeing someone else.

Finally, after a week during which Portia and Merlyn give me some Yuvana Labs money 'by way of compensation' to tide me over (thank god, as I am seriously down to my last pennies), Laure posts on the group chat. Her messages are always perfunctory, and I can't help but cringe at what she must think of us all. I wonder what it must be like to be a 'no messing' sort of person who always has a banana in their bag and donates to charity without even telling anyone about it.

'Rosamund can be in London on Tuesday next week, for twenty-four hours only.'

'*Eccellente!* All hands on deck,' writes Merlyn in reply.

And so, after everyone has left various comments, a plan is made to let ourselves into Yuvana Labs and between us, carry out the procedure. Holy crap. This better work. Otherwise that croft in Scotland with the tartan headscarf and basketweave might be the best option. I'm certainly not staying here to spend my days kissing adolescents and playing video games about silage. And besides, I need to see Mother Pells, and sharpish.

—

At nine p.m., we all arrive separately at the square in Kensington. We have to wait until it's dark, in the hope that the rest of the building is empty, but also because it's more difficult for anyone to spot us coming in. I stand under a cherry tree in the warm breeze, waiting for my signal on the group chat. There are six of us, seven including Professor Brandt. Peach Jumpsuit goes in first, as she has the keys, then the rest of us go in one by one, from different parts of the square, so as not to attract attention.

Merlyn is next – I think she wanted her outfit to look like a cat burglar but from where I am standing, she looks more like a mime artist. Then I see Cassia, who also got the memo about wearing dark colours but being an influencer and/or decadent couldn't resist making that a giant black shawl and a hat that makes her look like one of the Pilgrim Fathers. I roll my eyes watching Peach Jumpsuit let her in, and wonder, as I can't see from where I am, if Peach Jumpsuit is wearing a black jumpsuit. Next is Professor Brandt, looking business-like as ever, then Laure and Josie, who appear to have Héloïse with them for some unknown reason. Then it's my turn and, hopefully for the last time, I cross the square and head up the steps.

Inside, we all stand whispering in the reception area, which is in darkness. The screens have been removed from the walls, the blue velvet sofas are gone, and there are document boxes strewn everywhere. It feels cold and echoey, so different from the first time I came here in my puff-sleeved dress, full of excitement. How naïve I was.

Josie hugs me, then Héloïse sees me too and throws her arms around my waist. 'I'm happy that you will be my Erica again,' she says, before saying that the room smells 'of post offices'. For a change, I get what she means.

'Sorry about bringing this one,' Josie says, stroking Héloïse's cheek. 'We couldn't get a babysitter.'

Everyone shakes their heads to show it doesn't matter, and Josie stays in reception with her as we all go through to the treatment room. Peach Jumpsuit puts some of the lights on, and although it's dim I can see the treatment table and all the equipment around it. I feel a slow, prickling fear creep over me that reminds me of when I had to wear itchy woollen polo necks under my Brownie uniform when I was a child. Nobody has any experience, apart from Peach Jumpsuit I suppose, but Professor Brandt created the technology in the first place, so she must know what she's doing. Hope so anyway.

Peach Jumpsuit makes Laure, Cassia and Merlyn wash their hands and put on masks and gowns, then gives them various jobs to do, holding things, cleaning things, screwing things into other things. Then she leads me behind the screen to put on a surgical gown. I'll have to be sedated again, so Cassia has volunteered to take me home afterwards, which is both kind of her and the least she can do. Once I'm ready, I get up on the treatment table, and Professor Brandt puts a cannula in my hand. She's not making any Spice Girls jokes today, in fact she's not saying much at all, and is clearly unimpressed by the lot of us. Thank god for potato soup, is all I can say.

She explains that just like the treatment itself, the effect of the reversal isn't immediate – although the process will start as soon as I have the implant removed, the full reversal will take around ten days.

Just as she is about to administer the sedation, we hear a sound from outside the room. Laure rushes over to the door and pokes her head out into the corridor. We can hear her talking, then she returns, saying that Josie has heard people upstairs, and lights have gone on, so we need to hurry. Great – I do so love my neurological procedures to be in darkness, and rushed.

Merlyn the mime artist holds my hand as the sedation kicks in. Her words are muffled by her mask, but I can hear her say, '*Brava*, Erica.' As I go to reply, I realise my speech is slurring but I manage to say that if this works, she has changed my life for the better. Hearing myself say that out loud makes the tears come. Then, as the sedation takes over, the random thoughts fill my head... Paul Hollywood is shaking my hand... Carol's rabbit is back home after all these years... and I am making yarn with a Spinning Jenny, and it's coming out bloody perfectly, as if I've been spinning all my life.

Chapter Thirty-Eight

Cassia Carver has left the chat

Kaleidoscopic dreams of a weird cosmetic surgeon, Simon's compost toilet and the face of Gabe Dix bring me to the morning of the next day. The first thing I do is touch my nose, which is still covered in a large dressing. The pain in my head is identical to back in January, like I've leant forward on a pencil, so I reach over and grab some ibuprofen from the bedside table. I can barely remember getting to bed, but I think Cassia helped me.

Right on cue there's a knock on the bedroom door, and there she is in a perfect *#OOTD*: Zara jeans, white Veja trainers and an oversized blazer. If she hadn't been so kind to me, I would tell her to influence off for looking so put together when I look so... pulled apart.

'I'm going to go now, Erica, do you need anything?'

I didn't actually know she'd stayed the night. 'Erm... no. Thank you.'

'You're welcome. Remember to keep us updated on the group chat,' she says. 'Professor Brandt said it went as well as could be expected so... good luck, sweetie. See you on the other side. The right side.'

And she's gone.

It's quite humbling (by which I mean maddening) to be schooled by someone like Cassia, but I admit she's got the whole ageing thing sorted out a lot better than me. And now, I wait. It's the weirdest feeling. I know I won't be welcoming back the old parts of me like I welcomed the bouncy, youthful skin. But with my jowls, lines, cellulite and all of that, comes a chance to return to my old life and do it properly. I'm like a perimenopausal version of Scrooge on Christmas morning.

—

Make Erica Old Again
Group: Six Members

24 August

> **09:20 Erica Pells**
> Thanks @Cassia for staying and keeping an eye on me. And thanks everyone else for last night. Fingers crossed now...

> **09:22 Cassia Carver**
> So welcome sweetie!

> **09:24 Merlyn Vye**
> Buona fortuna Erica!

> **09:26 Josie Gauthier-Magennis**
> Sending lots of love @Erica from all of us.

09:29 Laure Gauthier-Magennis
How is your nose today? Mon Dieu, that thing went up quite far.

09:31 Josie Gauthier-Magennis
I'm sure Erica doesn't want to hear that @Laure. Are you still in the shop? Can you get Helly some Hula Hoops?

25 August

06:28 Laure Gauthier-Magennis
I think we should send Rosamund a thank-you gift.

09:54 Portia Crump
Might be better to wait and see if the reversal actually works? @Erica any signs yet? <GIF OF MR BEAN IN A FIELD LOOKING AROUND>

19:08 Erica Pells
Sorry for silence. Feeling a bit despondent as I don't look or feel any different. I really need this to work.

19:10 Cassia Carver
Make yourself a Corpse Reviver sweetie. You'll look ten years older tomorrow after a few of those.

19:11 Erica Pells
Thanks @Cassia very helpful.

26 August

08:12 Erica Pells
Morning everyone. I have a couple of grey hairs around my temples.

08:35 Merlyn Vye
Eccellente!

09:02 Josie Gauthier-Magennis
Great news @Erica!

09:10 Cassia Carver
You'll need to embrace the grey this time. #silversisterhood

09:12 Erica Pells
I'll get back to you on that @Cassia.

27 August

> **11:17 Portia Crump**
> How are you getting on @Erica? <GIF OF RACHEL FROM FRIENDS WAVING>

> **12:05 Erica Pells**
> I'm completely knackered today and slept really badly last night. Also finding all my clothes really tight, which is a 'good' sign.

> **14:13 Cassia Carver**
> Shall I drop round some clothes for you? I've just done a Free People try on.

> **18:47 Laure Gauthier-Magennis**
> Any update on the gift for Rosamund? Just trying to smooth things over at work.

> **20:09 Erica Pells**
> @Cassia thanks but we're not really the same size.

> **20:10 Cassia Carver**
> @Erica it's no problem, they sent me the plus size stuff too.

20:11 Erica Pells
THIS MESSAGE WAS DELETED

28 August

07:45 Merlyn Vye
Any news, Erica my dear?

09:12 Erica Pells
No, and I'm really concerned that the treatment has somehow reset me permanently. Apart from feeling knackered and a couple of grey hairs, that's about it. I would say I look 35, or 30 after a difficult year. If this is the extent of the reversal, it's not great. I really need to go and see my mum and look like ME. And not just that, Gen Z are bad enough, I don't want to have to make friends with Millennials. I want to get back to my real life, and my real friends. @Josie I'm sorry again.

09:18 Josie Gauthier-Magennis
You've apologised enough Erica, it's OK. And you need to give this time. It's only day five. @Merlyn do you agree?

09:23 Merlyn Vye
Absolutely!

12:34 Cassia Carver
I can totally relate Erica, when I tried to kick my Shellac habit it took much longer than I expected to see a difference.

12:35 Erica Pells
THIS MESSAGE WAS DELETED

29 August

11:16 Laure Gauthier-Magennis
I've taken the liberty of buying a Thermos for Rosamund. It has a separate section in the lid for tea bags and snacks.

14:28 Erica Pells
The lines on my neck are back everyone. I used to call it my nematode neck because they look like worm segments. I'm trying to think of something more positive, so I don't hate them all over again. But to be honest, I'm just pleased it seems to be working. In fact, I just messaged my mum to say I'll be in to visit her soon.

12:34 Cassia Carver
How about calling them Legacy Lines? We could make it into a hashtag and do a reel together! Thoughts?

20:09 Erica Pells
THIS MESSAGE WAS DELETED

30 August

08:12 Erica Pells
Hi everyone – just to let you know I had a terrible night's sleep as befits a woman of my age, and was walking like Homo habilis when I got up. Also, the jowls are back, and a couple of extra chins. Mixed feelings.

08:35 Merlyn Vye
It's difficult Erica, I understand, but remember the benefits will outweigh the downsides.

09:02 Portia Crump
This is good news, Erica. I suppose you're not Baby Spice anymore? <GIF OF EMMA BUNTON>

09:03 Erica Pells
No! But you'll always be Posh, @Portia.

09:04 Cassia Carver
Sorry to butt in! It's just if Portia is Posh, I'm guessing @Laure is sporty, so that wouldn't really work, as then I'd be Ginger.

09:05 Erica Pells
@Cassia she does seem to be the remaining Spice Girl, yes.

09:09 Cassia Carver
@Erica I wore that Union Jack dress ONCE, and it was part of a paid promotion.

09:14 Portia Crump
<GIF OF TUMBLEWEED>

09:18 Cassia Carver
THIS MESSAGE WAS DELETED

09:25 Cassia Carver has left the chat

31 August

09:24 Portia Crump
Has Cassia left the chat? <GIF OF SOMEONE EATING POPCORN>

09:25 Erica Pells
Yes, it's fine, it's just Cassia, she'll get over it. Least of my worries right now to be honest.

16:12 Merlyn Vye
A peacock spat in my tapenade – of course I want my money back.

16:13 Merlyn Vye
Disregard above message, wrong group.

18:47 Laure Gauthier-Magennis
@Erica are we feeling pretty confident about the reversal working now – keen to give the Thermos to Rosamund if so.

20:09 Erica Pells
@Laure I think so. I was watching GBBO last night and Paul Hollywood was either having an off day (unlikely) or there's something wrong with my libido. Might make a GP appointment for some HRT when I get home.

20:10 Laure Gauthier-Magennis
@Erica 'TMI' as Héloïse would say.

1 September

10:28 Merlyn Vye
How goes it, Erica my dear, are you nearly there?

13:06 Erica Pells
@Merlyn you know that scene in Indiana Jones where the German soldier drinks from the wrong cup and then gets old and turns to dust in about 20 seconds? It's a bit slower but basically that's what's happening to me.

13:08 Portia Crump
<GIF OF SAID SCENE FROM INDIANA JONES>

13:09 Erica Pells
Thanks @Portia.

13:11 Josie Gauthier-Magennis
Hope you're OK @Erica. I'm going to make your favourite chicken with potatoes and prunes when you get home. Keith says tell his girly-pop he can't wait to see her beautiful frown lines.

13:13 Erica Pells
Thanks @Josie.

2 September

09:24 Portia Crump
Day 10 Erica! <GIF OF LEONARDO DI CAPRIO RAISING A MARTINI GLASS>

09:25 Erica Pells
Yes, well, it's definitely worked alright. I ventured out this morning and was royally ignored by humankind in general, and when I got back into my block of flats a neighbour asked me if I was 'lost, dear?'.

14:47 Laure Gauthier-Magennis
Rosamund really appreciated the Thermos, everyone. @Portia she was also asking if she can get written confirmation that the WULT® brand has now ceased operating as per the conditions of helping Erica.

14:50 Portia Crump
@Laure email on the way to her.

15:01 Merlyn Vye
Are you OK, @Erica my dear?

15:05 Erica Pells
Yes thanks Merlyn. When I say I feel like my old self again, I really mean it. But new adventures await and I had an interesting email this morning. And at least now I can go and visit my mum. And my best friend, if she'll see me. Thanks everyone. I'll delete this group now. Love Erica X

Chapter Thirty-Nine

Just some middle-aged woman

The following day is my last day at Devon's. After gaffer-taping shut the last box (there aren't many, I didn't bring that much), I write a note apologising for breaking one of the deckchairs and leave the Fuchsia Frenzy bodysuit for her. This could possibly be construed as a strange thank-you present (especially as I put it in the only gift bag I can find, which has SANTA HAS BEEN! written on it), but it doesn't fit me anymore and it still has the gusset sticker on so I think it's okay. I'm also skint, so at this point it's the best I can do. Merlyn is arranging to have all the filming equipment collected, and for the boxes to be taken down to Wiltshire, so apart from that, and a desperate attempt to resuscitate the wilting monstera, I don't need to do anything, just leave the key on the kitchen island and make sure everything is switched off.

And then, finally, thankfully, I can get back home and see Mother Pells. I'm not going to visit her in hospital because tomorrow, she is moving into the new retirement flat, the one Simon and I went to view with the *very* low walk-in shower threshold. I can't wait. I don't remember ever feeling like this before about seeing my mother: it's strange, and new. But I want to hug her, and make her feel safe, and loved – which is how she has always made me feel, I was just too much of an idiot to notice. That goes for a lot of other things too.

Merlyn has also arranged for her driver to take me home. She's been messaging me a lot to make sure I'm okay, which has got me wondering what she and Cassia thought of me to encourage me to have the treatment. They must have seen me as so lost and sad, so desperate, so unhappy. But then I think back to the me that would rather wear an omelette to a party than show her face, and realise that's exactly what I was – all those things. But I didn't see it. Who would I go as to that party now, I wonder as I Dyson cracker crumbs from under the couch cushions. I know just the person: I'd go as Margot from *The Good Life*, and who cares if the twenty-five-year-olds didn't even know who I was.

The interesting email was a reply from Maxine, Gabe's friend, who heard I was 'a hoot' and would love to meet up about 'collaborating on some ideas'. The timing of this couldn't be better as I needed some good news. Even though the reversal has been successful, I have no work coming in, and have no idea what I'm going to do when I get back to Wiltshire. But I can't help wondering if she knows anything about me and Gabe. Or maybe there isn't much to know, which is even more depressing. But it's realistic: not a lot had even happened between us – he's probably forgotten about me by now.

I take one last look out across the view, still unsure which is the Gherkin and which is the Shard, pick up my bag and head for the door. I'm wearing some clothes that Cassia dropped off, clearly ones that she didn't want as they're quite big and not that interesting – an M&S grey jumper and some Free People rust-coloured trousers with an elasticated waist. I'm glad of them though, partly because it's feeling autumnal, and partly because the alternative would be a floral shorts co-ord that nobody, including me, wants to see on a forty-eight-year-old woman with cheese curd thighs.

Walking past the hall mirror, I spot a new chin hair. How did that sprout up so quickly? JEEZ. I look like a nanny goat. I remember that hair – it used to be a regular. I might have to name it. Maybe Portia, for old time's sake? I try to pluck it with my fingers, which never works, so decide it's definitely one for the GripMaster Pro Tweezers when I get home. Then I look at my whole face – *really* look, something I've been avoiding ever since the reversal was complete. Of course I liked looking young. Who wouldn't? But this face and I – we've got history. And from now on, every time I see bits I don't like – the jowls, forehead lines, crepey lids… that long list I used to obsess about – I'm going to remind myself that this is what I am meant to look like. These things are not 'wrong', or in need of 'fixing', in fact, I now see they come with benefits. Belly laughs with friends, and a family who loves me – needs me, even. Could this be actual wisdom? I don't feel ready to call myself a Wise Woman, but I'm definitely wiser.

Thinking about Cassia, I dig my phone out of my bag and look at Instagram, realising I haven't opened it all day. She's doing a 'Live': her weekly vintage cocktail, which this week is in the 'library' (three shelves of self-help books and from what I can see a user manual for a robot vacuum). I know for a fact she lives in a new build in Sidcup, so I feel this is disingenuous. But isn't all social media? The cocktail itself is a Last Word, apparently gin-based and from the Prohibition-era. I don't know if Cassia sees me join, but suddenly she says that her 'last word on a certain matter' is that getting older isn't easy, some of us find it easier than others – and that the best thing we can do as women is stick together. So, for the first time ever, I leave a comment: '*#wisewomen* look after each other'. Who even am I? She likes it straightaway, and replies, 'That's my mantra, Erica!' Yes, Cassia, that's why I said it. Anyway, that's enough Cassia for a while I think...

Merlyn's driver messages to say he's outside, so I pull the front door shut behind me for the last time, then get in the lift. Two floors down, Zoe and Jamal get in. They're deep in conversation talking about a game and don't acknowledge me. I'm pretty sure it's because they don't recognise me, or even bother to look that closely. Or both. Why would they? I'm just some middle-aged woman. After feeling invisible for so long, I'm realising that perhaps I was only invisible to those I didn't need to be seen by.

As I get in the car, Merlyn messages me.

> Safe travels back home, Erica my dear.

> Thanks Merlyn.

> I wanted to let you know that Dr Marcus was tracked down in Mauritius and is handing the patent over to Professor Brandt. She's settling out of court. And as Yuvana Labs has gone into liquidation, the technology can now hopefully be put to its intended use.

> That's good news.

> I believe it is, my dear.

> I know it can help a lot of people now but

> But what?

> I also want you to know… that it helped me.

> I am so pleased to hear you say that. Oh and Erica… one last thing: my driver just gave Nandita a lift to the pub – I believe Slay PR are having leaving drinks for Saskia. I just thought I'd let you know. Baci!

We pull out of the small car park in front of the block of flats, and I see another car coming in. A girl gets out with three huge suitcases. She's tall, with honey-coloured hair in a high ponytail and looks like Blake Lively. I know immediately it's Devon. The old me would have looked at her with envy. But this me, the new me? Well, there's a bit of envy, come on, I'm only human, and she is stunning. A snack, even. But for the most part, I smile, and I think, it's her turn. We get one go at youth each. Just one, if we're lucky. Same goes for middle age – if we're even luckier.

And if we're really, really lucky, we get to stay till the end of the night. And yes Keith, that's when we have the best stories to tell.

—

Twenty minutes later, Merlyn's driver pulls up on Old Compton Street and calls out that 'this is the place, Miss'. He tells me he'll wait for five minutes, and I thank him and get out.

It's an *aperitivo* bar with seats on the pavement and loud music coming from inside. It's rather too cool for an M&S jumper, but I'm here now. I feel like I haven't really prepared for this though. As much as I can't wait to see Nandy, I'm worried she'll tell me I'm a twat. She's not generally shy of calling people that.

I stand outside the bar, trying to build up the courage to go in, watching passers-by. Two young women walk past in trench coats and baseball caps. A man stands vomiting in a doorway, and when he sees me, shouts, 'What are you looking at, grandma?'

I take a deep breath and go in. The doors to the bar are open and I can see Nandy before I even cross the threshold. She's sitting on a high bar stool with a purple leather seat, one of many lined up along a wide shelf along one wall, and chatting to Mei-Ling, one of the beauty assistants from Slay PR.

I feel a rush of love when I see her. It's been so long, and I have so many things to tell her: about the Gen Zs, the gaming and the toys, and the club I went to with Channing, about Simon and the microdosing, about Kofi and what he told me, Cassia, what happened in Geneva, about Mother Pells... so many things. And I want to tell her how much I've missed her. And that I'm sorry I was stupid enough to put looking young before any friendship, but especially before ours.

I walk slowly towards her, and she looks up.

It takes a second, then her expression changes, from confusion, to disbelief, and then that huge smile I know so well spreads across her face.

'Evening mofo,' she says, looking me up and down, taking in the cardi, the grey hair, the face sliding down my neck like a Salvador Dali clock. 'So, the rumours are true. You came to your senses?'

I nod.

'You look fucking brilliant,' she says. And she stands up, and she throws her arms around me.

Chapter Forty

Right here, right now

Through the living room window I can see Mrs Belcher's budgie (not a euphemism), and Lucas, the postman, pushing his red trolley towards my front door. I get up off the floor and adjust my kimono, although I'm fairly certain Lucas doesn't think – or indeed hasn't ever thought – that I am trying to flirt with him.

'Good to have you back, Ms Pells,' he says when I open the door.

'Thanks Lucas.'

He roots around in his trolley and hands me a very thick A4 envelope. 'I saw that news article about you last month. So I suppose that wasn't your niece?'

'No, Lucas. It was me.'

'She wasn't as friendly as you,' he says, looking at his phone-meets-scanner device and holding it out for me to sign.

'She wasn't very happy,' I say.

He looks confused for a second, then smiles politely, turns, and heads up the road towards Josie's.

When he's gone, I go through to the kitchen and sit at the table to open the envelope. It's a script that Maxine has been working on – she wants me to 'make it funnier'. Tucked in the envelope is also a book called *Laughter Lines:*

A Primer on Crafting Comedy, which (sorry Josie) looks a lot more interesting than a story about a plucky wartime Irish girl. But also, holy crap. It was easy enough to come up with punny headlines when nobody even asked for them, but this is a whole different kettle of fish. Or barrel of laughs, should I say. Maybe that was funny? Maybe it wasn't though. This is a minefield. An exciting one though. If minefields can be exciting... JEEZ.

My phone pings.

> Good luck at your mum's new flat today. See you tomorrow, 3pm OK? Héloïse is making churros xx

> Thanks Josie. 3pm great. See you tomorrow. Xx

> Oh, I meant to say, now you're back, you should check out what they've done to the old FILLINGZ on the high street.

> Will do x

My phone pings again. It's a sticker from Nandy, of Cassia drinking a cocktail, with the caption 'Your new bestie'. I snort with laughter. Nandy is coming down to stay this weekend and I can't wait. We're having dinner here and Keith, Stephen, Josie and Laure are all coming too. Josie wanted to invite Peach Jumpsuit but although she has a Senior Railcard, which makes it cheaper for her, she doesn't like travelling after dark, so I'm not sure she'll come. Thankfully Nandy will be doing most of the cooking. Come to think of it, I must check my oven for any cremated remains.

What was I thinking, to turn my back on these people, my people. But they have been patient with me, and waited, and they might have told me off a bit, but they aren't bearing a grudge, not one of them. After Nandy hugged me in the bar in Soho, I must have said sorry about thirty times. She called me all sorts of names (and yes 'twat' was indeed one of them), but once she'd got it off her chest, she was really tearful and said that she hated the fact that I had wanted to change myself so much. I told her I don't anymore, and that I didn't realise how bloody lucky I am. I also told her Cassia and I got drunk together, which she couldn't believe, and when I told her I was wearing a *Teletubbies* onesie throughout, she nearly fell off her bar stool.

—

The removal men are just leaving when I arrive at the retirement flats in Bristol. Simon is giving them a tip out the front and sees me pull up in Josie's Kia. I get out and walk towards him across the car park, clutching a bunch of chrysanthemums and a card. By the time I reach him, he's on his phone and barely looks up.

'I've got someone called Subhan dropping off his paddleboard, so I need to wait out here.'

'You're renting a paddleboard? For Mum?'

'No, Erica. For Sam.' He looks up at me. 'I see you're back to your original human form.' Why does he make everything sound weird?

'I see you have a new obsession,' I say, watching him tap furiously into one of his sharing economy apps. This feels more like the me and Simon I am used to.

'Mum's waiting for you inside. She's excited to see you.' His face softens slightly as he puts his phone in his pocket. 'Erica... I get why you did it, you know.'

'You do?'

'Of course I do. We're all looking for something, aren't we? What happened with Interpol, and then the microdosing, made me realise I don't always get it right either.' He laughs, and in a moment of unprecedented self-awareness says, 'I keep trying though.'

I think he's going to hug me as he leans forward slightly, so I put out my arms. He doesn't though, and instead takes both my hands so it looks like we're doing some kind of Regency dance. It's awkward. But it's a lot better than usual.

Inside, the flat is piled with boxes and Alannah is unpacking in the tiny kitchen with the radio on. 'Your mum's in the bedroom,' she calls out to me.

I put the flowers and card down on a chair and walk into a small but bright room off the hallway, with white cornices and pale cream walls. The John Lewis clock is on the chest of drawers, and it fits perfectly. There are two alarm cords and a bed that moves into a sitting position, like the ones you get in hospitals. I feel that protective feeling again. She is old. She really is. Maybe this was *The Inevitable*, nothing more.

Mother Pells is examining the mirrored walk-in wardrobe. She looks round when I come in, and I can see the remains of a scar on her forehead. 'So much storage space, Erica, whatever will I put in here?'

I hug her, harder and longer than I can ever remember doing so.

She looks faintly surprised, so I release my grip a bit. 'Dad would have loved the flat, Mum. He'd think it was a very good choice.'

'I thought that too darling.' She pauses, looking carefully at my face. 'Sometimes I keep it to myself, you know, talking about your father. I don't want to upset you. I know you were his favourite.' She pauses. 'And he was yours.'

I don't – can't – say anything.

She strokes my cheek. 'You're wearing a lot less make-up than usual.'

I nod. It doesn't feel like a criticism though.

'Where have you been, Erica?'

'Time travelling, Mum.'

'I wouldn't mind going back in time.' She laughs and sits down on the edge of the bed with a sort of groaning sigh. The bed hasn't been made up yet, so it's just a bare mattress.

'It's not all it's cracked up to be,' I say. 'In fact, I think that right here, right now is probably the best place to be.' And that's the Fatboy Slim song firmly planted in my head.

She pats the bed next to her. 'Now, tell me what you've been up to.'

I sit down and hold her hand. We've not been this close to each other for a long time. Her skin feels so loose, like it's completely separate from what's underneath. I stare at it, and notice that my hand looks really young next to hers.

'I'm having a change of career, Mum. A bit late in the day but...'

'We're proud of you whatever you do, Erica. Me and your dad.'

'Thanks Mum. I know that now.'

—

Later that day, I'm on the high street, grabbing some Settlers Wind-eze Plus from Boots and a few things from Sainsbury's to make my cupboards look slightly less bare for Nandy coming to stay. I can see Je Suis Belle up ahead, and the shop unit where FILLINGZ was, and can just make out a different sign over the door. Remembering what Josie said, I get closer to have a look.

What does it say? I can see curly white writing on a wooden sign. It seems pretty stylish, and not in a try-hard 'hip-hop' kind of way. Also, thank god it's not another cafe selling instant coffee and lardy cake. I draw level with it and look up. It says, Brie My Guest. It's a cheese shop. Glory be.

I can see it's not quite open yet and there are a couple of men inside fitting fridges and units, and painting. I peer in and one of them turns around. His face is smiling, expectant, genuine.

It's Gabe.

He sees me, then puts down the drill he's holding and walks towards the door. He's wearing a blue t-shirt with paint splatters all over it, and jeans. I notice it's not just his hands that are freckly, it's his arms as well. Please don't let him be angry with me, I think, although he has every right.

We stand in the doorway looking at each other.

'You're a sight for sore eyes, Erica Pells.' I think he's pleased to see me, but he's guarded. I notice the hand that was holding the drill is now clenched. No wonder, I suppose; last time we had a conversation, I stormed off.

'So are you, Gabe Dix.' I try to sound breezy but here comes the fizzing feeling in my chest, which I know now isn't my arteries.

'And what's this, a cheese shop?' I say.

'It is. My very own. When FILLINGZ closed, I saw that as a sign from... I don't know. Whoever dispenses signs.'

I look past him into the shop and can see a counter and some chalkboards with the names of local cheeses written on them. The walls are a broad bean green, like Gabe's eyes.

'You miss out on all the news when you swan off to London.' He pulls a bit of wood shaving out of his hair. He's definitely hotter than Gary Barlow.

'I swanned back. It was very much not what it was cracked up to be.' I'm trying to read his face. 'Look, Gabe. I'm really sorry.'

He looks more serious. 'You should be, Erica.' I can tell he means it kindly. Well, for the most part.

I smile. Thankfully I'm not wearing that stupid contour that made me look like a Cubist painting, so it doesn't matter what angle I put my head at. I mean, don't get me wrong, I'm keeping up my skincare, obvs. I haven't had a complete personality change. But I've reached an understanding with my beauty products now. They're just to make me feel better – not change my life. I'm also doing my YouTube workout with that Bethany woman again, with similarly low expectations, and yes, using the doorstops as weights.

There's a pause, during which Gabe puts his hand on my arm and smiles too. 'You look so much better than when I last saw you,' he says. 'This is the face that makes me laugh... I mean, in a good way.'

'Even with the wear and tear?' I say, suddenly conscious of looking old enough for that vomiting man to call me 'grandma'.

'Especially with the wear and tear. You think I don't have any of that myself?' He points to his face, which is admittedly 'craggy', and his hair, which could never be described as 'luxuriant', but as I recall, Gabe is aware of that.

Someone shouts out from inside the shop, and Gabe calls back that he'll just be a minute. He turns to me again. 'Erica, are you working at the moment? I've still got a few students I'm teaching, so I need someone to help out here. You would be perfect.'

'Well, I'm doing some comedy stuff with Maxine, so I could do with the cash as I can't see that paying anything, for a while at least. Thank you for putting me in touch with her, by the way – she's great.'

I realise it sounds like I only want to help for money, so I add, 'And I'd love to. I really like...' I go to say 'you' but feel this is a bit much, so change it to 'Brie' halfway through, resulting in 'ye', and suggesting I am a frequenter of medieval battle re-enactments.

'GABE!' calls the person from inside the shop again.

'I have to go,' he says. 'See you at The Perch at the weekend?'

'Yes please.' I mean it this time.

Gabe goes back into the shop, and I head along the high street, grinning like an idiot.

There's no kiss. Sorry, but this isn't a rom-com. There might be one at some point (I bloody hope so), but that's another story. As for this story, instead of a happy ending, how about happy-ish? I've come to realise that's a good thing to aim for: happy-ish. Just happy isn't really what it's all about – it would be a pretty boring existence if there was only one emotion available, wouldn't it?

I think that's what I was after though, some kind of utopia where I got up every morning, surveyed my youthful face and just smiled all day because of it. But life is messier than that, and so it should be. It has puns and cheese and belly laughs, but it also has bingo wings and hangovers and grief. And what will get me through it isn't how sharp my jawline is, but having the right people around me. Because when they're the right people, they don't care what you look like anyway.

A Letter from Eleanor

Welcome to *Turn Back Time*. I can't tell you how happy I am that you're either holding or listening to my debut novel. I really hope you love reading it as much as I loved writing it.

As a former beauty blogger and journalist, and as someone who has always been interested in the beauty industry, I've become increasingly aware of the pressures and double standards women face as they get older.

Some progress has been made, it's true. But I don't think the way we feel (and are made to feel) about how we look as we age is something that will change in a generation, or even in two or three. We are all doing our best in different ways until we settle into a new normal somewhere in the future. I hope that one day this new normal will mean women can do exactly what they want – and look exactly how they want, too.

In the meantime, we're muddling through. Sometimes it's funny, and sometimes it's really not. And that's the backdrop for this story.

Turn Back Time is dedicated to my mum, but it's also for my girlfriends. Not just the ones I know and love, but for every middle-aged woman out there who like me (and Erica) has looked in the mirror and thought, *what the hell happened*? If you've never done this, I applaud you and hope you might enjoy the book anyway. If you have, then dive in – but be gentle with Erica. Like many of us, she is just searching for her place in middle age.

I'd love to hear that you laughed along with this story. I'd also love to hear that it made you think, or even cry a little. And if you're a literature fan, there are ten Thomas Hardy Easter eggs tucked inside the book for you to find. Just think of me as a perimenopausal Taylor Swift.

If you'd like to get in touch or find out more about me, you can do so on Instagram (@eleanortuckerauthor) or at www.eleanortucker.co.uk. And if you enjoy *Turn Back Time*, please do leave a review – it makes a huge difference for a new author like me. You can do this on Amazon and Goodreads, or by sharing it on social media.

Lots of love,
Elle

Acknowledgements

I didn't plan to write fiction, but I am so glad that I did – it has honestly been one of the most transformative experiences of my life. To that happy accident I owe the support of my agent, Emily MacDonald. Emily – knowing you're always just an email or call away with your insights and advice, your brilliant editing and all that dark-art agent magic you do, makes me feel so looked after and incredibly lucky to have you in my corner. Thank you for everything. And also thanks to the whole team at 42, especially Eugenie Furniss for championing this project in its formative stages.

A big thank you to my publisher, Hera. Jennie – your early emails to Emily about this novel made me cry happy tears. I felt from the start that you really got me, and it was such an easy decision to have you bring this book into the world. Kate – I really appreciate all your help and support with publicity.

The writing community is incredible, and although too many to name individually, I'd really like to say thanks to everyone who has cheered me on, particularly on Instagram, and also the No.1 Women (both Media and Author) – you know who you are. Special thanks to Daisy Buchanan – your early read of the manuscript was a gamechanger and I am so thankful for the endorsement you gave me. Matilda Battersby – you made a real difference that day. Thanks also to Sam Baker for your wise counsel, and to fellow writers Emma Steele, Sarah Robinson (my script co-writer and partner in wine crime), Brendan Shanahan and Andrew Tibbs.

Huge gratitude to my girlfriends, who have been not just supportive of, but interested in, what I'm doing, and also very understanding when I disappear down the writing rabbit hole. And Scott, because you'll never not be mentioned in any acknowledgements of mine – my friend for life.

There's one friend who gets her own paragraph: my best friend Fiona. Fi, right from the start you helped me work this book out and gave me honest and helpful feedback and ideas. You read a really scrappy first few chapters (when you have so much else on your reading pile), cheered me on and celebrated with me every time I had a win. This is true friendship, and 37 years on (eek), I feel so lucky to have you by my side.

I also really want to thank my family for their support and encouragement with my writing career. My mother Di (who this book is dedicated to) has been my biggest fan on my writing journey – always front row at any book events. This pride in me makes me feel very loved – thank you, Ma. And my dearest big sis Ros, my in-laws Heather and George, my beloved Auntie V (who has a real Merlyn in her life), my cousins Verity and Rod, and my nephews and nieces, I appreciate you all so much. And Pops, of course, who I know is grinning away somewhere about all this.

Jake and Phoebe, stop being brilliant – you're spoiling my snarky comments about Gen Z. Jake – thanks for all the cups of tea and hugs along the way. Phoebe – you're my right-hand woman and you've patiently listened to me reading chapters out loud to you. The thought of making you both proud – and inspiring you to work hard for your dreams – drives me to open my laptop when I don't even feel like it. I love you both so much.

And lastly, my brilliant husband Andy, the person without whom I wouldn't have been able to do any of this. Writing a book is a solitary business and I've frequently had to disappear into rooms (and even away for the weekend). He didn't just hold the fort but actually taught himself to cook so that it wasn't nachos every night. He also encouraged me when I was feeling fraught, talked me down off a ledge when I was on sub, read early drafts and helped me when I was stuck, and supplied a good few jokes too – notably the sea lion belter in chapter twenty-three. Thank you darling, for always believing in me, and of course for liking the wear and tear. There's nobody else I'd rather grow old with.